HASH TAG

A Novel

Eryk Pruitt

Rock and a Hard Place Press

HASHTAG: A Novel
by Eryk Pruitt
Copyright © and ™ 2015

Cover by Heather Garth
Edited by Susan Jessen

ISBN: 979-8-9991000-9-2 (Paperback)
ISBN: 979-8-9938836-0-1 (eBook)

10 9 8 7 6 5 4 3
First publication: 2015 by Immortal Ink; Reissued in September 2017 by Polis Books, LLC; Reissued in November 2025 by Rock and a Hard Place Press

Published by Rock and a Hard Place Press, an imprint of Rock and a Hard Place Press, LLC
Woodbridge, NJ.
rockandahardplacemag.com
amazon.com/~/e/B08WPQG5YV

DEDICATION

To Lana

If Not For You

Introduction

The first thing I've ever read by Eryk Pruitt was a short story called *Houston*, originally published in the tenth issue of the now-extinct crime journal *Thuglit*. In a nutshell, it tells the story of a motley crew of simple minded, small-town Texas kids trying to get into the big city drug trade. A *Dazed & Confused* meets *Scarface* with a juvenile and self-deprecating sense of humor kind of deal. I loved it immediately.

One pattern you quickly discover when you read as much as I do is what I call *the romance of the outlaw*. An emotional reverence to criminal characters who live by (or claim to, anyway) some form of moral code. I don't know what's going on with writers, but most of them think that thugs, bullies and sociopaths are somehow deeper than the rest of us, that their violent ways are just a metaphor for a complicated soul. It's basically the Hallmark Channel version of bad behavior and I gradually lost all the patience I had for it over the years.

The romance of the outlaw is almost completely absent from Eryk Pruitt's writing. He writes like a man who knows a thing or two about what kind of people end up on the wrong side of the law. Not every kingpin is Walter White, and not every serial killer is Dexter Morgan. In fact, none of them are. Most criminals are just people with hair-trigger tempers or a weird sense of entitlement, convinced the universe owes them a freebie because life kicked them in the teeth once.

These are the criminals Eryk Pruitt is writing about and that's why they feel infinitely more real to me than any self-proclaimed badass saving a busful of kids or whatever.

Pruitt's characters are flawed, funny and firmly hanging on to that abstract, but extremely relatable feeling that their lives are on the cusp of a lucky break. You've met them. They're the coworkers you talk shit about at lunch time. Your best friend's shitty ex. The assholes that cut you off in traffic like it's a personal statement. That client who acted super melodramatic for no apparent reason. The protagonist of *Houston* is the idiotic little brother of at least ten people you've known. Chances are you've been one of these people at some point or another.

Whether you want to admit it to yourself or not, you've been the bad guy in someone else's story. At least once, but we both know it's probably more than that. No one's above their bad behavior. No one's above catastrophic life decisions. Any self-respecting adult should be at peace with that and yet none of us are.

That liminal space between who we think we are and who we really are is the perspective where Eryk Pruitt writes his novels. He's an observer of people who claim to be observers of the human condition. A man scientifically interested in the stories we tell ourselves. That's why his novels have such a strong personality. His characters firmly believe in their own romance of the outlaw, but he doesn't believe in it himself. Even when their circumstances couldn't be any more removed from your own, you share with them that unspoken, lingering feeling that you'll be the one to get away with it and there's a voyeuristic and sometimes even empathetic pleasure in that.

Eryk Pruitt's novels feel like something that happened to someone you know, but don't necessarily like. It's the craziest story you hear at the coffee machine. That's why I enjoy reading them so much. I love these stories.

Another trait of his writing that I find endlessly fascinating is his depiction of the American South. If anything has been more mythologized than criminality or violence in popular culture, it's the South. It's either painted as the last wild frontier where only the strong survive, or as a sepia-toned wonderland for "simpler living." So-called serious novels haven't done much better: the South is usually trapped in one of two caricatures: either seduced by its own haunted beauty, or reduced to a backwoods hellscape that eats its young. Pruitt doesn't play either game.

From Texas to North Carolina, his South is lived-in, flawed, and modern, full of people wrestling with whether their savage folklore will define them or bury them. It is the South of a man who lived it all his life. A place with two rulebooks: one written down by institutions, and another unwritten one you just know. His characters don't just understand what'll get them arrested. They know what'll get them a beating, or a shovel to the back of the head.

Pruitt's characters are streetwise. Not in the way private detectives are. Not in the way Marlon Brando's tough guy is in *On the Waterfront* either. They are the way people are in small towns, where everyone knows the history of every family, and the social order is as fixed as the weather. They can read the room before they even walk in, or, if they can't, Pruitt will do it for them and narrate their inevitable collapse. His books are funny, sure, but there's always this pulse of danger underneath. In his South, people live (and usually die) by the ties that bind them. His outlook is rooted in history, but his stories keep staring the future straight in the eye.

Which brings us to the book in your hands: Pruitt's sophomore novel, ***Hashtag***. Hard to believe, but it's already been ten years since it came out. And if you were alive, functional, and even half-paying attention a decade ago, there's no better time to read, or reread it. Because **Hashtag** is set in a world that feels strangely foreign now: when the Internet still had a sense of wonder, when we actually experienced uplifting moments together in real time, and when literally anyone could be the hero of the day. In hindsight, it was our digital version of the mythological South, a place where legends were made, stupid decisions went viral and sometimes the biggest fool in the room got exactly what they wanted, just because the timing lined up.

Sweet Melinda Kendall is the quintessential Pruitt character: brash, too confident by half, and riding chaos like Kelly Slater catching waves in a hurricane. Odie Shanks isn't far behind, just a small-town pizza shop manager with a dim grip on reality and a desperate craving for attention. Together, they stumble into creating a digital spectacle that feels like digging up the corpse of the American Dream and forcing it to dance for clicks.

If this is your first time reading **Hashtag**, I envy you. If it's your first encounter with Eryk Pruitt altogether, I envy you even more. Because you're about to get hit with a novel that's equal parts savage and hilarious, full of violence that's way too plausible, and characters so dumb-yet-recognizable they might as well be your neighbor, your cousin, or the guy in front of you at the DMV.

Enjoy, reader.

This isn't one of those novels where everything ties up neatly in the end because real life doesn't and Pruitt sure as hell knows it. But I'm guessing you already sensed that. You're the kind of person who leans toward primordial chaos instead of tidy resolutions, who knows the world is too messy to be fixed with a bow. You're in the right place. You've made the right choice.

And here's why **Hashtag** still matters: it captures that fleeting moment when the Internet felt infinite, right as the algorithms started to fence it in. Just before outrage became the default currency. It reminds us how fast stupid ideas can become folklore, how quickly ordinary people can be turned into myths or monsters, and how funny and terrifying that process can be. That hasn't changed. If anything, it's only gotten worse. Which makes this book less of a time capsule and more of a warning flare.

Benoit Lelièvre, editor of Dead End Follies
September, 2025

#PROLOGUE

S am McCarthy stopped just shy of picking up his newspaper. They had been at it again, right there at the edge of his property. Flowers, crosses, other crap. They'd mounded them all together and lit candles, candles that dripped wax all over his yard, and who'd be responsible for picking up all that mess? Why, it would be him, and no amount of reasoning with anyone would ever change that. He'd done this before.

McCarthy made his way across his yard, down near the street, where sat the wall. Folks around Lake Castor grew up knowing about that wall. Six feet wide, four feet tall, and two feet thick. Time and nature giving it a lovely overgrowth. His wife—who had long departed to her Kingdom—planted a willow oak behind it, and the mighty roots snaked up from under, but still it wouldn't budge.

Nothing moved that wall.

McCarthy, forgetting his paper for now, leaned his walking stick against the concrete. He had to pick up the wreaths. Who else would do it? Who else would pay a hand to come out and scrape all that wax off the wall? The city never came to clean those skid marks off the road. Sure, they sent a wrecker to remove the junked-out, totaled cars, but it would be Sam McCarthy responsible for having the bits of windshield picked out of the grass and the blood sprayed off the street in front of his house.

And those damn vigils! They'd start coming at five, just after the workday. One by one, lining up outside his house at the wall, armed with candles and holy hymns. Most often, it was a kid. Somebody from the high school, trying out their wheels, trying to go fast, faster . . . and having heard about the hairpin-curve on Creechville Road and its horrible reputation, trying like hell to prove they could beat it.

Before the wall, they drove into his living room. The McCarthy house sat on the bend on an S-curve that originally had been designed to skip around a watering hole that had since run dry. The first one was a baseball player, a shortstop with a mean bat. He'd gone off the road and into the McCarthy house and ended his career with a broken arm and punctured lung. His girlfriend had been decapitated. Three more cars missed the curve and, tired of repairing his house, McCarthy poured the concrete that would kill its fair share of Lake Castor youth.

McCarthy gathered up the photographs of the two boys laid at the base of his wall, stacked them one on top of the other, and wadded them up. He collected as many of the flowers and floral bouquets he could with his two hands and, leaving his walking stick at the wall, stalked the distance of the yard to the trash cans.

A car inched down the street, extra slow, and McCarthy knew what they were looking for. He stuffed the flowers into the garbage and stomped down the street to head them off.

"Are you Sam McCarthy?" the driver asked, not getting out of the car, only slowing. McCarthy didn't recognize him, thought him dressed a little better than someone from around here.

"You best drive on," McCarthy replied. He picked up his walking stick at the wall and waved it at the road. "This is a dead end, so you'll be good to turn around right now and go back the way you come."

The car stopped, but the man didn't get out. "Is this where Dean Hergenrader and Oliver Churchill were killed? Is this the wall?"

"You hear me tell you to get on down the road, mister?" McCarthy let his hand slide down the cane, making sure the driver of the car got a good look at the head of his stick. It was a gilded skull that John Parton'd made for him long, long ago and it was heavy enough to knock the snot out of whatever he swung it at and he thought it fair to let the stranger know he toted it.

"Easy sir. Take it easy. I don't mean any bother."

"Well, you're bothering me."

"I just want to ask you a few questions about the other night."

McCarthy drew closer to the car. "I don't want to answer no questions. I ain't going to tell you again to get on down the road."

"Look, I work for the paper over in Tucker. Those two kids are big news over there. Their parents are making a lot of noise. They say they aren't going to stop until the city has you take down this wall. People over in Tucker are real interested to hear your side of the story."

"I'll tell you what I think about the people over in Tucker, mister." McCarthy took his walking stick and swung it hard onto the hood of the car.

"What the hell are you doing?" shrieked the man in the car. He fumbled into gear, to get the hell out of there.

McCarthy didn't wait. Unsatisfied, he stomped around to the front of the car and smashed out one headlamp, then the other.

"I don't give a good hard shit what the people in Tucker think!" He came around to the passenger side and eyeballed the windshield, but the driver collected his wits and spun into reverse, barely missing McCarthy and screeching his tires, adding his black skid marks to those already marring the asphalt.

The car came to a stop, the driver feeling he was at a safe enough distance from McCarthy.

"You're a crazy old man!" he called through his windshield. "They're going to make you take down that wall."

McCarthy started towards the car, and it lurched forward, then sped the hell out of there. It never flashed its brake lights once as it tore back up Creechville and toward the highway. McCarthy watched after him, made sure he didn't come back. He knew he'd never see that guy again. He'd probably go into town, looking for a policeman to cry to, but he wouldn't find one. Not one that would do a damn thing. The people over in Tucker didn't get it. They never did.

This is Lake Castor.

#ODIE
SHANKS

1

Nothing jazzed Odie Shanks more than a busy night at work. When his co-workers melted down, started running this way and that, calling each other names and screaming . . . when both phones were faced down on the counter and the girl hired to answer them could only be found crying behind the giant ovens . . . when it seemed folks still lived in Lake Castor all up and took root in the front lobby, Odie found a peculiar Zen. He'd buckle down, fall silent, and box the hell out of some pizzas. Trouble was, busy nights didn't come along often enough for Odie. Not anymore. Most nights were spent cleaning some shit they'd cleaned a thousand times already. Staring at the wall. Talking shit and smoking cigarettes out the back door. Standing around. Making plans or telling dirty jokes.

So when Commissioner Rodenhizer threw a ribbon-cutting for the new Walmart out on the highway, and Clarence Bossey fell sick and couldn't smoke up the hogs he'd promised, Odie found himself with an order for forty pizzas. All this on top of a regular Saturday night dinner at Maggie's Pizza Pick-Up. Maggie herself flew into a tizzy and called in a couple of extra kids to help with the rush, but Odie took a breath, settled in, and got right to work.

Once he slid the last pizza, sliced and steaming, into its box, he took off his Maggie's Pizza Pick-Up hat, slapped it against his thigh to dust off the flour, and told no one in particular he'd be out the back door for a minute or so.

That's where she found him, leaned up against the railing of the small loading dock, sucking a Winston and staring up at the water tower.

"It's inventory night tonight, Odie," said Maggie Hornbecker, his boss.

His shoulders slumped. "We counted your inventory last week."

"A woman needs her inventory counted more than once a week." She figured the matter good and settled, then disappeared back into her restaurant. Odie wished the cigarette was longer. He fell back against the railing and spit smoke into the stars.

Maggie fancied herself something special. Something refreshing for a woman in her early fifties. She loved the outdoors and thought herself something of a rebel by running her own restaurant in gym shorts and sweatbands. Her body was slick, toned, and defined. Odie thought she looked like Richard Simmons.

The dinner rush ended, and one by one, Maggie had him send home the rest of the employees. First, the counter girl, then the high school boy who looked after the ovens, then finally the dishwasher. In no time, they were alone, and Odie's stomach fell into fits.

She waited for him in the walk-in cooler. He'd gone in to put away the onions and bell peppers and found her atop the cases of tomato sauce, trying to maintain her seductive pose despite the blasted chill. She'd rustled up a black, frilly camisole and smuggled it in under her clothes, but now resorted to her discarded britches as covering from the cold. All the same, she struggled like the dickens to compose herself as Odie opened the cooler door.

He had no recourse. He never did. She was his boss. She told him what to do, and he did it, as he had done every inventory night for the past five years, since back when he was only seventeen. He forced other things into his mind, focused on how cold the walk-in cooler was, rather than what it must be like to have sex with Richard Simmons. She told him to pull her hair, so he pulled it. She liked to suck on his fingers, so he let her. He was very careful not to free-style, as this could give her the fidgets. She was set in her ways, so he simply followed instructions and waited for it all to end.

But Maggie liked to cuddle, so they lay there for a bit until she declared it was too cold and asked to relocate to the stack of flour sacks in dry storage, swaddled in a couple of dough-caked aprons. Back in the early days, Maggie acted hard, mechanically getting up after sex and dressing, hoping it made Odie feel cheap and off his game. But she soon sensed he preferred it that way and immediately altered her approach. Maggie reckoned sex no fun unless someone were uncomfortable and that discomfort was prolonged.

"What'd y'all do last night?" Odie asked her. He lay with his back flat on the flour sacks, her nestled into him, head on his chest. She tickled the small sprouts of hair on his belly with her bony finger. She had hands like a man, he thought, then tried to think it no more.

"Went to the movies with Glenn," she said. She gave him a little peck on his nipple.

"What'd y'all see?"

"I don't know. I didn't pay much attention to it."

"Oh yeah? Y'all screw in the theater or something?" He didn't care. He tossed forth words to take his mind off things. Odie couldn't think of a damn thing said after sex that mattered a hill of beans, but that evening his mind raced, and he didn't like where it kept taking him. Thinking about his car, still broke down and on the side of the road over in Deeton. Thinking about where he was, what he did. Thinking that if someone bothered to make a movie about his life, what would the audience think of this scene before them, him post-coitus with Maggie Hornbecker, some thirty years older than he. Thinking about that tomato stain on the wall next to him and how he couldn't decide if it looked like Africa or South America and why it hadn't been cleaned before the other employees left.

"No, we didn't screw," she said. "I just don't like all that action movie crap. Hookers, guns, and firetrucks. I like stories about women. About self-discovery."

"You seen *Thelma and Louise*?"

"I don't like movies about lesbians," she groused. "The world's got enough problems without showing pictures of a bunch of deviants." She sat up and fished through Odie's discarded pants pockets for his cigarettes and Zippo, lighted up. "I think Glenn's a queer, you know."

"You always say that," said Odie, already bored. "He ain't a queer."

"How do you know that?"

Odie wondered if telling her he'd seen Glenn chatting up the counter girls more than once would actually cheer her up, convince her that *at least there was a chance*. He thought better of it. Maggie got hers. Glenn got his. Odie reckoned he had his own damn problems.

"You can just tell with some guys, that's all," he said.

Maggie smiled. "That's called *gay-dar*, you know. It's like *radar*, but only the gays have it. They say a gay fella can walk into a bar and spot another gay fella, just like that. Even if the chap don't know he's gay. Freaking *gay-dar*."

Odie looked sideways at her. "You got no idea what you're talking about."

"Now, if it would have been you on that movie screen," she cooed. "I sure liked watching you back when you was acting in them plays. You were like a little Bruce Willis. I'd sit there in the audience, and you'd get me to stirring up there on that stage."

A shiver ran up his spine. "I was in high school."

"And I knew even back then that you was going to grow up into something special."

She smiled at him, blew smoke into his face.

"He sure as hell don't take advantage of this, not the way you do," she said. She took a quick, last drag off the cigarette, then dropped it to the floor. She arched her back. Leaned in to steal a smooch. She set to tinkering with his undercarriage and wanted another go. *Dammit.* It was quarter past ten, and he wished he could ask for overtime.

"Don't you love him?" asked Odie.

"Do what?"

Odie tucked his hair behind his ear. "Glenn. Your husband. Don't you love him?"

"Of course, I love him." She worked at him with her hand under the flour-caked apron. "Why do you think I make you wear a condom when we do inventory?"

And with that, she kissed his throat, then his chest, his nipple, and soon set upon his solar plexus and headed south. Odie put his hand over his eyes and did what he could, but that weren't near good enough, and she popped her head back alongside his and asked what was the matter.

"I guess making and boxing forty pizzas affects me different," he said. "That's all."

She opened her mouth to say something, but thought better of it and returned her head back to his chest. She kept quiet a while before she said, "And you? You don't normally get a Friday off. Did you do something nice with it? I mean, after the funerals?"

Odie didn't answer right away. A million things hit him at once, and he took his time sorting through them. His phantom arm rose from behind her head and lightly stroked her hair.

"I had car trouble after they put Dean in his hole," he said. "I walked up to the All-Niter Café where I spent the rest of the evening trying to fetch a ride home."

"That's awful," she said. "What a lousy Friday off."

"Weren't so bad. I met somebody, and we got to talking."

"Oh?"

He heard the smile in her voice. "It weren't like that," said Odie. "Weren't like that at all."

"Were you real close to those boys? Those two that died?"

Odie shook his head. He hadn't been close to Dean Hergenrader or Oliver Churchill. No closer than he'd been with any of his other classmates. But that didn't mean it didn't sock him good in the gut when he heard they'd been killed joy-riding down Creechville Road late Tuesday night. He'd stood there a good long while after the Mexicans started shoveling dirt atop old Dean's hole, wondering if this is what it would come to—him buried under six feet of Lake Castor soil, ruddy, ruined earth that had been there for all of creation—and he had no plan of ever being anywhere else.

He changed the subject. He talked about the ribbon-cutting out at the new Walmart, about the blind commissioner, about how folks came expecting Bossey's BBQ and instead got pizza pies that Odie himself had sliced.

"Some folks say you poisoned him so you could serve your pizzas," said Odie.

"Some folks can kiss my ass," said Maggie.

Odie reckoned she must have started thinking about counting all the money she made on the deal because she set to twitching again and rubbing her smooth, stone-cut legs against his and, in no time, was back at it. On the wall across from them hung a mirror. Odie found himself staring into it, much like he'd stared into those graves the day previous, placing his own hand on Maggie's shoulder, when, from the front lobby sounded the little *ding* signaling that someone sure as shit had come in looking for some pizza. Countless cigarette breaks and long story jokes had broken up over the years thanks to that *ding*, but Odie could think of no time more inconvenient.

Neither could Maggie.

"What the hell?" she spat. She was up and threw a finger to his face. "You didn't lock the fucking door?" A cloud passed over her for sure. She was well-known for having her turns.

"I didn't get a chance to—"

"You ignorant *retard*," she hissed. "What the hell is wrong with you?" She scrambled for her britches. First only her blouse which she threw on, then later a bra which she held until she located her pants still in the walk-in and then a shoe, then the other under the dishwasher. She pulled her unkempt hair together, but it was beyond repair. As she headed up to the lobby to see after the customer, Odie gathered his own britches, himself in no particular hurry. Found his Maggie's Pizza Pick-Up polo over by the cooler door, pants beneath where Maggie had been lying, socks scattered here and there. He picked up Maggie's discarded cigarette and finished it atop the flour sacks, when he heard Maggie scream.

Over the years, he'd heard her shout plenty, but never before *scream*, so he was caught off-guard and dropped the cigarette stub to the tile. He left it to burn as he one-hopped—wearing only a single shoe—around the pizza ovens and the pick-up window and into the cashier's station where he found himself face-to-face with a masked gunman.

2

Jake Armstrong had never seen such a mess as that kid who came into the diner just around sundown. He looked like he'd pitched a doubleheader, as sweaty and rumpled as he was. The shirt probably used to look nice and more than likely, not that long ago. He carried the suit jacket in his hand and his necktie, half-undone, hung from his pants pocket. He wore his hair just past his shoulders and slicked it to the side of his head.

The air conditioner hit the kid like a kiss from a sweet woman and he took time to take it in. A short minute, because he set sights on the stool next to Jake and fell on it like a madman in from the desert. He dropped the suit jacket to the floor and sunk elbows-first to the counter.

"Water," he said. "Please."

The older woman with the nametag 'Frances' came and dropped water from a pitcher into a plastic glass. She held a menu at arm's reach before the kid.

"You got money tonight, Odie Shanks?" she asked. The kid nodded while swallowing whole gulps of water, ice and all. "Show me you got money, and I'll give you a menu."

Odie slapped the water glass back to the counter and fussed around in his trouser pockets until he fished out a wallet, opened it for her to see. Eleven dollars. A tenner and a single. Jake turned his head back to his chicken-fried steak. The woman refilled his water and left him with the menu.

The kid was too young to be a hobo. Dressed too nice to be a degenerate and way too sober to be a drunkard. Jake would have paid him no more mind had he not shuffled up to the jukebox and started dropping quarters. The last thing Jake wanted to hear was country, so he'd gone to sopping gravy with a roll when he heard the beginnings of Stevie Ray Vaughan's 'The Sky Is Crying.'

Jake waited for the kid to take his seat before telling him, "You know, I seen him play. Back before he was famous. It was in a bar in Austin, long before he died."

"I didn't know he died," said Odie.

"Oh sure," said Jake. "About twenty-five years ago, I reckon. In a helicopter crash. He's buried right outside Dallas."

"I didn't even know he was from Texas."

"How could you not know he was from Texas?" asked Jake. "He's got songs like 'Chitlins Con Carne' and 'Texas Flood.' He's about as Texan as Dr. Pepper and the Alamo."

"I didn't even know Dr. Pepper was from Texas," said Odie.

"Sure it is. It's from Waco."

"That's where them crazy religious folk got themselves killed by the government, right?"

"Yes," said Jake. "Texas is also the birthplace of two Presidents and the home of the greatest football team on the planet."

Frances walked by and asked the kid what it would be. He'd never so much as looked at the menu.

"Hamburger," he said. "No cheese. Add me some bacon." He shook a fork and knife from the rolled up paper napkin, then swiped his forehead with it. She'd refilled his water, but now he nursed it. He looked to Jake. "I'm guessing you're from Texas then."

"What gave you that idea?"

"Just speculating," he answered. "You ain't stopped talking about Texas since you started talking and that's usually a dead giveaway. Next I imagine you'll quote your father."

"How's that?"

"People from Texas always quote their daddies. 'My daddy told me this' and 'my father once told me that.' I'm fine with Stevie Ray Vaughan, and I can deal with Willie Nelson in spurts, but if you start quoting your daddy, I'm going to have to take my business over to one of them booths."

Jake had never known his daddy but felt that was a bit heavy for polite, casual conversation. Instead, he pointed a finger to the kid's get-up.

"A little dressy for bumming on the highway, you reckon?" Jake asked him.

Odie scowled. "I was at a funeral, and my car broke down. It overheats every now and again, but normally I can get it to the gas station in time to fill it up with water. Not this time."

"You ought to get that fixed."

"I'll take that under advisement," said Odie.

Jake popped the last of the roll into his mouth and said while chewing, "Didn't nobody from the funeral procession offer you a ride?"

The kid said something under his breath while he added cream and lots of sugar to his coffee. He tasted it, then shook another spoonful or so into the cup.

"I didn't even like them boys that was killed," said Odie. "Classmates of mine. I only went because I figured some of the girls we went to school with would come in from out of town, and I could see who got fat and who stayed good looking. And this was my best suit, too."

He and the kid talked plenty, and Jake couldn't help feeling for him. He couldn't explain, but something affected him. To him, it was like looking through old photo albums, seeing shit which might cure something he didn't know needed curing. He saw someone in a fix, someone stuck, and he recalled it wasn't that long ago, he was in a similar situation.

His parole officer had been a fat guy, a seedy piece of shit. Thinned, greasy streaks of hair combed over a shiny pate. Bushy moustache. Licked his lips a lot. Did so several times when last Jake'd seen him.

That's when, after a stretch of nineteen years in the state prison, he'd been handed down his real sentence: A nine-to-five at an electrical parts warehouse in Knoxville, Tennessee.

"I know a guy," said the parole officer. Licked his lips. "He runs the place and he don't mind hiring you ex-cons. That is, until you miss work. Then he minds it quite a bit."

"One question," Jake had asked him, pointing a finger to the ceiling. "Does it got to be Knoxville?"

The parole officer looked at him a minute, then put both his meaty arms on the desk. "What's wrong with Knoxville?"

Jake hemmed and hawed, shifted his weight in the chair a bit, then said, "Everybody that's anybody knows there ain't no good barbecue in Knoxville. Now it's my understanding that when I get there and report to the halfway house, you folks won't be too keen on me getting out of town to stretch my legs a bit, am I right?"

"Damn skippy," said the fat man. "We don't want you so much as a foot outside Knox County, you know what's good for you."

"You can't find me nothing over in Shelby County?"

"That's clear over the other end of the state," said the parole officer. "What's so all-fired important about Memphis?"

"Man, I read about one joint they got over in Memphis that's been smoking hog since before Robert Johnson sold his soul." Just thinking about it gave Jake the fidgets. "Ribs, pulled pork . . . sauces both spicy and sweet. They got that kind of cole slaw that—"

The parole officer would have none of it. He punctuated his words by jabbing his finger onto the desktop. "There ain't no way I'm moving you clear across the state just so you can eat barbecue, you hear me? Knoxville is where you're going and Knoxville is where you'll stay. I'm sure if you look around some, you'll find suitable lunch plates out there."

Jake stared hate-fire at the wall across from him. Picture of a grinning fool President and some fella he could only imagine was the governor. They all had it in for him.

"I need you to understand something, Mister Armstrong," The parole officer licked his lips again. "The state of Tennessee recognizes you as a murderer. And they ain't none too happy about you getting out, but you did, and they expect you to behave a certain way. And that way is to keep your head down and to do it over in Knoxville. Stay put. Work your job. You understand me?"

Jake told him he understood him just fine, and when they finished up with things, Jake shook his hand and boarded the bus headed east. Somewhere along the way, at one of the stops, he got off and never got back on.

"There I was," he told Odie Shanks. They'd moved to a booth where Jake bought two slices of pie. "At some gas station washing a colored boy's Caddy for a five-spot. You see, my father was a railroad worker, and I guess I got some of that in me, because I have a hard time not moving around. I knew I couldn't never be what it was the parole board or the prison system wanted. I could only be what I was."

"You robbed that gas station, didn't you?" asked Odie.

"Yes, I did." Jake nodded. "I made out with sixty-three dollars from the till, a carton of smokes, and a full tank of gas in that colored boy's Caddy." He rubbed at the stump where the ring finger on his left hand used to be. "And I ain't never looked back."

Odie said nothing. He seemed to divine whether or not he was being bullshitted.

"What about you?" asked Jake.

"What about me?"

"There something you always wanted to do? Something you wished you could do but ain't never done?"

Odie shook his head.

"Nothing?" Jake took a bite of meringue. "I don't believe it for a second. Everybody's got a dream, even in a shit town like this."

"You'll laugh," said Odie.

"No I won't."

Odie pushed his pie plate away. "Sure you will. It's stupid."

"Let me be the judge of that."

Odie looked around the room, as if the old-timers and truck drivers gave half a shit about what the two of them said or did. He leaned forward, real close to Jake, and said in a low voice, "I always wanted to be a Hollywood actor. I always wanted to be in the movies."

Jake said nothing at first. Odie shifted this way and that in the bench seat and pretty soon, worked himself into a fury, then said, "See. I told you it was stupid."

"No," said Jake. He looked at the kid like he was something he had never before seen and, for all he knew, neither had anyone else. "I don't think that's stupid at all. In fact, I think that's about the coolest thing I've ever heard."

***

Jake remembered that. The way the kid looked when he told him he wanted to act in movies and be a big star, how he'd seemed so vulnerable and small. Much as the kid looked later, the next night when he came bounding around the pizza ovens and saw Jake, masked and armed, pointing his gun at the screaming woman who owned the joint. The kid threw up his hands and looked like he might throw up much more, given the chance.

"Don't try nothing funny, kid," said Jake. He moved the gun on him and prayed Odie was as good an actor as he claimed to be. "Stay right where you are. You don't plan on being no hero, do you?"

"No, sir," said Odie. "Take what you want, just don't hurt nobody."

Up to then, the boss lady had been some degree of composed, backed into the corner with her hands up about chest high. Never taking her eyes off Jake, she snapped.

"Hush up, Odie," she said. She raised a finger to Jake's face. "Listen here, when you're in my restaurant, it's me that tells you what you can and can't take."

Jake turned to face her, followed with the gun. Slowly. Pointed it between her eyes. He saw Odie flinch and look away.

"Fair enough, bitch," said Jake. "Then you can open the register and put the money in one of them to-go bags."

A shadow crossed her face. The skin around her eyes tightened until they were nothing but creased slits for her to peek through. Her jaw set. She took a step forward and said, "I don't know which of these mouth-breathing, white-trash inbreeds in this town raised you, but you don't dare call me a *bitch*. I came up in hard times with next to nothing in a world that didn't respect women. I carved out a business in a community that didn't want change, and I made them change, and made a good living. I am married to a *homosexual* and jog ten miles a day and don't take kindly to some common hood calling me a *bitch*."

"Not another step . . . *ma'am*," said Jake. He clicked back the hammer with his thumb. She had the good sense to stop, but Jake had no idea for how long. "I will decorate your lovely pizza ovens with those liberated brains of yours if you come any closer." He turned to Odie. "Kid, grab the cash out of the drawer and stuff it in those bags. Do it now."

Odie moved to the register. Maggie was on him like a skunk on a cricket, got between him and the drawer, then shoved him to the ground. She opened her mouth to say something ungodly, but Jake didn't waste time. He jammed the gun barrel to Maggie's temple. Hard. She quit talking so tough. Became more flexible.

"This could have been easy," said Jake. He wanted to tell her how if it weren't for the kid, she'd be a grease spot. Instead, he said, "When I die, I want to walk with Jesus. That's all I want. But I ain't going to get to walk with no Jesus if I keep calling people motherfucker and shooting women in the head, am I?"

Her answer came as a weakened, resigned squeak. She collapsed against the wall and didn't say nothing as Odie scooped up first the dollars, then the coins from the register and slipped them all in a to-go sack. Once finished, Jake asked did they have a cooler.

"Beg pardon?"

"A cooler. A walk-in. Some place you put stuff you want kept on ice."

"Yes, sir," he answered. "In back."

"Let's walk old Maggie's Pizza Pick-Up back there, get her locked up good and tight," said Jake. He motioned with the gun like there wouldn't be any arguments and so none were made, and the three of them stepped to the back of the restaurant. Jake directed her inside the cooler.

"What about him?" she asked.

"He's coming with me," said Jake.

"That's not necessary. Leave him with me."

Jake shook his head. "If it's all the same, you've thrown enough monkeys in my wrench. You wrangle your way out of this here cooler and, for all I know, you'll make things sticky for me during my getaway. No, I think I'll need some leverage."

"That's ridiculous," said Maggie. "You'll only make things worse for yourself with a hostage."

"Good thing I got the gun then, ain't it?" said Jake. "Step inside."

She did so. She turned to Jake and looked him dead in the eye. "Run," she told him. "Do me that favor. I want you to run because I will have fun searching every trailer park in this county. I will burn every shithole bar. I will be in and out of every welfare office, and when I find you, I swear—"

"Close the door, kid," said Jake. For the first time that night, someone obeyed him immediately, and once Odie had engaged the lock, Jake ripped off the ski mask and said, "That one's rougher than you said."

"She'll freeze in there," said Odie.

"She'll be fine," said Jake. "She's got enough hate burning to cook a chicken. Besides, she should be the least of your worries right now."

"She is." Odie sighed. "You really think you're going to pull this off?"

"I don't see why not," said Jake. He stuffed the ski mask into his pocket and waited for Odie to collect his other shoe, slip into it. "Don't puss out on me now, kid. This was all your big idea."

3

B ack before he went away to prison, Jake lived with a guy by the name of Rob Winchester. The two of them were in the weed business together. Primarily, they kept the street-level guys happy and rarely carried quantity that could make things federal, but every once in a while Butchie would call in a favor. Butchie was the guy who sold them the shit they sold to other people. Sometimes Butchie needed a driver, someone to travel out of town and haul back the shit. While Jake and Rob both appreciated several levels between them and the Mexicans, the extra cash could be nice. On occasion, they would make the drive.

This one time, they drove to south of Dallas. He and Rob laid low in a fleabag motel, just down 67, in a little town called Cleburne, to wait for the guy to call them. The guy was a man named Chicken Bone and, despite his name, was very serious. He didn't like to smile and resented anyone who tried to make him. Chicken Bone ran the lines between Memphis and Nashville and had ambition, so folks had a pretty good idea he wouldn't be doing that for long. Chicken Bone was what you'd call a 'can-do' guy. Shit went dry in Memphis, and he said no problem, let me find someone else who can get it for you. Hence, Rob and Jake's little drive south of Dallas.

This was the 90s. The best way to get a hold of folks back then was a system involving beepers and payphones which, Rob argued, could be managed from anywhere, especially outside the confines of a seedy, shag-carpeted motel room down in Cleburne. He suggested while they waited, to take a drive to blow off some steam. Maybe have some drinks, hunt up some pussy, or raise a ruckus.

They found a Holiday Inn up the highway in a little place called Duncanville. Rob chatted up damn near every girl he could, but finding nobody by last call, resigned himself to the long ride back to the motel. They had a nice buzz on and thought it wise to stop at the first place to grab something to eat for the drive, something to help get their heads back in the game.

They chose a grocery store just off the highway. Maybe it was the cocktails, maybe it was the fresh air. Hell, maybe it was just being in a town where didn't nobody know them, so they felt a bit festive, like being on a vacation of sorts. Maybe it was all of that, but more than likely, it was the joint they smoked before walking into the grocery store that got them laughing and feeling good and falling into each other as they walked up first this aisle then that one, never able to settle on anything to buy.

Rob had a time with it, as he was known to do. He shook boxes of Macaroni and Cheese like they were Mexican *maracas* and held the kielbasa at about groin-level and gesticulated. He ran from one side of the produce aisle to the other, sliding some on his knees and nearly taking out a display of avocados. Jake, being of sounder mind and body, thought it best if they vacated the premises before someone got antsy.

That's when things got hairy. They hadn't taken all of three steps out of the grocery store when three corn-fed Texans in smocks and aprons surrounded them. Formed a ring. Behind them stood a smaller fella who Jake could only assume was the manager. Backed by his army of burly beef-eaters, the manager pointed a finger to below Rob's mid-section and said, "Let me see it."

Again, the two of them had made quite a night of it. Rob couldn't divine if it was time to laugh or act indignant, so instead he simply asked, "See what?"

"I want to see the meat," said the manager. He jabbed at the air with a finger pointed toward Rob's belt. "Take the meat out of your pants."

"Beg pardon?"

The three Texas boys closed the circle in around them.

"Take the sausage out of your pants now, boy," said the manager, "or I'll have them take it out for you."

Jake wanted to tackle Rob. He wanted to throw him to the ground and stop him from doing what he knew Rob wanted to do, which was fetch out a laugh. Jake reckoned something broken in Rob, because the man would chase a laugh even though there weren't one to be chased. Sometimes Jake could stop it in time; sometimes he couldn't.

There in the parking lot of that Duncanville Minyard's was one of the instances Jake couldn't get there in time. Rob, laughing like a deranged child, thumbed open his belt and pants and exposed his self to those beefy boys from the grocery store. He pivoted himself this way and that, just to make sure each of them got a good look at it, the manager too. Even asked if any of them would like to give it a kiss.

Turned out it was all a misunderstanding. The boys from the Minyard's thought Rob and Jake were two fellas jacking product from the meat market. They thought Rob had slipped that kielbasa down his pants, and that he aimed to make off with it. But misunderstanding or not, it's best not to show off your pecker to a Texas redneck, because next thing they knew, both Jake and Rob had their asses kicked and were booked in the Duncanville jail.

"And then what happened?" asked Odie.

Rob looked at him sideways. You see, nineteen years passed and while Jake went to prison, Rob went to the bottle. His sense of humor was first to go.

"What do you mean, *then what happened*?" Rob eyed the kid sideways. "We went to jail, then we got out. That's what happened."

Jake cut in. "Chicken Bone heard tell where we were and came to bail us out. He gave us an earful, man. Then he called Butchie back in Nashville and gave it to him, said he shouldn't be sending a pair of clowns to Texas to pick up his weed."

Jake got more of a kick out of the trip down memory lane than his buddy Rob. Rob didn't look to be the kind of guy getting many kicks any more. When they arrived at his door late that Sunday afternoon, Odie's first thought was this didn't look nothing like the fella Jake had described. Years of drinking had sent him to shit.

"You going to invite us in, Rob?"

Rob looked the both of them over. "I'm a married man now, Jake," he said. "I can't afford to go bringing up old troubles."

"No troubles, Rob." Jake turned back to Odie and winked. "I'm just passing through is all. Me and the kid here are driving out to Hollywood. Figured you could help me with something."

Rob held open the door a little wider and stepped aside. Nearly tripped over his own bathrobe. They entered. Jake whistled low. The place was a shambles. Ashtrays needed emptying. He could fill a trash bag with beer cans. The air smelled of cat piss, despite nobody having so much as seen evidence of a cat.

"I thought you said you was married," said Jake.

"I didn't say she lived here no more," Rob answered. He closed the door behind them. Slowly he walked to a hutch with broken hinges. He pulled free the liquor cabinet door and set it on the rug at his feet.

He had a half-dozen bottles of this or that, and he retrieved something brown. "Can I get you fellas something to drink?"

Jake shook his head, told him no thank you. He looked to Odie, encouraging him to do the same. Rob nodded and made to help himself, then stopped. Indecision tinkered with him until he finally shook his head and poured a couple fingers into a small, cloudy glass. He held it just shy of his lips and, for the first time since they'd stepped inside, looked Jake in the eye.

"So what gives, Jake?"

"Just come to see an old friend is all."

Rob swallowed that drink. All of it, then said, "You do what you got to do. Whatever you think is right. I reckon you've had time to settle on that." He helped himself to another.

"I come to see about a car." Jake came around from the window, used a finger to nudge back the curtain and have a peek outside.

Odie wondered when Jake had slipped on those black, leather gloves. "The one I've been driving is nice, but I stole it off a lot way back in West Virginia. Figured it's high time to trade it in, get something a little more my style. Something still has a tape deck, maybe."

"I see." Rob sounded tired and weary. He sloshed a bit of the bourbon as he crossed the room and collapsed into the easy chair. "That all you came for? A car? After all this time?"

"Way I remember it," said Jake, "is couldn't nobody rustle up something like my old roommate Rob Winchester. I told Odie some stories the whole way here to Columbia. About the time it was Sunday and all the liquor stores was closed, but them girls wanted rum to hang out with us, and low and behold you got your grubbies on a couple bottles of rum. Or Percocets, whatever."

Rob lazily rolled his eyes over to Odie and said, "And who is this new friend of yours?"

"My new partner," said Jake.

Rob poured a little more into his tumbler, then held it up in the air. "That's nice," he said, in mock toast. He swallowed it down. "Partners is nice."

"You got to trust somebody," said Jake. A cat couldn't have been quieter than Jake walking across the living room, coming up behind the chair Rob sat in. Lowering himself to just below Rob's ear. Whispering, "And if you can't trust a partner . . ."

Rob closed his eyes. The hand holding the whiskey bottle shook a bit. Then it calmed. All of Rob calmed. As if something that had scared him shitless his entire life turned out to be far less terrible than he'd imagined. Or maybe he was right all along, and it was just as terrible, but at this point so little could actually be done, and that put him at an odd sense of ease. His shoulders pulled back. His chest sucked as much air as it could hold. His lips parted.

Time, and everyone in that dusty den, held their breath.

Then slowly, they could hear the clock ticking from the kitchen. A car outside and down the road, honking at one thing or another. A crow laughing at some cosmic joke only it had been let in on and eventually, the sounds of each of them exhaling, inhaling. Rob opened his eyes.

"If you ain't here to kill me," said Rob, "then what exactly did you come here for?"

Jake leaned against the wall. He slipped the .38 around behind him, put it away under his shirt. He tilted his head to the ceiling and studied constellations in the textured, popcorn finish.

"Like I said, old friend: I come to see about a new car."

"And your partner here?"

Jake nodded to Odie. "Him? What about him?"

"What is it he wants?"

Odie squared his shoulders, suddenly realizing it was him being talked about. He'd let himself become a touch distracted by the undercurrents and tension in the room. He noticed the both of them waiting for his answer, and he found himself able to do little more than quiver his lower lip.

"Didn't I tell you we was driving out to Hollywood?" Jake smiled. "Odie here . . . all he wants is to be a movie star."

4

It was a truck stop, one of the newer-fangled ones, complete with a convenience store stocked with all anyone could ever need, a few shower stalls in the back, some payphones, and a little diner. The diner couldn't offer much more than coffee and whatever could be slapped on a flat-top grill, but nobody should be looking for much more than that at a truck stop on a Sunday afternoon.

Apparently nobody ever told that to Jake Armstrong.

The waitress placed coffees in front of him, Odie, and Rob Winchester, then set the sugar caddy and tin of cream at the center of the table. She shook a pad of tickets from her apron and held her pen at the ready. She never saw it coming.

"What you got back there that's fresh-made?" Jake asked her.

"It's Sunday afternoon," she said. "Ain't nothing fresh-made."

Jake pursed his lips and nodded. "Fair enough. You got hamburgers, right?"

She nodded.

"You make those here or do they come frozen? In a box?"

"The meat gets shipped to us," she said. "Darryl, in the daytime, makes them into patties."

"He freeze them?"

"No," she said. A trucker a few booths up waved his empty coffee mug, but she kept eyes up front. "We can't keep them in stock long enough. Hamburgers is popular."

"Perfect," said Jake. "I'll take one of them."

"How you want it cooked?" she asked.

"Bloody to rare. Just brown it up if you don't mind."

"North Carolina law says we got to cook it well to medium well."

He massaged the bridge of his nose with his thumb and forefinger. "I break laws for breakfast, baby. How about if I promise not to tell nobody."

"Can't do it. State law." She scribbled something on her pad of tickets and looked sideways at him. "So how you want it cooked?"

"What the hell does it matter how I want it cooked if it only comes well or medium well?"

She shook her head. "Because Hank on the grill back there wants to know how he's supposed to cook your burger."

"There ain't no difference," snarled Jake. He looked at Odie and Rob and bared teeth. "Well or medium well."

She glanced around the room. More than one of the truckers and other folks had eyes their way. Odie twirled an eddy in his coffee with his forefinger.

"Are y'all going to order something to eat or what?"

"I'll have a burger," said Rob. "Medium well."

"Same for me," said Odie. "But make mine well."

Jake tossed his plastic menu on the table. "I ain't hungry," he said. "Just the coffee is fine."

The waitress muttered something sounded like 'don't need this shit' and toddled off with the coffee pot to tend to other folks.

Rob had been somewhat sour since leaving the house. More than once, Odie thought being away from the dingy domicile would cheer the man. So far, it had yet to dent his demeanor. He slouched and sighed and gave nary a shit to anything in his direction, unless it was repeated. He'd especially taken an interest in Odie and what the hell he was doing with his former roommate.

"Hollywood, huh?" said Rob once the burgers came. "I think that's a big mistake."

"How's that?" said Jake.

Rob shrugged, took a bite of his sandwich. Didn't wait to swallow before speaking. "I mean, I can see it maybe a couple years back, but that hen done flown the coop. Your best-looking years are well in the rearview. And you're too old to start an acting career. Maybe consider being a writer. Writers don't have to be good-looking."

"I can't write worth a lick," said Odie.

"Best I can tell, that don't matter neither in Hollywood."

Jake put both hands on the table. "Quit ribbing the kid," he said. "Me and him have plenty of miles between us and California and I'd prefer him in good spirits, if it's all the same."

"What the hell does O.D. stand for anyway?"

"It ain't *O.D.*," said Odie, his voice gaining volume. "It's *Odie*, like the dog in the comic strip."

Rob's eyes arched up, well into his hairline. He popped a fry into his mouth and leaned back in the booth. Odie's face burned bright, but he said nothing more, for he'd recriminated himself plenty.

"What time's this guy of yours coming?" Jake looked at his watch, then looked this way and that. Outside, a semi pulled up to one of the tanks and the air filled with the clanks and whirrs and other cacophony with which those things were associated. Inside was quiet, except for the waitress, laughing in the kitchen.

"Directly," Rob said. He rose a finger to Jake. "You got to toughen this guy up. He's going to have to take a lot more than a good-natured ribbing if he's going to ride with you, right Jake?"

Jake finished his coffee and craned his neck, searching for that waitress.

"Guy's got to have thick skin. That's all I'm saying."

Odie spoke up. "I ain't a pussy, if that's what you're driving at."

"Sure you ain't." Rob did his level-best to keep his voice down, on account of the other folks in the diner. "No, you're a hardened felon with an itchy trigger finger and shit taste in music. Oh wait, that's not you. That's the other guy. You're the baby-faced pizza manager with . . . Remind me again, what kind of gun are you carrying?"

"Kenner toys."

"My point exactly." He turned to Jake. "This ain't 1996, Jake. You can't climb inside a time machine and go back there again. It's over, man. You grow up and move on. It's been nineteen years. You should know better than anybody."

"I do."

"Then act like it." Rob leaned forward, well into Jake's side of the table. The light caught him right, and Odie saw how much older he looked than Jake. "You come blowing into town with some kid, saying you need a car so you can rob gas stations clear to California. You ain't aged a day."

"Guess I got more sleep than you did over the years."

The waitress dropped by and refilled coffees. After she was gone, Rob said, "I slept plenty, Jake. I slept like a goddamn baby. I did so the night you went up the river, and to be honest, it was the first time I slept so well in years. I've done so every night since."

"You sure don't look it."

"Go fuck yourself," whispered Rob. "I done what I did, and I'd do it again. And you listen up good. If I hadn't done it, you'd be dead right now, so yes sir, I sleep just fine, and I'll sleep even better when you finally man up and say *thank you*."

Jake chuckled to himself. He wiped at the tip of his nose, and Odie once again made note of the missing ring finger on the man's hand. Jake's other hand sank below the table, and Odie wondered was he getting after that .38 or just scratching his belly and thought to say something about it just to make sure, when suddenly Rob's phone rang.

"That will be your car," said Rob. He fished the phone from his jeans and flipped it open. Odie never took his eyes off it. Rob half-turned in the booth so that his back was to the others. He spoke in a low voice and kept it short. He took the phone away from his ear, flipped it shut and destined it soon for his pocket, when Odie reached a hand across the formica and touched his elbow.

"That phone you got there," he said soft and meek. "Does it have Internet on it?"

"Yeah, why?"

Odie's eyes went puppy-dog and his breath stuttered some. "You think maybe I can take a look at it, just for a minute?"

"Knock yourself out," said Rob. He slid the phone across the table, then climbed out of the booth. "Your car is here. If you don't mind, I'm going to take care of this business."

"Make sure it's got cruise control," Jake called after him. Jake watched him cross the length of the diner floor, pass through the convenience store, and step out into the parking lot. Next to him in the booth, he found Odie scrolling across the screen of Rob's phone. "What are you doing?"

"Checking my email," he said.

Jake slapped the phone from his hand. "The hell you are," he said. He poked at the phone with his coffee spoon until it was good and on the other side of the table. "Do I need remind you that folks should be operating under the assumption that you were kidnapped? That both you and a sum of cash were liberated from that pizza restaurant back in your home town, both against their will?"

"About that . . ." Odie looked at the phone a moment, then up at Jake. "How come there ain't no news stories about the kidnapping? I mean, you'd think there'd be some sort of ruckus over something like that, wouldn't you?"

Jake shrugged. "Not necessarily. The whole thing went down pretty late, and I reckon it would be even later before anybody went rooting around in that cooler to let out that old lady boss of yours. No, I'd say we bought ourselves a considerable head start, so don't get your panties bunched and damn sure don't go checking your email. It's best if folks just forgot about—What the bloody hell?"

Jake dropped his spoon and jerked not only Odie but the whole damn diner into the direction of his angry gaze.

Outside the wall of plate glass, out in the parking lot, Rob Winchester chatted it up with a black fella, one with a do-rag on his head and his britches half-off his ass. The guy was tall and lanky and wore a plain white tee hanging down to about where his belt should be. They did a series of tribal hand gestures, palms slapping and fists bumping, and Jake swore he saw the guy slip Rob a set of keys.

"I'll be goddamned . . ."

He lifted himself from the table with a pair of dropped fists that further aided the clamor. He'd barely gotten so much as his ass from the booth bench, when Odie grabbed his shoulder and helped him back to his seat.

"What's gotten into you?" he hissed. He looked this way and that at the other diners, all of whom in the same boat, wondering exactly what gave.

"You can't tell me it's gotten that bad." Jake shook his head. "I mean, I could tell, you know, by standing around at his place that things had gone to shit, but I had no idea that—"

"I don't get what's eating you," said Odie. "Ain't he getting us a stolen car?"

"Sure he is, but take note of where he's getting it."

Odie looked back to the parking lot. Rob said something to the guy, and the guy laughed. Odie said to Jake, "I don't understand."

"Look, it's one thing to elect one of them president, but it's entirely another to—"

"Whoa whoa whoa whoa . . ." Odie couldn't silence him quick enough. He looked around the room, but needn't bother. South Carolina still considered itself occupied territory, and the other patrons appeared to have similar concerns. "You ain't serious, are you?"

"If you've seen what I seen, then you'd—" Odie still didn't care to hear him out. He put up a hand. "Look, man. I know prison has encased you in amber, but the world has changed since '96. You can't go carrying on like that anymore."

"I beg your pardon, but before I went inside, it was a free country." Jake spoke more to the table than to Odie. To the salt shakers. To the forks and spoons. "I can and will say what I choose." He crossed his arms. "I worked with them before. It's a bunch of watching your own back because the second you turn it, they stick you. All about cheating each other and calling names. Turning your gun sideways. No thank you."

Odie's mouth hung open, and his attempt to muster forth words proved an utter failure. He was stuck much as so when Rob returned and dropped the set of keys to the table. He felt as if he'd wandered into the middle of something and looked to both their faces as to ascertain just what. He stood there a bit, never taking his seat, waiting for one of them to speak.

"That about does it, right?" he finally said. "Maybe we should move along, now that you've got your car."

Jake held out long as he could, then turned to his friend from days long gone. He opened his mouth to speak, but was interrupted by the timely arrival of the waitress.

"That going to be all for you, fellas?" she asked, check already in hand.

Rob nodded yes ma'am, followed by Odie. Jake, on the other hand, was far from done. He turned his head to the woman and asked her if she had any good pies.

"Pies?" she asked.

"Yeah, pies."

She thought a moment. "We got a cobbler. Peach. We're fresh out of ice cream, though."

"Who made the cobbler?" asked Jake.

"My momma," said the waitress. "She works in the kitchen in the mornings, cashier in the evenings."

"She make it today?"

"Yesterday, sir."

Jake closed his eyes a second, then opened them real slow and reverent. "May I please have some of your cobbler?"

"Just the one?" She looked to the others at the table. Rob shook his head and she was off.

"What was you going to say, Jake?" Rob sighed. He realized this little excursion down memory lane still had a ways to go, so he dropped himself back inside the booth and got comfortable again.

The waitress returned and slipped a piping hot bowl of cobbler before Jake. He lowered his head and took in the smell. Generous chunks of peaches, oat-strewn topping, sugary steam wafting from just below his nose . . . Jake closed his eyes and picked up his spoon with a trembling hand.

"Jake?"

Jake took a bite, and with a full mouth said, "It don't matter, Rob. I don't reckon it matters at all."

"What don't?"

"You ever had a frozen cobbler?" Jake asked Rob across the table. Rob said nothing. "Trust me, you can't imagine a frozen cobbler to taste good. You get off a desert island, and someone offers you frozen cobbler, you best ask to be set back on that island."

Odie and Rob both settled in and let Jake enjoy his cobbler in silence, both of them well aware—despite the great chasm in time either had gotten to know the man—that silences were few and far between. And for that reason, they too enjoyed his cobbler though they took nary a bite.

5

To hear Rob Winchester tell it, he reckoned that day Jake dropped in to be about the lowest point of his life, second only to the last time he'd seen him. That one night, nineteen years earlier and well after dark. The moon barely a crescent shattered in the ripples of little Lake Watauga. Nobody nowhere to be found in all of Centennial Park's darkest nooks and crannies, save for them.

Them was Rob himself and two folks much like him. Also guys who knew Jake well enough to spot him in the dark. Unlike him, more likely to squeeze off a shot soon after he'd step out of the shadows, hopefully before giving him the chance to do the same. Rob shivered, despite the mercury hanging high into the sixties.

That night, he'd wanted to be anywhere rather than where he was. He'd done all he could to keep from it. Twice Butchie had approached him and twice Rob had told him to go fuck himself. The second time even, Butchie'd showing with his left arm in a sling and face good and bandaged. That second time, bringing two friends with him, the smaller popping open a blade to rest just below Rob's chin.

"I had a date with me," Rob later told Danny Yeager. "I finally got that girl from Gallatin to agree to go out with me. You know how she said she'd never date no thug, and I told her over and over I weren't no thug, and I even brought flowers to prove it. Took her to that steak and spaghetti joint and then to a movie instead of one of them honkytonks down on Broadway, like where I take the others. And then comes Butchie with those two guys and now I can't get her to pick up the phone."

Danny Yeager was a guy who knew nothing of girls not picking up the phone. He was incredibly tanned for a man in a state so landlocked. He wore penny loafers, but never any socks. Hair forever blond. To him, all of life was a breeze; those smile-lines were too deep set to say anything else.

But Danny Yeager did not picture himself forever selling little baggies of coke to undergrads. No, he was an up-and-comer, and Butchie didn't need to ask him twice or bring around a couple of other fellas. Sure he'd been friends with Jake, but there were other currencies Danny Yeager valued above friendship and, as he slipped shells into his shotgun, he counted those currencies on two hands.

He was the one who'd brought along Eyeball McBreen. If Danny, Rob, and Jake were small-time, Eyeball McBreen was smaller-time, just a kid who liked weed more than he liked attending class at Vanderbilt and soon found that to no longer present a conflict. A kid of about nineteen who only darkened doors on campus to sling shit for either Danny or Rob and had a good time doing so. Eyeball got his name because one of his rolled a little wacky, due to a car accident, when he was but a child. He now approached a time in life where he needed to find a calling, and Danny offered him a suggestion.

"You and me will lie in wait while Rob draws him out," Danny explained to Eyeball. "Rob's the only one he trusts. Can't nobody else draw him out, and once we're sure it's him . . ."

"I don't like having anything to do with this," Rob told them both.

"I told you we got very little choice," said Danny Yeager. "Jake done this to all of us. Hell, Jake done this to all of Nashville, when he rode out to Memphis and shot Chicken Bone and his boys. Thanks to him, all of Davidson county has run dry. He didn't ask none of us if we wanted to be dragged into the middle of this. You reckoned he gave you or me or Eyeball here a single consideration, when he drove those two hundred miles down Forty, or even the three hours back? No, I reckon he didn't."

Still, Rob had his reasons. For one, he and Jake were friends. For another, Rob never reckoned himself someone who would kill a guy or even flush out a guy to be killed, nevertheless a friend. But Danny shot down each and every excuse Rob offered and did so each and every time it was offered. Danny wasn't known to bullshit, but was more likely to 'offer dialogue'. He spoke of words like *synergy* and *best possible outcomes*. Often, with arguments, he was prone to provide photographic evidence, but this time laid it out plain and simple. "They're going to get Jake for what he did," he said. "With or without us. It's best if we're on the right side of history in this matter."

Rob told himself as much all that night, standing in the darkness of Centennial Park. The profile of the Parthenon just up the hill before him. And out of that profile came a silhouette, and that silhouette was Jake Armstrong. Behind him, he heard Danny Yeager shushing Eyeball, heard the sound of him racking the shotgun. Rob closed his eyes tight and hoped when he opened them, he was anywhere in the world but where he was.

Jake's memory of that night ran slightly counter. It wasn't Danny's face he saw waiting for him in the darkness, nor was it Eyeball's. Rather, he saw Rob standing just out of the yellow-hued pool of light cast down by yonder lamppost, saw that even in the shadows his expression soured, tense. Rob moved jerky, slurred his speech as if maybe he'd needed to drink up a little courage. Jake was far from relaxed after he laid eyes on his long time buddy.

Jake remembering the phone call; Rob on the other end saying they needed to get together. Rob could work something out. Jake saying he couldn't hide any longer, he needed to get out of town. He needed money, and he needed a ride, and he needed a place to get to. and even somewhere to stay once he got there. Rob told him he'd handle it.

Jake, over the course of nineteen years, could look back on that night and see where he might have gone wrong. Missed some signs. Zigged when he damned well should have zagged. Should have asked himself how Rob suddenly had connections to get him out of town. Should have asked himself why they were meeting over in Centennial and in the dark. Most of all, should have wondered why Rob didn't joke around, like he was known to do, or had been drinking heavy, which he wasn't.

But no, that night he didn't think any of those things, was just happy to hear his friend's voice, to see his face. Happy with the promise of this whole thing going away. Since Jake lacked the power to go back and unkill the people he'd killed, he'd have to settle for getting the hell out of town and, at that moment, he was more than happy to do so. He stretched out both his arms and moved in on his friend for a hug.

"Stay where you are, Jake," Rob told him. Jake never heard that tone in his friend's voice before. He stopped dead in his tracks. "Just . . . just don't move."

Jake looked this way and that. A cool breeze moved through a set of shade trees over yonder and the rustle sounded too much like rattlesnakes for Jake to be calm. That was the moment he knew he was fucked. He didn't know it then, but he had plenty of time to know it later.

"Who got to you?" asked Jake.

Rob said, "Either way, somebody's feelings are getting hurt. And hell, Jake, Memphis has got way bigger guns than you, so that's the choice I got to make."

"You sound like Danny Yeager." The gun in Jake's waistband never felt so heavy. He'd never get to it in time.

"Funny you should mention that," said Rob. "Because he's right over—"

Rob might or might not have finished what he was saying, because that's when things got noisy and drowned him right out. His lips moved, but all Jake heard was sirens and hollering and tires screeching. Somewhere beyond the poplars *whup-whupped* a helicopter, and it wasn't long before that white hot beam fingered him from the sky.

Voice through a bullhorn said, "Jacob Armstrong, lift high your hands or you will be shot." Voice said it one or two more times, which turned out to be oddly necessary.

Jake remembered it being very important to him that Rob see just how he felt. No sneer, no smile, no simple roll of the eyes would ever do as far as Jake was concerned. If given his druthers, Jake would fly forth, wrapping both hands around Rob's throat and squeezing until his fingertips touched, but he knew he'd get no further than two steps before the coppers cut him in half. No, he'd have only his eyes for damage, and he spent every night for nineteen years wondering if he'd done himself justice.

And finally he could say to hell with that night nineteen years ago and all the nights after where he'd practiced and plotted and regretted everything he'd done and hadn't done, because here before him stood Rob Winchester, his friend of many years who'd taken sides against him, and now had nary a gun in his hand. The look on Jake's face spoke volumes, but it was Rob's that Jake would forever remember. It was Rob's turn to suck shit.

But Odie could have known none of this yet, so all the history and nuance and subtext were shelved as he watched the scene unfold before him. Rob, not bothering to turn on the lights as he pushed open his front door and trampled the carpet to that busted hutch of his. He again pulled free the cabinet door, and this time didn't set it gently at his feet but dropped it and stabbed his hand inside. He moved perhaps a bit too quick, because Jake had his gun on him and jabbed into the back of his head. That's how they stood when Odie first entered the house.

"Not another inch, old friend," said Jake. "You think I'm stupid?"

Rob stopped just shy of the bottle of brown, his hand frozen in mid-air. Rob's head committed the slightest of nods—just to the left—so as to say to his buddy, "Regardless of my answer, I'm reaching for this booze. I ain't stopping until it's good and inside me. Keep that in mind while you reckon on whether or not to pull that trigger."

Rob grabbed the neck of the whiskey bottle and turned it up into his mouth. First one, then two gulps and then another for good measure.

Jake lowered the .38, but didn't dare put it away.

"Some things can't be forgiven," said Rob. He held the bottle just beneath his nose. "That's the way, isn't it, Jake?"

"Nineteen years," he answered. He repeated it.

Rob took another drink.

Odie realized he'd stopped in mid-step, his foot still dangling an inch above the flattened shag. He set that foot down, but made not another movement. He felt fool standing there with his mouth open wide but feared he'd catch hell if he shut it.

"It was you, tipped off the cops," said Jake. He kept the revolver at his waist, pointed down.

"Yeah," said Rob. "It was me."

"And you know you got to pay for that, don't you."

"I've always known," said Rob. "And I've always paid for it."

"And you're okay with this?"

Rob set the bottle back into the cabinet but didn't remove his hand just yet. "I am now," he said.

Jake nodded. His finger eased itself into the trigger guard.

Odie took a step into the room, kept a good bit of wall between him and the action. Wondered if Jake saw him, maybe would he cool down some. Wondered if that should even be what he wanted.

"Why did you do it?" Jake asked.

"Not that it matters," said Rob, "but if I didn't, you'd be dead."

"Oh?" Jake spoke through his teeth. "And what makes you so sure of that?"

Rob's hand left the liquor bottle. He brought up his eyes to his old friend. They'd gone watery, more from drink than despair, but he held them fast at Jake. "I know it," he said, "because we was coming to kill you."

Jake's gun hand trembled, but everything else cooled. Rob left the liquor cabinet and rounded a ratty old couch which he fell into. Crushed an aluminum can somewhere deep within a cushion. He stared at the wall across from him.

Jake stepped up behind him, stood at the back of his head.

For a second, Odie half-thought he'd reach out and stroke his old friend's hair. Maybe pat him on the shoulder. The other half readied itself for something much, much worse.

"I am sorry," said Rob. "You have no idea. But I called the police and made sure they got to you well before we did."

"Nineteen years," said Jake.

Rob nodded.

"Nineteen in a cage," said Jake.

"You ain't been the only one."

Jake turned his head to his left shoulder. "Odie, why don't you run on out to the car? Wait for me there?"

"Nuh-uh," said Odie. "Why don't we both go? We got a lot of ground to cover."

"That's right." Rob closed his eyes and smiled. "To Hollywood, remember?"

"Odie," said Jake, "I ain't going to tell you again."

Rob said, "Yes, Odie. Listen to your partner. *Partner.*"

"Word means something different to each person, turns out."

"I reckon it does," said Rob. "I wonder what partners meant to Nick Fuller."

Jake rose higher the gun. He didn't point it at Rob, but it was up all the same. Maybe he meant to strike at the back of Rob's head, a blow that would shut him up and drop him to the floor, but leave him alive. Or perhaps it was to put a couple rounds into the ceiling, but rather he simply held it up, suspended at just about Rob's ear.

The entire time, Odie didn't so much as suck a breath.

Jake turned to the liquor cabinet. This time it was he who picked up the bourbon bottle, but not to drink. No, rather he scooted it aside and there, behind a variety of candied cordials, he retrieved a gun, a 9mm. Jake checked the chamber for bullets and set it on the back of Rob's couch, no more than an inch from his head.

"I will turn my back on you," said Jake. "And it will be for the last time, you son of a bitch."

Rob didn't so much as move. He said he understood. He got it.

"Let's go, Odie," said Jake. He brushed past him as he walked briskly to the door. He hesitated before cracking it open. Stood with his back to both of them.

"I left you something," said Rob. "I hope it helps with whatever you have to do."

Jake opened the door and slipped into the night with Odie right behind. Odie had to trot to keep up with Jake, and no sooner were they at their new ride before they heard the gunshot. Odie, caught off guard, first dropped to his knees and threw up his hands. No, that report came from the house and had not been fired upon them, and he hopped quick to his feet, charging toward the door when Jake caught him by the arm.

"It's time to go, Odie," he said. His grip had no give. "Hollywood is waiting for you."

Jake's eyes said a lot of things. They said he wasn't getting back into Rob's house. They told him if he was going anywhere at all, it was into the passenger seat of that Hyundai. They told him Jake gave nary a shit any longer about what Rob did or got away with or pulled over on him, and he'd now closed this chapter. Odie quit struggling and let his arm go slack in Jake's hand. Jake let go and rounded the car, jingling the keys.

On the dash was an envelope. By the time Odie slipped into the passenger's seat, Jake had ripped it open and yanked free a sheet of paper. He read it, then leaned forward as he stuffed it into his back pocket. He started the car.

Odie asked, "What is it?"

"It's an address," Jake said.

"Who's address?"

Jake eased the car from the curb and got them back on the road.

"An old friend," he said. "One we're going to look up and go see."

6

In Odie's mind, nothing perked a heavy heart quite like a pretty girl, and that's exactly what he had sitting in front of him. A blondie. Curls. Sunny cheeks and disposition to match. All that plus a ring on her danger finger, winking like a highway hazard. Odie collected the change from the fifty and his soda bottle, then sidled up next to her and her friend.

Her friend was much more down-to-earth. A girl who needed that chili dog like she needed a hole in her head. She stopped chewing and—without swallowing—demanded to know what Odie thought he was up to.

"Keep working on your lunch," said Odie. "I just want to have a word with your friend here."

The pretty girl sitting in back of the gas station and snacking on a paper tray piled high with nachos from the kitchen, blushed. The old lady at the register watched him with a wary eye, perhaps used to fellas sniffing around a girl such as that. Odie considered the ring again, then fancied it best ignored from there on out.

"What's your name?" he asked her.

"Kara," she said. She smiled back. "What's yours?"

"Odie," he answered.

"What kind of name is Odie?" asked the fat girl.

Odie turned to her and said, "You going to eat them fries?"

She harrumphed and sat back in her chair, squeezed her phone from a pocket in her jeans. Typed something with her thumbs. Odie's eyes lit up.

"Will you take a picture of me and your friend?" he asked the fat girl. He scooched closer to the blonde and slipped an arm around her dainty shoulders.

"You're a bad man, Odie," said the blonde.

"And I bet you've made a lot of poets' pens run dry," he said, back at her.

About that time, in walked Jake Armstrong. More than a little miffed because Odie never went to the door to give a signal. He saw Odie there with the girl and knew right away what was what. His lips curled into a tight sneer, and he liked to have changed his mind about where to point the gun.

"You forget something?" he called across the room.

Odie turned and arched his brows. "Sorry," he called back. "But it's all in there. Plenty of bills, just the way you like it."

Jake liked to have exploded. He puffed his cheeks and balled his hands to fists. The lady behind the counter never moved. She watched Jake as if she knew it was coming, didn't want to miss it. Odie reached out and put his hand on the girl's. Rather than scream, Jake yanked the gun from his waistband instead. He stuck it in the woman's face.

"Money. All of it. Bag."

She got right to work.

It wasn't until later that Jake gave him the business. He'd said nothing between the gas station parking lot and the brisk drive through town, but no sooner had they hit the feeder road onto the Interstate than Jake launched into him, pounding the steering wheel for emphasis.

"You can't clown around when we're doing these jobs," said Jake. "I want you down with this before you find yourself on the wrong end of a gun."

"Can I ask how much you got from that register back there?" Odie asked.

Jake looked sideways and answered, "Seventy-four bucks and a carton of Parliaments."

Odie turned in his seat, smile smug and secure.

Jake drove a bit, then turned and asked what that had to do with the price of grits in Georgia. Odie answered by holding out his palm. There sat the girl's phone, setting next to a scrap of paper.

"What the hell is that?" asked Jake.

"Her phone number," answered Odie.

"Not that," hissed Jake. He nodded and said, "*That*."

"It's a phone," said Odie.

"I know what it is. I want to know what you're doing with it."

Odie grumbled. "Figured maybe I'd check my Facebook feed. If weren't nobody talking about me on the news or nobody trying to email me, sure enough they'd be talking about me on Facebook. I mean hell, now with it Monday and two days since, you'd have to reckon that—"

"They can track you down with those things," said Jake. "Get rid of it."

Odie refused. He fiddled with the touchscreen and did what he could to access her menus. "Damn passcode," he said. "I can't get hold of nothing without her damn passcode."

"Throw it out the window," said Jake. "I ain't going to tell you again. If there's one thing I heard plenty of over the past couple of years, it's how some dumb joker or another got a free ride to the pokey, because he carried a cellphone he should have long gotten rid of. Now throw it out."

Odie tossed it free from the open window. He watched it explode against the asphalt then rolled up the window.

"What on earth are you doing?" Jake demanded.

"Rolling up the window. It's hot as blazes outside."

"Of course it's hot," said Jake. "It's summertime. So leave it down."

"To hell with that. Turn on the AC. This is ridiculous, man."

Jake shook his head. "It ain't natural for a man not to want to sweat."

Odie fell back into the passenger seat. Suddenly he felt returned to high school or on a trip up to Richmond with his parents. Things no longer near as fun. He crossed both his arms and stuck out his lower lip.

"Pout all you want," said Jake. "But this here is a job. You know what it ain't? A laughing matter, that's what it ain't."

Odie told him weren't nobody laughing, but Jake kept on.

"You walk into one of them gas stations and you got just a couple seconds to figure out does the guy have a scattergun below the counter. These days, it seems like it's nothing but Arabs back there, and those bastards play from a whole different deck."

"Arabs? Really? Dude, you need to—"

Jake continued, "You got just a second or two to figure out: Is there a camera. Is there a drop-safe? Do they have enough cash in the till to make it worth your while? Is Joe Bob Shitkicker hunting up a twelve-pack on the back aisle going to play hero or will he lie down on the floor like a good boy? You know what you ain't got time to do? Clown around. No time for that shit at all."

Odie watched out the window a bit before saying, "We just don't have to be so serious all the time, is all. You know, there's plenty chances to hate life and mope, and then there's time to have a ball. I just broke out of the lamest town in all of America, and I'm on my way to Hollywood to be a big movie star. If I ain't the picture of a success story, then I don't know who is. If ever there's a time to pop a bottle of champagne, I'd say it's now, wouldn't you?"

Jake kept eyes front. He gripped the wheel a bit tighter, then, he said, "Look, I don't mean nothing by it. Just I want you to know there are stakes here. It's hard to communicate that to somebody carrying a toy pistol."

Odie pulled something from his shirt pocket. He held it close to his face and eyeballed it some, then smelled of it. A soft smile came to his lips. He held it back close to his eyes.

"What's that?" asked Jake.

Odie held it up. It was the blonde girl's shiny ring.

"How the hell did you get that?"

Odie shrugged and looked out the window.

"Clowning around, I reckon."

7

To hear Danny Yeager tell it, he thought it only fitting that Jake Armstrong would go so far out of his way to hunt him up. After all, nineteen years ago Danny had moved heaven and earth to find Jake. So there he was in the sports bar south of Atlanta that he'd bought with ill-gotten money, because he'd done the one thing a man known to sling cocaine was not wont to do, and that was grow old gracefully. There he was, holed up in his back office with things that all seemed to be nicknamed.

His right-hand man and restaurant manager nicknamed Smoke, all because of some incident once involving a girl named Fire. The sawn-off Danny kept by his desk, they nicknamed Mary Lou after the former Olympic gymnast. They called the wooden Indian in the corner Chief, and the shit lined up in skinny rails across the mirrors they all called *yay*, especially on the telephone, because who knew when somebody was listening.

Danny'd eased off the stuff long ago. He didn't like what it did to his looks. His life-long adage being, once it messes with your face, you're done with it. But desperate times, yeah yeah yeah . . . He never let Mary Lou get more than two feet away from him, for all the pacing he did across the room.

Smoke tried to be more reassuring. "What makes you figure he'd come here?"

"You've been nothing but a real good guy to me," said Danny, again bending over the tiny mirror positioned atop his desk, "but sometimes I don't think you have the brains God gave a mole rat."

Smoke lowered his head and crossed those massive arms across his barrel chest. No, Danny Yeager didn't keep Smoke around for his brains. Those steel-cut muscles stood a distant second to Smoke's lack of moral conscience as to just why Danny Yeager loved him so. For a man whose compass pointed so absolutely toward self-preservation, Danny was a man who loathed to be without a partner in crime. Over time, he'd discovered the best cohorts to be those with nary a second thought as to orders handed down.

Take Eyeball McBreen, for instance. Nineteen years ago, Danny couldn't have asked for a better side man. Eyeball, all of nineteen years old, young dumb and full of what-have-you, and ever since he'd left school on a whim, he'd found a peculiar need to assert himself somewhere. Back then, if Danny had trouble moving any product, he'd dump it on Eyeball and ask him to haul it up to Vandy. No problem, no questions, just Eyeball showing up a few hours later with an envelope full of cash and a burning desire to be useful.

It was this burning desire that Danny Yeager decided to tap that night after Butchie came at him. Eyeball still lived on campus, despite not attending classes for most of the semester, so Danny showed up at his dorm room at three in the morning and told his roommate to hit the bricks. Once they were alone, Danny leveled with the boy.

"You heard about Jake? About that stunt he pulled over in Memphis?" asked Danny Yeager. Not many in certain circles hadn't heard. "Folks over in River City won't deal with Butchie no more until we hand over Jake, dead or alive."

Eyeball nodded. Behind those still-sleepy, slightly stoned eyes was a man who knew what knocked at his door. A college dropout. Options limited by taste or design. A growing predilection for trouble and fast living. What was he going to do, go look for a job? Type up a resume? A fork in the road appeared before Eyeball McBreen and here stood Danny Yeager in his dorm room, stretching out his hand.

"What are we going to do?" asked Eyeball.

"We're going to go fetch him," said Danny, and that was that. It took some doing, but two days later, they'd found him and, if things had gone according to plan, both of them would be set for life.

But things hadn't.

So here he was all that time later, sweating and pacing and hoping like the dickens things would hurry along and work themselves out. Because goddammit, Danny Yeager had better things to do than hide out in the back office of the sports bar. He paid good money to folks to make sure he didn't have to dirty his hands with that place and hated the smell of fry oil and the sound of that shit music they played and hated even more having to spell things out for his good man Smoke, but one thing he loved about the place was the stable of waitresses and pretty young bartenders staffed to keep the Yellow Jacket humming. Loved the shit out of them, despite their problems and those problems could be legion.

The first one ran by the shut office door in a cacophony of choking sobs and Danny Yeager first got the jitters, then calmed at the all too familiar noise. The second one raised more of a ruckus with the pounding on the door of the Ladies Room. Danny jerked his head to Smoke who opened the office door, slow at first, then all the way so as to show Danny the goings-on.

"Come on out, Cassie," pleaded the one waitress. She beat on the door some more. "Just remember, you need this job. Get your shit together, girl."

Danny considered the scene for a moment, then decided he felt much more comfortable in a panicked state, so he rushed headlong to where he thought he'd left Mary Lou then again over to where he'd actually left it, resting against a dusty file cabinet. He stood just before it, shielding it from the two girls, but wrapping his fingers around the barrel for comfort. Smoke took charge.

He stepped out into the skinny corridor where the drama unfolded and demanded to know just what in god's name was going on.

The cocktail Missy turned from the bathroom door and sucked air. "I'm real sorry, Smoke. It's Cassie. She's having a real time with a fella out there being rude, and she's crying."

"She's in the bathroom?" Smoke asked. Missy nodded. "You ever thought maybe she wants to be alone so she can deal rationally with her emotions?"

Missy looked at him as if he'd sprouted a horn in the center of his forehead. She hadn't considered this. Her face flushed, and she stepped gingerly from the door. To add insult to injury, as soon as the path became clear, Smoke pulled open the door, revealing Cassie standing awash in her own tears.

"All that damned fuss?" Smoke nodded for Missy to scoot, and she did. He led Cassie out of the bathroom and said, "You want to tell me what all this is about?"

Cassie blubbered and choked air. Before long, she managed to string together a sentence or two.

"There's a man out there being real mean," she said.

"Imagine that."

"No, Smoke. He's above and beyond. First he says he wants tea, and I ask him if he wants it sweet or unsweet. He says that's an awful dumb question to ask on this side of Atlanta. Then he tells me forget it, he'll take a coke. So I bring him a Coke, and he gets all mad because I didn't ask him what kind of coke we got. I mean, the man said *coke*, so that's what I brung him. He says, what if I wanted me a Sprite? I tell him he should have asked for a Sprite, and that got him really mad."

Smoke rubbed his cheek. He put his other oversized hand on her shoulder.

"That got you carrying on like this?"

She shook her head. "No, sir. Then, after all that, he orders a chicken-fried steak basket, and I ask him if he wants rolls or hushpuppies. He wants to know how many of each he gets. So I tell him he gets two rolls or eight hushpuppies. He says he wants one roll and four hushpuppies. I tell him we can't do that, and he tells me to find someone with half a brain to come wait on him."

From inside the office, Danny said, "What's this man look like?"

"Huh?"

"His looks," snapped Danny. "Describe them."

She ran it through her head, then said, "Kind of handsome, I guess. Thin. Mean-looking. Old."

"Old?"

"Yes sir," she sniffed. "About your age, I guess."

Danny winced. He turned his back to the door, faced his desk. Eyed the mirror over yonder with two skinny rails left and plenty powder to make maybe a half another one. Suddenly felt it the last thing he fucking needed in all the world.

"Let me ask you something," he said over his own shoulder. "This guy, is he alone?"

"He's got somebody with him. Early twenties and with long hair. Kind of cute."

Danny nodded his head. He sucked in a breath and held it some.

"Don't you worry about that fella," Danny told her. He turned around and looked her in the eye. Despite it all, he could be quite comforting to the women and could still turn on that old playfulness with so much as a wink. His hair, still blond, not yet gone to gray. He'd found himself a way to make money in which he could still wear khaki shorts and penny loafers with no socks. He had every intention of that being still a ways off. Danny Yeager put on airs that all of life was a beach and worked damn hard to make sure folks still believed him when he said it. "I'll take care of it."

He sent her on his way. Smoke closed the door and told the boss maybe he should sit down, maybe he should let him fetch him a Crown and ginger. Maybe he should let him run out and take care of this unruly customer, teach him how to talk to a lady.

"That isn't an unruly customer," said Danny Yeager, carefully putting away the mirror in the top drawer of his desk, those last lines untouched. "And if he's anything like he used to be nineteen years ago, we're going to need to call in a couple more guys to handle old Jake Armstrong."

***

Jake Armstrong, on the other hand, thought it rather funny to find Danny Yeager much as he left him all those years previous: Sweaty, bug-eyed, and whipped into a frenzy. Danny sat connipted, in his desk chair in back of the Yellow Jacket, feet propped high on the desk and trying like the dickens to put on airs, but his thumb tapped restless against his thigh, and he chewed his lower lip like a squirrel after a nut. Jake reckoned he must be thinking about what Jake would do to him, were he not equipped with the big fella Smoke and the bar's bouncer, both standing between them and the door.

"Were they carrying anything?" Danny Yeager asked the big fella. Smoke answered him by setting Jake's thirty-eight on the desk. Danny picked up Odie's little plastic gun by the trigger guard with his thumb and forefinger. "What the hell is this?"

"The kid had it on him," explained Smoke.

Jake said, "You know, I never met so many bad and broken people than when I come East."

"Oh, I'm sure they had plenty of them back in Texas where you was from," said Danny.

"They had them, all right," answered Jake. "Only thing is, in Texas at least some of the people was good and solid. In fact, some of them was *too* good, which of course presents its own set of issues."

"I can see how that would be a bit of a bother." Danny licked his lips then turned to Smoke. He said, "Jake here is a real old friend of mine. Me and him go way back. But it seems Jake has something of a bone to pick with me. Maybe a little chip on his shoulder."

"You'd be surprised how easily I can say bygones is bygones," said Jake.

"Is that so?" Danny wiped at his forehead with the back of his wrist. The Crown and ginger before him did wonders to take off the edge. He smiled. "Bygones is bygones is something easy to say when somebody's taken your gun from you."

Jake looked over one shoulder at the bouncer, then over the other at Smoke. Then back to Danny. "And here you was, using words like retired. I reckon there to be way too much pussy out in that bar for there not to be any cocaine traveling through."

"Did I say retired?" Danny asked. "No, I believe what I said was I don't dirty my hands anymore. You see, I invested rather well. This place here is a kind of retirement plan. It's the shiny red Corvette to my mid-life crisis. Too many fellas I know wound up either dead or in jail, all holding tight to tiny white baggies, and I had no intention of being somebody else's sucker. No, I pay good money to have other fellas dirty their hands for me."

Jake said to Smoke, "I guess he means you, right?"

"I use plenty of soap," answered Smoke.

"Among other things, I'm sure," said Jake.

"You've yet to introduce me to your friend here." Danny Yeager pointed a rickety finger to Odie.

"Forgive me for being such a bastard," said Jake. "This is my good friend, Odie Shanks. Go along and remember that name, fellas. You see, he's going to be a big-time movie star and you can all say you knew him when."

Odie slipped a lock of hair behind his ear. His eyes flipped between folks in the room like they were TV channels. Head sometimes going with them, sometimes not. Jake felt for the kid. Figured hell, the kid signed up for a trip West and maybe a little excitement. Reckoned two out of three wasn't all bad.

"Usually Rob was the comedian," said Danny to Odie. "But those two were a real hoot, back in the day. Always goofing around, never taking anything serious. Giving those of us who did quite a case of the cramps." Danny sipped from his drink. "Tell me, Jake, how is Rob lately?"

"To be honest, I'd say his mood has been better."

"Me and him would talk on the phone every now and again," said Danny. "He had a harder time than me when it came to moving on.

We kept up, all the same. Talked about you getting out. Funny . . . our conversations stopped quite recently."

"I should take my fair share of the blame for that."

Danny Yeager nodded. "And then you came here."

"And then I came here." Jake took a step toward the desk. Smoke and the bouncer took a step along with him. Jake then stayed where he was. "Maybe I've come to see about getting work."

"We got all the bartenders we need, Jake." Danny said something to Smoke with his eyes, then said to Jake with his mouth: "But I tell you what. I think we got something you can do for us."

"Oh really? Like a job?"

"Sure," said Danny. "Like a job. And if it works out for you, maybe we'll have something else for you to do. You see, we got this friend of ours who cut some shit he sold us with B12. It happens, but I didn't pay for stuff cut with B12, so that means he owes us some money, and he's been a little hesitant to pay it in full. Why don't you and Smoke run up there and ask him nicely to pay up?"

"If it will help bury the hatchet between us," said Jake, "then I'm more than happy to do it. But listen here, that sounds like a fairly simple operation, so why don't Smoke stay here, and let Odie and I handle it ourselves?"

"No can do," said Danny Yeager. "I need Smoke there, because fucking people up is one of his favorite parts of the job, and if I gave it to somebody else, well, he'd be heartbroken. And Odie can stay here. Give us time to get to know one another."

"Let me guess," said Jake. "This place you need me and Smoke to go. It's somewhere out in the woods. Somewhere ain't nobody around."

"See what I told you?" asked Danny Yeager to his two big fellas. "Jake here is one of the smarter ones."

"Can I have back my gun?"

Danny shook his head. "Let's let Smoke hang on to it a little while, why don't we?"

Jake sucked his lips inward. He put both hands in his pockets and looked over toward Odie. "Odie, I'm fixin to ride. You don't get too drunk on Danny's free liquor, hear?"

Odie didn't cotton to it. "Jake, I don't think it's a good—"

Danny Yeager came alongside and slipped an arm around Odie's shoulders. "Don't you worry about a thing, Jake. I'll keep an eye on Odie."

The bouncer held open the door. Smoke nudged Jake with his own gun, the .38. Jake took one last look at Odie and followed them out of the office into the sports bar. Into some Hank Junior, David Allan Coe bullshit coming from the jukebox. Into a world of haven't drank much, but man it's high time I get me something stiff and quick. Into the day's last heat as it turned quick to night.

Jake reckoned this would be a lot harder than he thought.

8

J ake wasn't gone two minutes before Danny excused himself, said
he needed another drink. Odie knew he had to act fast. He'd never
get another opportunity like this again. No sooner had Danny Yeager
closed the office door than Odie rushed the length of the room to the
desk, where an age-old computer sat dusty in the corner.

First he googled his own name. When that proffered no more results than usual, he entered his name alongside the words *Lake Castor*.
Nothing. He tapped in "Maggie's Pizza Pick-Up" and "Lake Castor
kidnapping." Still nothing.

Sweat beaded across his forehead, and he was in the middle of
pointing and clicking here and there, when in walked Danny Yeager
with two cocktails, both copper-colored, but one in a highball glass
and the other in a plastic cup. He handed the second one to Odie.

"What is it?"

"Whiskey and ginger ale," said Danny. "Drink it."

Odie drank it. Tasted like piss. He soured his lips and pushed the
drink to the opposite edge of the desk. Danny narrowed his eyes, then
took a seat across from him on the Naugahyde divan located in the
corner of the office.

"What is it you're doing on my computer," asked Danny Yeager.

"I was looking up the news," said Odie. He put his face into an upturned palm. "Did you know they got all kinds of crime going on in the United States right now? They got this one guy who had kids with one lady but married another. He chopped up his baby mama and got the other lady to help ditch her parts in a creek. They got another girl in Louisiana who robbed two college boys and put fish hooks in their ball sacks after stealing their car and all their money. All these sick bastards running amok across the Internet but not a single story about me, getting kidnapped out of my place of employ and robbing a gas station."

"Sounds like you need an agent," said Danny Yeager.

"What I need is a picture of my mother crying tears over her missing baby," said Odie.

Danny Yeager took a drink. He'd mellowed some since Jake left. Asked what Odie thought of Atlanta.

What did Odie think of Atlanta? There were things he thought and things he said and there was plenty of room between the two. Odie said Atlanta was a beautiful, cosmopolitan center of commerce in God's blessed South, but what he *thought* was there could be no worse hell in all the world. Billions of miles of concrete, stretching into the unknown, all named Peachtree Street and cram-packed with coffee shops. Banks. He and Jake had spent a good part of the afternoon struck in traffic, all the while Jake telling him which rib joint was the best, where they should eat.

Odie couldn't have felt worse about his opinion on the city, not more than when they pulled over and asked directions. The first guy stopped what he was doing and walked to the curb, pointed this way and that and told them streets to avoid. And sure enough, when Jake went his own way and got them lost again, the lady they hailed behaved in much the same manner. Nice as could be and full of information, whether asked for or not. Odie thanked her and when he'd gotten back in the car had said, "Wow. Folks in this town sure have their glasses half-full, don't they?"

Odie returned to the computer. He tapped once, tapped again, then asked Danny Yeager:

"Who is Nick Fuller?"

Danny looked like he'd been caught off guard. His mouth hung open a second, then he collected his bearings. A smile snaked up, faraway and alone.

"Jake told you about Nick Fuller?"

"No," said Odie. "It was something your buddy Rob Winchester said. Said it before he . . ." He thought it best to let his words trail away.

"Ah, yes." Danny was no longer sentimental. "You see, there was an upscale joint up in Belle Meade, a place we had no business in but Jake rode with me to that side of town to drop off some shit. We stop for a drink, and this girl Ruby is a cocktail waitress there. Those two hit it off and guess what, now every time Jake wants a drink, he's got us driving out to Belle Meade, which is some place we got no business in, unless we got business."

Danny sucked down the rest of his cocktail, then rattled the ice cubes a minute. "This lady was a real pro, man. If there's ever anything coming between a man and what he's supposed to do, it's a fucking woman, and she snared him good. Pretty soon, where you saw Jake you saw her. She was like a redneck Yoko Ono."

Odie nodded. "And what does this have to do with Nick Fuller?"

"Nick Fuller was her husband."

Danny Yeager snatched the plastic cup he'd brought for Odie and poured the watered-down contents into his own glass. The divan squeaked as he returned into its cushions and nursed his new drink.

"You want to hear stories about Jake Armstrong?" he said. "I can tell you stories. Man, have I got a doozy."

To hear Danny Yeager tell it, he'd run every possibility through his mind, the whole drive from Nashville to Memphis. There were all sorts of reasons why Jake would be calling him at just before midnight—a coke dealer's busy time—demanding he drive to an address to meet him. Sounded distressed. Maybe he had some girl who couldn't handle her shit and needed help getting her to the ER. Maybe he needed a wingman. It could be anything, Danny told himself, but he'd never prepared himself for what it actually was.

"I walked in the place, and it looked like the Manson family," said Danny. "Blood on the walls, blood on the floor. I mean, when you sling yay, you get used to seeing crazy shit, but I'd never seen anything like that. Jake's on the far side of the room, sitting in a La-Z-Boy. He's got a gun in his lap and this oh-shit look on his face. To my left are two guys I've seen around. Friends of Chicken Bone's. I think one of them was named Charlie something or another, I don't remember. These two are duct taped together, and they've had the shit beat out of them but that ain't where all the blood's from. They were pissed, sure, but they were still in one piece."

All the blood came from the guy face down in the middle of the living room. Six bullet holes in his back. Danny Yeager knew who it was without bending down for a better look but did it anyway. The dead guy was Chicken Bone, Butchie's connection. Danny jerked backwards like thrusting himself out of a fire. He felt his world ending.

"What the fuck is this, Jake?"

"I don't know what to do," said Jake.

"You call your buddy Rob for this kind of shit," Danny Yeager had told him. "Call anybody except me. I ain't the guy you call for this."

"I never killed anybody before."

"Well you picked a hell of a guy to start with." Danny looked at the other two, connected in several places by thick strips of silver binding. "Jake, these guys aren't going to let you get away with this."

Jake put his head in his hands. "I don't know what to do." He said that a couple more times.

"Y'all see I just got here, right?" Danny asked the other two. He'd knelt before them, as if praying for mercy. "Y'all see I got nothing to do with this?"

Neither man took eyes off him. Eyes full of hate. Eyes saying they knew Jake had made a ruckus over the past week, saying he was gunning for Chicken Bone. Eyes saying it was all a matter of time now, it was all a matter of time.

Danny put his face in his hands. He rubbed like maybe he could erase all of this all by himself and then figured maybe he could, so he reached into his jeans and tugged free the little snub-nosed he'd brought with him. He rose to full height and popped each of those other two, one bullet for each. Killed them dead.

***

"We couldn't leave those two alive," Danny told Odie, all those years later. "They'd seen Jake and, worst of all, they'd seen me. To be honest, I should have put a bullet into him and been done with it, but I didn't. I didn't, and here I am nineteen years later and still regretting it."

He'd finished his drink some time ago. Odie regretted not keeping it. He settled for a cigarette, but it took some time lighting it, due to his hands shaking so.

"Why did Jake kill that guy?" asked Odie.

"Chicken Bone?" Danny stared at the tiled floor of his office. Outside, in the bar, someone turned up some shit hip-hop music, and it got a bunch of girls cheering. "Danny killed Chicken Bone because of that woman. That cocktail waitress. The one he'd been carrying on with. Didn't I tell you she was trouble?"

Danny continued. "We ransacked the place so maybe they'd think a couple coloreds did it, but it was no use. Jake had made so much noise before he'd driven out to Memphis that pretty soon, guys from Houston were in town. Once guys from Houston hit town, it was all over. You see, the job is to put as many people between you and the Mexicans as you can while still making money. Jake removed one rung to the ladder and fucked us all."

"They wanted Jake dead for killing Chicken Bone?"

Danny nodded. "And only three people knew I was in that room that night. Two of them were dead. So when Butchie said Jake needed to go, I figured the secret would die with him."

Odie nodded. He'd forgotten all about the computer. He'd forgotten all about wanting a drink. Something tugged at his mind like a leper woman at the feet of Jesus, and he couldn't shake it. His stomach had gone to fits, and he looked up to Danny for an explanation and feared that he might have found it.

"So why are you telling me about it?" asked Odie.

Danny's eyes—impossibly blue—sparkled as he stood from the divan. He nodded at the empty glass in his own hand.

"You know what I'd like?" he said. "I'd like to see about getting something sucked on tonight. How would you feel about that?"

"Beg pardon, sir?"

"Getting something sucked on," repeated Danny. "All them young things we got dancing around out there in the sports bar by God get me good and worked up some nights, and I tell you, after two of these

Crown and gingers, it gets hard to throw on the brakes. What do you say?"

Odie didn't know what to say. He shook his head, then nodded, before finally shrugging.

"You should let me introduce you to Mary Lou."

It all happened so fast. Danny pulled the sawn-off from around back of the Naugahyde divan and put it up to Odie's face. All Odie saw was Danny's eyes, wild with blue frenzy and the shotgun barrel out of focus due to proximity. He threw up a hand out of instinct, but Danny slapped it away with a hand of his own.

"I could paint my walls with you," said Danny Yeager. "And wouldn't nobody hear it over that shit music they play out there. And clean up? I got Mexicans washing dishes who'd do it happily for an extra forty bucks. I'd call *La Migra* and have them shipped back to where-the-fuck and take our little secret with them."

"What do you want?"

"I want you to put the barrel of this shotgun into your mouth."

"Beg pardon?"

Danny slapped the side of Odie's head with the shotgun. "I ain't a warden, so quit begging me for a pardon, you hear me? Put the barrel of this shotgun in your mouth or I'll pull the trigger. Do you know what I could do to you from this distance?"

The barrel didn't jut out more than four inches from the forestock, but Odie got all four into his mouth. His lips wrapped around naturally, and he did his best to move his tongue off the barrel, but no going. Whoever'd sawn it off had done a lousy job and cut it at an angle, never filed it down. Tiny, razor filaments got him here and there inside his mouth, and his entire world tasted of gun oil. Metal. He couldn't close his eyes, not even to blink.

"Suck on it," said Danny.

Odie said something unintelligible but sounded enough like "beg pardon" to rile Danny up fierce, so he tilted the gun upward as if preparing to fire. Odie screamed from behind the gun barrel. He moved his lips quickly and obediently along the gun barrel.

"Good boy," said Danny. His pulse didn't seem to change. He watched Odie calm and cool sucking on the stubby barrel of his sawn off, then said, "Come on, man . . . use your hand some. Ain't you never had your pecker sucked before? Don't you know how to do it?"

Odie's eyes bugged. He put his hand near enough to the forestock but didn't move it any closer, for fear of . . . hell, for fear of anything. He just left his hand, a dangling idiot, next to the gun as Danny began to gyrate, sticking it further into Odie's face and sliding it further out.

"That's right, boy," said Danny Yeager. "You could do this for a living. I could get good money for you down in Midtown. You got that long hair like a woman . . ."

Danny reached his other hand around back of Odie's head, pushed the gun further into him, ramming the forestock into his lips.

"You see, Jake was dumb as shit for coming back around here. And I know it ain't your fault he's a dumb shit, but when they find his body washing up out in the South River, I can't take no chances."

Odie said a lot of things in that moment or tried to say them but it wasn't any use. All the deals and promises and oaths he swore, none of them made it around the barrel of that shotgun, and he saw the skin around Danny Yeager's eyes tighten and the flesh in his neck turn to knots, and finally Odie found strength to close his eyes and over the *thump-thump* rhythm of that shitty music off in yonder sports bar and the waves of screaming and cheers came all of it even louder and in a rush that filled the entire back office but never came close to drowning out the sound of the first gunshot, the second one or even the third as they exploded all around him and finally, for the first time in all of his twenty-two years, he wished he were back in Lake Castor.

That thought, more than any other, shook him.

And still with the noise and the music and the girls screaming and Odie realized he no longer held the stubby barrel of the sawn-off in his mouth, that it had been ripped free and more than likely taking plenty of his face with it. A tooth. Still that music and he wondered if the soundtrack to hell sounded anything like a fraternity party.

"Odie, get your shit and let's go."

Jake's voice. Odie thought of worse hells.

He opened his eyes.

Jake stood over him. Again he held his .38 special and this time the sawn-off as well. Danny Yeager lie dead on the floor, awash in his own mess, those blue eyes staring off yonder. Jake slapped Odie good in the face.

"You hear me?" he said. "We got to go. We got to go now."

Odie, clearly in shock, said the only words rattling around his head:

"Beg pardon?"

9

They'd gone to sleep in a rest stop parking lot just inside the Alabama border, rather than spend any cash on a room. Odie reckoned it to be about five or so in the morning when Jake nudged him from the backseat, told him to wake up.

"What's the matter?" asked Odie. Sleep was the furthest thing from his mind. He'd reclined the passenger seat almost level and thought maybe he'd squished Jake's leg some.

"I got to talk to you about something," said Jake. "It's important."

"I don't want to talk about it," said Odie. He looked at himself in the rearview and put a finger to the spot on his mouth where part of his lip was missing. "I don't never want to talk about it."

Jake let that sit, then said, "It ain't nothing to do with that."

"What then?"

"What do you reckon to do about your accent?"

"Beg—" Odie's chipped tooth gave him pause. "Do what?"

Jake leaned up on his elbow. "Your accent," he repeated.

"I don't got to do nothing with it," said Odie. "All my friends say I don't have an accent. It's what they call a *non-accent*, like newscaster fellas use."

Jake put a cigarette into his mouth. "Your friends told you that?"

"The part about not having an accent, yeah. Not the part about the *non-accent*. I saw that on the Internet."

"I hate to be the bearer of bad news, Odie: You have an accent. And it's as Southern as stone-ground grits."

"What are you talking about?" asked Odie, trying like hell to erase any inflection or nuance to his speech, his words suddenly more crisp and self-conscious. Odie wiped sleep from his eyes and looked around to see if perhaps the rest stop had a vending machine with coffee. No such luck. The lot was spotted with cars, but no people. The sun threatened to rise any minute, but currently was only a purple sliver slipping before the black, on a horizon miles and miles away.

Jake said, "You know, the fact you don't think you got an accent concerns me a tad. Granted, it's nowhere near as pronounced as say, mine, but you're definitely sporting some twang. Mine's more of what they call a *drawl*. Now, when I hear you talk, I'm not thinking Southern Virginia like some of the other assholes in your hometown, but I'd definitely put you out near the Carolinas."

"You ain't—er, *aren't* making me feel any better."

Jake sneered. "It ain't supposed to make you feel better."

"So you're telling me I should work on dropping the accent?"

"Hell no," said Jake. The backseat lit orange as Jake flicked his lighter to the cigarette, then plunged them back into darkness as he pocketed it. "That's the last goddamn thing you should do. Wear that shit like a badge, brother. You know what chapped me more than anything while I was inside that Tennessee jailhouse? We didn't get to watch movies but every so often and when we did, and they'd put on a movie supposed to take place in the South, they toss in assholes from California or what have you to dumb up an accent and make them sound like we don't. I can't stand it. The movie reigning supreme in the Southern pantheon is *Gone with the Wind*, but Clark Gable is from Ohio, and Vivien Leigh is a British chick born in India. I call bullshit on all that business, but it's business and you should know that going in."

Odie thought about it a bit longer than he should have, staring out the window at a sky turning into a mess of pastels. After a while, he heard Jake's breathing become snoring. Odie looked into the backseat and found him asleep, cigarette still burning in his hand. Careful not to topple the pillar of ash, he removed it. Jake stirred.

"It's a sinking ship," muttered Jake, who then rolled over in the seat and returned to sleep. Odie took the last drag, cracked the window, and chucked the butt.

A few hours later and Jake still came off a bit surly. When a plate of hash browns didn't cheer him up, Odie thought it best if they find a gas station to rob. Something to lighten the mood. They drove around the outskirts of Birmingham, cruising in and out of parking lots until they found one without much traffic. Jake parked the car on the far side of the property, next to what used to be a phone booth.

"Wait in the car," said Jake.

"Hold up a minute," Odie said. "Don't you think it's high time I go in there and see what I can do?"

Jake cocked an eyebrow. "This ain't an audition, kid."

"From here on out," said Odie, "everything's an audition."

"Fine, kid. But all you get is the toy gun."

Odie climbed out of the car and slammed shut the door. "That's all I'm going to need."

When Odie half-jogged across the asphalt to the gas station, he reckoned he could expect anything on the other side of the door. Anything, except what he found, which was a giant mirror. Not a real mirror, per se, but a figurative one, because the kid behind the counter could have been him or, in some alternate dimension, perhaps it was.

Like they were on some different time thread and Jake had driven him to the convenience store at the world's end.

The kid behind the counter had shoulder-length hair that hadn't been brushed in a while, ratty and thrown back into a tail. He'd been reading a magazine off the rack. Maybe he'd just smoked a joint, because his lids never fully opened and he couldn't be bothered to give more than half a shit, only lifting a finger as Odie entered through the door.

Odie fought not to sick up his breakfast. There was no way this kid was a mirror of him. Despite the hair, the build, even the fuck-it-all around the eyes, this kid had never been forced to fellate a sawn-off shotgun, and Odie suddenly felt if this were a mirror, if this were some grand reflection of where he was to stand against where he'd come from, then he could do a lot worse than smashing it to a million pieces.

He rushed the counter quicker than the cashier may have been accustomed to things moving and yanked that toy pistol from under his shirt. He jabbed it into the kid's face. He thought more than once about telling that kid to wrap lips around the plastic barrel but before the words could shit forth, he pulled the trigger five or six times and wasted him, blasting his insides across the poorly-swept floors.

Wait . . .

No, he did none of that. Instead, he stood at the back beverage aisle with a root beer in his hand and watched the stoner kid slowly turn the pages of his magazine. Not even reading. Odie felt it welling up in him. What did this kid know? Maybe he was on summer break from some state college or another, but more than likely he wasn't. More than likely he'd do just what Odie would do after work which was go home to his parent's house, watch a movie or play games on the goddamn computer until along came somebody to bust him free, because he damn sure wasn't going to do it by his lonesome. No, he'd be contented to sit and rot in this bullshit town, cashing bullshit checks from his bullshit job. Never knowing what it was like to zip through the pages of a road atlas. Never knowing what it was like to make somebody his bitch.

No, Odie stood there seething in the candy aisle until he'd worked himself out of that frenzy and approached the counter, slipping across both the soda and the fifty dollar bill. The kid looked up from his magazine and, hopping off the stool, rang up his customer. He didn't care about making change and sure enough, he hadn't made a safe drop in a while. Couldn't be bothered with it. He slid out the change, and when he looked up, Odie told him to put all the money in a plastic sack.

"Dude, what are you talking about?"

Odie lifted up his shirt and let him see the butt of the plastic gun jutting from the waistband of his britches.

"Do I got to pull it out?" he asked.

"No, sir," said the kid. He got right to work. With incredible focus, he slid coins and slapped bills from the drawer, then dropped them all into a plastic sack. He kept eyes to the floor, didn't dare look Odie in the eye.

Odie snatched both the root beer and the sack of money and high-tailed it out the door. Jake pulled the car around close to the building, and Odie barely had time to shut the car door before Jake got them the hell out of there.

"How'd it go?" asked Jake as he swerved down this back road and tore up that one.

"I'd say I passed the audition," said Odie. "Looks like I got the part."

***

To hear Ruby Fuller tell it, there was little point in acting surprised when she answered her doorbell and found Jake Armstrong at the patio. For behind her sat three cartons of what she last remembered Jake to smoke. She herself had quit the habit nearly a decade ago, but when she caught wind of Jake's release, she reckoned she'd need to play catch up. She also stood awash in the rich smell of hickory wood from the barbecue she'd run out to Decatur to pick up in anticipation of his arrival.

Furthermore, she'd gone to the beauty shop to have her hairdresser wash out the gray.

So to act surprised would have insulted him when everything else threatened to give her away. She'd not even been caught off guard upon sight of the kid Jake had in tow, only that he wore a shiny, greased-up pompadour rather than hair down to his shoulders, despite what she'd been told.

And she'd been told plenty.

"You still play the harmonica?" she asked, instead of saying hello.

His lips curled back, and she realized it was his smile. "Your hair didn't used to be this red."

"Lots of things didn't used to be lots of ways." She stepped out of the doorway and into his arms. They hugged for a good, long while until she realized they were not alone together, nor had they been and for quite some time. She lived on a suburban street and had plenty of neighbors, none of whom knew jackshit about her beyond what they could imagine from peeking through lifted window blinds or parted drapes. And then there was the boy. The boy stood awkward behind Jake, trying like hell to look and act tough. He'd taken on a sort of sneer that she remembered well from her days with Jake, although he had quite a ways to go before he pulled that off. He looked left and right, as if some hired bodyguard, albeit one who would leave his back turned to the street.

"Is he yours?"

"Jesus no," Jake said. "That's one bullet I dodged."

As introductions went around, she looked at the boy and said, "I hear you still play with toys."

Odie blushed and looked to say something witty but apparently that well had run dry and instead he asked to use her bathroom. She put a hand to his shoulder and gently led him inside.

She fought the urge to explain her setup to Jake. She also knew he wouldn't ask after it. Long gone was the life she lived in the affluent Nashville suburb with Nick, her husband with a jailer's paycheck. But not the desire to live it. Her place now didn't come easy, but neither had it come hard. For once again she was Ruby Fuller, but until recently she took mail as Ruby Granger until that one died, but he'd changed her name from Stanton, which had been given to her by a man who made good money, but she couldn't overlook what he did with his secretaries, so she took half of it. Before that was another guy and even another guy before that. Sure, it was a sport and since she was good at it, she got trophies. This little house she led Jake and Odie into was her favorite of all those trophies.

But she had changed her name back to Fuller, which was the name of her first husband, Nick. She did it because, best she could remember, that was the time she was happiest. That was the time when things made the most sense. When anything was possible. But if she recalled it as thus because of Nick himself or of Jake, she couldn't really say. All she knew for certain was that all that happiness, all that certainty, all that everything came crashing to a halt at once when she lost both of them in one fell swoop.

That night, nineteen years earlier, when she came home from the hospital. She still wore the clothes stained with her husband's blood. From finding him shot three times and lying on their front lawn. His wife off and carrying on with some low-level weed dealer who—

That night, her opening the front door of their place in Belle Meade and dropping the keys to the linoleum and wandering dazed into the kitchen, unable to keep a single thought from rattling around in her head and barely remembering to turn on the kitchen light, but when she did and that brassy yellow pool came down from above, there sat Jake Armstrong in a corner chair, and he had been sitting there for quite some time.

"I don't want to see you," she had told him and then, because she didn't think it expressed enough by saying it only once, said it again and then again, and before she knew it, she was saying it and punctuating it by slapping him, hitting him, kicking him. He never restrained her. He let her do what she had to do until she was too beat to do it anymore.

And she lay there at his feet, exhausted. She wrapped herself around his ankles and wept. She thought if he sent down his hand to stroke her or arms to hold her, she'd rip him to pieces with anything she had left, but he never did. And that's how they stayed for a good long while.

She poured her husband's whiskey into a glass that had been a wedding present and set it near Jake. She sat across from him at their dinner table.

"Swear to me you had nothing to do with this," she told him in a voice barely above a whisper.

"Nothing," said Jake.

"Do you know how long he lay there in that front yard, bleeding to death?" She shook her head and couldn't see straight. "If I do my math right, while he was lying there . . . we must have been . . . We were—"

She closed her eyes.

"I'm going to find out who did this," Jake told her.

She sighed. "What does it matter now?"

"It matters to me."

"It won't undo it," she said. "Nothing can undo it."

He never touched the drink. "And when I find them . . ."

She didn't bother interrupting him. She realized she could search the furthest shadows of her soul and still have no idea what she was feeling, and she stumbled about as such for nineteen years, going through the motions, and not even certain if she felt anything at all, or if it had a name. Much like the next time she laid eyes on him, after opening that door and him standing there with the kid. For this time it was different. This time, he stood before her less one finger and less nineteen years between them and less any sort of closure they may or may never have had. Instead, he had upon him all the weariness and awareness and anger of someone in his situation, anger she never had to bear because Jake Armstrong himself had kept a promise, and the man who shot up her husband was dead and gone. Dead and gone and nobody's bother but the worms.

So now, Jake in her new home, far enough from Nashville but suddenly seeming so close. She popped open the go-boxes of barbecue and extra sauce just for him. Odie looked it over and turned up his nose.

"What's that white stuff?"

"I'll tell you later," said Jake. He never took eyes off her.

"How did you find everyone?" she asked.

"Prison had a library," said Jake. "You'd be amazed what all a fella can do when he's got time on his hands."

She looked to the floor. "I'm glad you're out of there."

He nodded.

"I heard you're up to some old tricks," she said. "And again, some new ones."

"You sure hear a lot," he said.

"When I care to listen."

Jake dipped a chunk of pork meat into a little plastic ramekin of white sauce. "You knew I'd come?"

She nodded.

"And you wanted me to?"

She took a second to do it, but she nodded again.

"You want to go out for drinks tonight?"

She smiled. "You boys will want to freshen up. You both smell like highwaymen, like you've been on the road for days."

The boy sniffed at himself then shrugged. She counted each bite he took of his lunch and reckoned he couldn't eat it near fast enough but once he did, she hurried him off to the shower.

She didn't realize until he'd got the water to running that she'd neglected to give him a towel, but by that time it was too late, because she'd already scurried down the stairs and into Jake's arms where they had at it like school kids right there at the dinner table. This the first time in nineteen years that either of them had been with someone they truly loved.

10

That next morning was Wednesday, and Odie found himself in the little kitchen, reading the newspaper. Ruby came down the steps quite disheveled but even still, Odie found it remarkable that time had lain such a gentle hand upon her. She drew her robe tighter and fell upon the coffeepot like a famished jackal.

"How you fixed for breakfast this morning, Odie?" she asked him.

"Don't sweat it," he said. "I helped myself to some of your bread for toast. I hope you don't mind."

"Of course not." She poured herself a cup and leaned against the counter. Watched him turn the pages of the paper. "Looking for something in particular?"

"Just something don't nobody seem to want to report on."

"Did you sleep well?" she asked.

"Well enough, considering the circumstances," he said. He looked her way, then off somewhere else. "Walls are thin."

True. He blamed himself. He'd gotten a good glimpse of what was to come at the bar the night previous. The three of them tried their hand at a game of pool, but Jake got grabby with her and every time Odie turned around, the two of them were making out.

The situation worsened later when, after they'd left the juke joint, Jake drove them to a drive-thru for some late-night grub and, as they waited in line behind other cars, he and Ruby couldn't keep their hands off each other. Kissing, goosing, tickling and the like. Odie sighed and grumbled in the backseat, wished for more of whatever the hell they'd been drinking.

"What's the matter, Sourpuss?" Jake kidded. "We gave you plenty of time to scare up a woman back at that bar."

Odie shifted about. "And I think I would have worked a little harder had I known I'd be spending the night in the backseat, forced to watch a couple old people make out."

"Old people?" Ruby's shoulders sagged. She slumped in her seat, back against the passenger door, and thought it over a bit. Odie wished he'd said nothing, but then she reached out with her foot and poked Jake's thigh. "Hey old man, what do you say you tickle me with that cane of yours?" And Odie really wished he'd kept his mouth shut.

"He's sleeping it off," she told him as she warmed her hands with the coffee mug. "If he's anything like I remember him, he'll be in that bed for a while." She smiled at some distant memory, then said, "Couldn't nobody get me heated like Jake Armstrong."

"So I heard."

Ruby didn't have time to be embarrassed. She looked Odie dead on and said, "Which are you referencing? The loving or the fighting?"

"Both, I reckon," he answered. "They seemed to alternate enough for me to wonder which was which."

She sipped her coffee. Sure, Odie had heard plenty. He was no pervert, but they'd do their share of talking too and he lacked enough pieces of the puzzle to be curious. Throughout the night, he'd hear his name mentioned, and he'd sidle up against the wall to hear better, only for them to start screwing again.

What he heard mostly was how Ruby disagreed with Jake's plan.

"Hollywood, Jake?" she'd said through the wall. "That's outrageous, even for you."

Jake didn't give in right away. "Ruby, there's three things you can count on me to do in life. Damned if I can't remember the first one, but the second is to keep a promise once I've made it. And the third is to see things all the way through to the end."

Odie never made out what she said next, but Jake answered it by saying, "While I was in that cage I learned a person frets more over what they don't do rather than what they actually do."

She'd lit into him a bit more, and then they got to giggling and, after a disturbing period of silence, there'd be moans. Odie would cover his ears with a pillow or step outside for a smoke, but soon enough, they'd be arguing again. Mostly her repeating over and over "It's over, Jake" or "Just let it go." Or the time she said, "One thing we all have in common is we've moved on. Every one of us. And another thing is you coming back to drag us all back into it."

Odie could tell the next morning that she still stuck to her guns. She helped herself to a second cup of coffee, and this time did not sit to drink it. Resolve burned into her face, and she remained in a perpetual state of seeming ready to say something, but never saying it.

Odie looked into the newspaper, drew his face closer to it. Squinted his eyes. He looked up and held up the page to Ruby.

"You care if I cut something out of here?"

She shook her head. "What is it?"

"This chick I've been hearing about," he said. He held his hand flat against the page while slowly and carefully tearing out the length of the article. "She's on a spree, same as Jake and me, I reckon. Says here she beat up some guy and left him tied up in a motel room. Took all his shit and ran."

"That's one way to do it," said Ruby. She sipped on her coffee.

"I'll say. Probably the only person in the world with a more exciting road trip than me."

She smiled. "You've got a ways to go before you realize there's more to life than wall-to-wall excitement."

"That's either an insult or a compliment, but I don't reckon I got enough sleep to go rooting out either one."

Odie didn't like the way she looked at him. He still wasn't used to the new haircut and worried it must look a fright after a night such as that last one. He ran his hand through it, the length or lack thereof still quite foreign. He hung his head and found something safe in the floor tile worth his attention.

"Odie, I worry about you."

"There are better things to occupy your mind," he said.

"Seriously. I recognize an anger in you, and I fear what you might reckon to do with it, if left unchecked."

Odie looked in the direction of the bedrooms and wondered when Jake might be joining them.

She noted the direction of his gaze and said, "And I don't think Jacob Armstrong to be the best of all possible role models."

"Funny," said Odie, "he thinks you love him."

"I do love him. I love him more than anything in this world. But he's hell-bent on something and carrying a load he best put down."

Outside a wind riled the wind chimes, then fucked off to some other part of town. Odie had a million explanations and justifications rattling about his head, but no one had asked for them yet, nor had they held open a door to let them out.

"For instance," continued the woman, "for all your talk about heading to Hollywood to be a movie actor, I ain't seen you carry so much as a book on acting or reading anything about where to go or get started once you get there. Instead, all I ever hear about is this gas station you've robbed or what that girl has done on a crime spree and what have you. Clipping stories from the paper about criminals."

Odie bit the insides of his mouth until they bled. "It's a long way between Alabama and California," he said. "I'm learning as I go."

"I'm afraid you're learning the wrong things."

Oh, he had plenty to tell her about things he'd learned. Most of which had struck him since walking into that vanilla house of hers way out in suburban Alabama, but he'd been raised different and wouldn't open his mouth to speak of them. Not then, no, but rather he'd wait until he got into the car with Jake, and he couldn't wait because there, there he'd have plenty to say.

Instead, he nodded and looked over the news clipping.

She put down the coffee cup hard on the countertop. The air sucked from the room. She said, "You and me, let's go for a little ride."

"Beg pardon?"

"A drive," she said. "Did Jake ever tell you about my husband, Nick?"

"Jake hasn't, no ma'am," he said. "I heard about him some from . . . From some of Jake's other buddies."

If she heard him, she didn't let on. Instead, she started for the stairs, stopping just shy of the bottom step.

"Get your clothes on," she said. "We're going on a drive. There's someone I'd like you to meet."

"Who?" asked Odie.

"My husband," she said.

***

Odie Shanks stared at the man and couldn't look away. He hadn't known what to expect the entire drive. Had she driven him to the graveyard or to a prison, he would have been ready for it. Hell, had she driven him to some crusty old man deep in the woods, telling nothing but old jokes and saws of wisdom, he'd have been more prepared. But looking down on the simple fella in the wheelchair knocked the wind clear from his sails.

His head had been shaved so as to maintain ease of care. Ruby described him as a "big man," so merely a shadow remained. He couldn't have weighed more than one-thirty, all muscle whittled down to strands of atrophied sinew. Ruby said they gave him physical therapy, but the movements were little more than muscle memory, since what once ran rampant upstairs now lay eerily dormant.

They'd left him simple. The one that got him in the head may have been the one that done it, but it could have been any of the other two. Who knows, considering the period of time that Nick had lain unattended and bleeding. He hadn't spoken a mumble in over a decade. When, and if, he looked up at his wife, there were no sparks of recognition or any sign that lights shone from his tower. No, he had the brain of a gerbil and would until the day he died.

He had been a jailer, simple as that. Not some connected guy who moved pounds and pounds of weed or some other shit. Not even a nickel sack. Just a jailer. He drank beer from cans and scratched off lottery tickets. Every two weeks, he cashed a jailer's check up at the bank. Folks would consider him completely unremarkable were it not for the woman he kept. Ask a guy like Nick Fuller what amounted to a happy life, and he'd tell you a good job, a good home, and a good woman.

Two out of three wasn't bad.

The way Ruby heard it was the Sheriff picked up Andrew 'Chicken Bone' MacMurphy for speeding and found a warrant somewhere, then ran him in. Chicken Bone would never spend more than twelve hours in any lockup, so he needed only bide his time. No sooner had they clanged shut the metal cage than some guard started mixing it up with him, and since all those rednecks live by the same code—fuck with one of us, fuck with all of us—Nick Fuller became a marked man.

Simple as that.

Chicken Bone never pointed any fingers at anyone, threatening revenge from some perceived jailhouse slight, never so much as raised his blood pressure. No one saw anything special go down between him and Nick Fuller. No, Chicken Bone merely took his lumps then returned to his cell and shut the fuck up until he was released only hours later. Had Nick minded his own business . . . Had Ruby been home instead of out gallivanting with her lover . . . Had any measure of things gone the way they didn't, Odie would not be staring at the man in the wheelchair.

"Jake swore he'd fetch revenge," she told Odie. "He said he wouldn't sleep until he found out who did that to my husband and, lo and behold, he rattled more than a few cages. No sooner did he find out who it was than he was gone, and the last I hear from him is a phone call telling me he'd taken care of it. Then everything went to shit."

Odie wanted to say something nice, but couldn't. Instead, he kept quiet and felt like an idiot, watching the fella in the wheelchair consider the floor tiles at his feet. In the ward were other fellas just like Nick. Some better, some worse, but none of whom Odie would ever want to trade spots. He heard their moans and grumbles as they shuffled to and fro, some on their own, others with the help of orderlies. He felt a violent gurgling in the stomach that he was able to quell for now but knew if he stayed, he may not be so lucky.

"Why did you bring me here?" he asked her.

"Why do you think?"

Nick's head twitched. Odie turned to her. "Can we please leave?"

"If you're ready to go."

"I don't want to sound like a dick, but this is a little rough for me."

"Ain't no picnic for me neither, Odie."

Outside, they found Jake smoking a cigarette. Said he reckoned he'd find them there. Odie felt like a bastard, so he didn't say much, opted instead to let Ruby explain. She asked if he'd been in yet to see him, and Jake said no, he hadn't.

"I don't think that would be my place."

"Maybe you ought to take time and think real hard where exactly your place is," she said. "We'll meet you back at my house."

They said nothing more and went back the way they'd come, and after a while of Odie watching TV and solving crosswords and generally wishing they'd be on their way, soon enough Jake showed up and in no mood to dick around.

"Let's go get some barbecue," Odie said to him, but got no response. "I read somewhere about a place out here that serves fried green tomatoes like nobody's ever seen, and I bet you'd hanker for those the rest of your life after so much as one bite. Right, Jake?"

Jake was having none of it. Instead he marched upstairs to where Odie had last seen Ruby and he figured he may as well settle in for a bit. He did his level best, but in no time found himself curious and tip-toed to her bedroom door and listened hard, hoping not to hear any funny business. But after the trip to the hospital, funny business did not seem to be the order of the day, and instead, Odie found himself eavesdropping on an argument in the works.

"I don't want you to leave, you idiot," she said. "I don't know what is so difficult for you to understand."

Jake's voice said, "Back then, I could have fought to keep you, but we both know it would be a fight, and since I always fight dirty, I reckoned to let you go."

"And now? What's your excuse for right now?"

"I ain't done," said Jake. "I got to finish what I started."

"No, you don't."

"I could never look at that face of yours and let it go," he said. "I made a promise."

No one spoke for so long, Odie thought maybe they knew he was on the other side of the door and planned to catch him. He tensed his knees, ready to attack the steps until he was downstairs until he heard her say:

"I got a million moves in my playbook, Jake. Moves I could employ to get what I want from a man, but something tells me none of them would work on you. I know you like to say it's me that can't be kept, but we both know it's you."

"I'll come back," he said. "I got those two promises I got to keep, and I'll be back. I'll handle things and drop off the kid, and I'll be back."

Odie thought for sure she'd give him the business right there, but instead she said, "Then I should tell you that McBreen is looking for you."

"What?"

"McBreen heard you were running about and figured it only a matter of time before you came here. He told me to put you two in touch. He'd rather it not be a surprise. I didn't tell you, because I was hoping I could talk you into staying . . . but that ain't the case."

Odie stepped away from the door. He felt like an immigrant in this world, but he knew well enough to collect his things and be standing by the car, so he did just that. In no time, Jake appeared with his shit and slipped into the driver's seat. It hurt like holy hell for him to say goodbye to her, but he'd made his way through it, and soon they were on the road. Behind them, the little Alabama neighborhood got smaller and smaller until they passed over a rise, and it disappeared altogether.

They drove west for a bit and were out of Alabama in no time and into Mississippi.

"I need to ask you something," said Jake.

"Go for it."

"What did you think?"

"Think about what?"

"About back there." Jake kept his eyes on the road. The fluorescent yellow dashes lining the center of the freeway blurred as they zipped beneath the hood and snaked behind them. They cruised through an abandoned construction zone where bright orange barrels stood sentinel over the area that tomorrow would be worked by men in hardhats. Orange cones dotted the landscape. "Back at the hospital."

"What did I think?"

"Yeah."

Odie thought a moment. He took it all in, did the math. He knew what Ruby Fuller wanted him to think. Wasn't that why she'd brought him there? Jake had a crazy life before. Once upon a time, Jake took action and look what happened. His true love's husband had been shot in the face and left simple. Now he partnered with Odie. He knew exactly what he was supposed to think in that regard. But that was not what Jake asked. Jake wanted to know what the kid thought.

"I think," said Odie, his words measured with pinkie nails, "that it's high time you let me hold the gun for a change."

11

Jake Armstrong stared over the Tennessee River when the shooting started. He jerked himself upright behind the wheel and reached for his gun long before his brain reminded him he'd given it to Odie, left himself armed with a plastic toy. Jake inhaled through his teeth. He slapped the car into reverse and faced the car toward the street, but his eyes remained fixed through the back dash.

Damn kid . . .

The door flew open and nothing would have surprised Jake had it come running out that door, except it was only Odie Shanks, whooping and hollering. He bounded all the way across the parking lot to the car in maybe three giant steps. Jake saw plenty of sweat but no blood and no sooner was the boy in the car before they tore down one road and up another and put plenty of miles between them and the gas station.

"What the hell happened in there?"

Odie panted for breath. He clutched the sides of the car seat as if to keep himself from hurtling off the earth's surface. Still that grin plastered across his face was just north of shit-eating, and Jake thought he might launch into him.

"Did you not hear me?" demanded Jake. "What happened in that gas station? Did that Arab bastard pull on you? Did you shoot him? Did he get you?"

"Naw," said Odie. He straightened his shirt, dusted off the thighs of his jeans. He leaned back in his seat and struggled for air. "Nothing like that. I'm okay. Everybody's okay."

"Okay? I heard gunshots."

"Yeah . . . that was me."

Jake squinched his eyes and anxiously rubbed his cheek with a flat palm. "What were you shooting at?"

"The ceiling," said Odie. "I just shot up in the air."

"Up in the air?" Jake blinked. "What in hell for?"

"I told him a joke," said Odie. "While he was fetching out the money, he looked awful scared. He kept saying these foreign words over and over. So I told him a joke."

"A joke?"

"Yeah. It calmed him down some, I think. I mean, the joke had Jesus in it, and on account of him being a Muslim, he probably missed the point. What I'm saying is he didn't laugh at it, so I shot the gun in the air."

Jake didn't say anything. His jaw clenched. He watched the road and weaved slower through traffic. The needle on the speedometer crept a little higher.

"I bet that's one guy that don't forget ole Odie Shanks, right?"

Jake nearly killed them jerking over the wheel and bringing the car to an abrupt halt on the side of the road. Horns blared past them as other drivers expressed discontent with Jake's driving. Odie bumped his head against the window and, as he righted himself, directed an expression most sour toward his partner.

"Are you crazy? What gives?"

"What gives? What gives is you're doing this all wrong. You don't want that guy back there to remember you. You don't want the girl whose ring you stole to talk about you on the Internet. You don't want to leave spent shells on the floor of the gas station you just robbed, not to mention rounds in the ceiling. Am I getting through to you? Do you understand why I prefer you to have a toy gun?"

Odie reckoned this had been welling up in the man for quite some time. He felt willing to give leave of it, but no sooner had he thought of Jake's side of things than he had an answer somewhere deep within himself, and that answer begat another and then another, and before he found the good sense to keep his mouth shut, he opened it.

"Look here," said Odie, "I ain't been nothing but a good guy through all of this. I ride with you all day long with no AC even though it's hot as blazes outside. I listen to your old-timey music and pretend I don't hear all the racist shit you say. And let's not even get started on your alternate agenda."

"Alternate agenda?"

"Don't play dumb with me," Odie hissed. "You said you was taking me to Hollywood so I could be a famous actor."

"Where the hell do you think we're headed?"

Odie, nobody's fool, smiled sideways. "We may be headed there, but you didn't say nothing about stopping off and killing anybody and everybody that ever done you wrong."

Jake said nothing. His eyes narrowed to slits, and he studied Odie for more than a minute. Behind them, traffic whipped past. Jake couldn't be bothered with it. After he reckoned his point good and made, he turned in his car seat and faced forward.

"You got no idea what they done to me," he said.

"You got no idea what I know and don't know," Odie countered. "I know plenty, and I ain't got out of the car yet, have I? No, I'm still in it, right alongside you. I get what you're up to and now I'm asking you to get what I'm up to."

"And what is that?" asked Jake. "Telling jokes when you're supposed to be on a job? Leaving evidence at the scene of a crime? Is that your grand scheme?"

Odie fumed. He stared out the window a bit before muttering, "I want people to remember me is all."

Jake felt for the kid. His voice shook, and he looked every which way except at Jake, as if eye contact might shake loose that tear dangling over his cheek. Out of respect, Jake found something else to look at, something outside the car.

Odie said, "You know, I done googled myself something fierce every time we stopped someplace. Ain't nobody talking about me going missing back home. Ain't no news reports about the kidnapping or pictures of my parents crying or nothing. I check my email and nobody's written me to ask if I'm okay."

"What have I told you about checking email?" said Jake under his breath. "There ain't no cause for—" Odie wasn't having it. "You know, there's some girl running all over Mississippi, stealing cars and beating the shit out of guys, taking their wallets. Everybody's talking about her. Everybody's trying to figure out her story. On Twitter, she has her own *hashtag*, for Christ's sake."

"Hashtag?" Jake furrowed his brow. "What the hell is a *hashtag?*"

"I don't have time to go into it right now," said Odie, "but it's big. 'Hashtag Sweet Melinda' is what they're using, and there don't seem to be nobody in the whole world curious about what happened to old Odie Shanks."

Odie turned his face to the window and said no more. Jake watched the back of the kid's head for a while and let him stew. Jake and his family never much mattered to each other and neither missed the other when Jake lit out, back when he was young. Sometimes it was hard for him to think that other folk's sentiments ran counter. He reached out a hand to the kid's shoulder, which Odie promptly shook off.

"You don't realize it right now, kid," said Jake, "but it's best if they don't know who you are. It's best if ain't nobody looking for you. I know it's hard for you to believe, but in time you'll be happy that you're anonymous."

Odie sniffled. Jake returned his hand to his shoulder and again, it was rebuffed.

"If it makes you feel better," said Jake, "we can look into what it takes to get you one of them hashtags, whatever they are."

Odie chuckled. After a moment, the chuckle developed into something heartier, and Odie turned back in his seat, facing front. He ran a finger along beneath his eye, then laughed some more.

"You're going to fetch me a hashtag?" Odie smiled.

"Sure," said Jake. "If it helps, and ain't too hard to get."

Odie quit laughing, but his smile stayed right where it was.

"Thanks, Jake," he said.

"You bet, kid."

Jake checked the road before easing them back onto it. He touched the knob on the radio, then stopped just shy of clicking it on. He motioned to Odie, to let him choose the station, if he wanted.

"You go ahead," said Odie. "I don't know none of the stations out here anyway."

Odie sat back in his seat while Jake watched new horizons unfold.

12

Eyeball McBreen had it all figured out. He drew a crude outline of the Office Supply store onto a flattened cardboard Bud Light box. He took time to look up from his work and meet both Odie and Jake's gaze with his one good, static eye.

"Friday nights for places like this are slow," he explained. "At night, they don't see any traffic after seven, seven-thirty."

The cardboard box was spread out over a pool table nobody was using. The pool table was in the back room of the bar where the only other living, breathing souls were the bartender and two saps hunched over chilly mugs of beer, their heads only inches above the counter. The bar was on the back half of Clarksdale, Mississippi, just off Highway 61.

It was a quiet day. Thursday.

Eyeball McBreen was nobody's fool. He'd brought with him a short, stocky fella named Stuart. Stuart ran a bit slow. Eyeball explained that Stuart had "whatever that thing Rain Man has." Stuart sat on a bar stool next to the pool table and watched the billiard balls, all racked up and ready to go.

"There are three employees on a Friday night," explained Eyeball. "A cashier, a manager, and a fella whose job it is to stock the shelves.

Only there ain't nothing for him to stock, so he's usually standing around, joking with the cashier or smoking a cigarette out back."

"No security guard?" asked Jake.

"They got a security guard," Eyeball answered. "He sits outside in a minivan. This minivan stays parked in the handicapped spot all night long. He's there even after the joint closes. He's licensed to carry a gun and he keeps pepper spray in his belt."

Eyeball pointed to various spots across the cardboard map. "Two ways in and out. One up front, one in the back. Four video cameras. Closed circuit."

"Say, if it's slow, chances are there won't be much cash in the register," said Odie Shanks. He pointed to the little rectangle Eyeball had drawn on the box, which was supposed to represent the cashier's station. "Chances are, they drop it into the safe throughout the day."

"Chances are you are absolutely correct," said Eyeball. "But since they were busy all day, the safe will be full."

"I don't know nothing about cracking no safes," said Jake.

"Which is why I brought my good friend Stuart here. Stuart may not seem like much, but when it comes to safe-cracking, he's a genius."

Both Jake and Odie turned to look at Stuart. Stuart sucked on two of his fingers and wouldn't take his eyes off the nine-ball.

"You're going to have to trust me on that one."

Odie shrugged it off. Over the past week, he'd heard crazier things.

When they first met up, Eyeball McBreen expressed a need to find a new line of work. He filled Jake in on the ever-changing business of weed and how the last nineteen years—while good to him—were the end of the "salad days" of that particular industry.

"It's a whole new world. They're regulating the shit. Decriminal- izing. You seen what they've done in Colorado and Los Angeles? It's over, man. I been doing this for nearly twenty years, so how exactly am I going to move on? What the hell do I put on a resume?"

Jake rubbed the stubble on his cheeks. "I'm just not so sure that an Office Supply store is the answer. There are too many variables. Too many nooks and crannies. Gas stations are smaller."

"And gas stations have smaller payouts," said Eyeball. "You'd have to hit twenty gas stations to get the payout we're going to fetch at the Office Supply. And think of the possibilities. We can move on, hit a couple more of these scores before they catch on. I mean, it's what's left of corporate America, so by the time they run it up the chain of command and catch on, we'll have robbed eight or nine of them and have moved on to Circuit City or Payless Shoes."

The thought of hitting one store instead of ten did something for Jake.

It did something for Odie, too. Especially after Eyeball McBreen offered his next suggestion.

"We're going to need to get a gun for this kid."

Jake shook his head. "No way. I'm nervous enough when he plays with that damn cap gun."

"We need another gun," said Eyeball. "Just in case. And we can't exactly outfit Stuart with a piece."

Eyeball explained there was no place better to get a gun quick and quiet than that part of the country. Folks armed themselves with Bible quotes protecting their second amendment rights. But among all the spots in the region, there was one above all for firearm procurement.

"Folks sell all kinds of shit in Tunica pawnshops," said Eyeball. "You'll get your pick of the litter."

So they found a spot just up Highway 61. A quiet little strip mall where every occupant except the pawn shop had gone belly-up. A place called King Louie's.

Odie got the feeling if it wasn't on the walls, in the aisles or behind glass at King Louie's, it couldn't be found. From chainsaws to lawn mowers to gold or diamond jewelry, King Louie's had it. He had no time for any of it, rolled instead straight to the back counter where the guns hung on the wall behind the register.

Jake, on the other hand, had different priorities.

The man running the joint was King Louie himself. He stood nearly seven feet, weighed about three hundred easy and had skin colored like coal. His voice had bass so loaded it could rattle windows.

"Say fella," said Jake, "you know any good rib joints around here?"

"You bet I do," said King Louie. He leaned his massive weight across the counter and pointed a thick finger out the window. "Go up one stoplight, then hang a right. Then take another right. It's out behind a pair of hemlocks on your left. If you hit the bass tank, you've gone too far. Maybe about five minutes or so."

"They better than what I'll find a little further into Memphis?"

"I can't say nothing about a little further into Memphis than fuck a little further into Memphis," said the large black man. "But that little joint is half the reason I bought this shop where I did. Besides the barbecue, they got gumbo so thick, it goes down like oysters."

Jake reckoned that good enough for him. He grabbed Eyeball by both shoulders and drew him near. "I'll run on up to that rib joint and pick us up three slabs of spares and some of that gumbo for the table. You help the kid with the gun." He hitched his pants and shot a sideways glance at Odie before ambling out the front door.

Odie and Eyeball got down to business. King Louie laid several pieces along the counter: a 9mm, a shotgun, and a .22.

".22 will clip a guy," said King Louie. "It will shut him down, but won't kill him."

He pointed to the shotgun. "This will make a statement. You can't hide it, nor can you hide your intentions. Walk into a place with a shotgun and you're basically giving folks two options. Leave the place on your feet or in a soup bowl."

Odie felt butterflies slam-dancing inside his belly when King Louie motioned to the 9mm.

"9mm is the go-between," said King Louie. "What you hit, you stop. It's bigger than a .22 but ain't quite a .44. You rack this thing and folks will stop what they're doing. If you have to fire it, it's going to put a body in the dirt. She kicks, but she kicks smooth and after a while, you'll find that you like it. She's a bad girl, but you ain't got to spank her none. No, she'll do the spanking for you."

"I think I love her," whispered Odie.

"She's one that won't break your heart."

While they waited for Jake to return with the ribs, Eyeball took Odie aside, out of earshot from the soft-brain, which gave Odie cause to wonder if it all was an act.

"Let me ask you something, kid," said Eyeball. "How serious are you about this Hollywood business?"

Odie cleared his throat. "Beg par—"

"This trip to Hollywood," said Eyeball. "To be a big-time movie actor. How serious are you about it?"

"Pretty serious," mumbled Odie. He had to confess, he hadn't given it much thought as of late. That shiny, coal-colored Beretta in the waistband at his back served as a sort of force field letting no stray thoughts enter his brain. He couldn't be bothered with anything before he stepped into the pawn shop and very little after. "Why do you ask?"

"Cause it seems to me you got a natural knack for this business," said Eyeball. He looked around the room, took his time getting out the words. "I think you'd make a good manager for an outfit like ours, and I don't reckon Jake there knows the proper way to go about using a guy like you."

Odie was humbled. "You know, I've been thinking the exact same thing. I like Jake and all, but he's from a bygone era."

For the first time in a week, Odie felt secure again. In a week that had been nothing but lights at the end of tunnels, he finally felt like he'd found a good, solid foothold.

"We don't have to talk details now," said Eyeball, "but I just want to hear that you're not married to old Jake. Like, if Jake wanted to go his own way, you might consider other options."

"I'd more than consider them," said Odie. He tapped his new toy tucked neatly under his shirt. "I think you and me could go far."

Eyeball slapped him on the shoulder and pointed out the window. Jake pulled the car into the lot, and the two of them stepped out into the hot Mississippi sunlight to help him with the go-boxes full of hickory-smoked madness.

For to hear Eyeball McBreen tell it, the only unforgiveable sin was to not see the writing on the wall. While he didn't believe in ESP or psychics or divinations, that did not mean he didn't think one could see into the future. He'd known for quite some time what was in store for him, long before those phone calls from Rob Winchester and Danny Yeager.

Only a couple days earlier, he'd gotten off the phone with Danny Yeager and known what was coming. No one had heard from Rob Winchester, and here was Danny on the other end of the phone, full of light and promises.

"I got him," said Danny Yeager. "I finally did what we should have done nineteen years ago, and there ain't no need for you to worry no more."

"Have you seen his body?" asked Eyeball.

"Don't need to. I sent him with my best guy."

"Your best guy ain't no match for a pissed off Jake Armstrong," said Eyeball. "This ain't over by a long shot."

"You worry too much." Eyeball reckoned it was true, but he still needed to see the body. "Call me when it's done," he said and hung up.

That was the last he or anyone else had heard from Danny Yeager.

Two hours later, Eyeball set his plan into motion. He called Ruby Fuller several times, each time emphasizing how he'd love to patch things up with Jake Armstrong. He pulled out old plans he'd shelved regarding the Office Supply store down South of Memphis. He called up Stuart Rimon, long considered one of the best safe-crackers in all of Tennessee.

He made sure he had plenty of bullets.

Eyeball McBreen heard Jake carried a kid with him. He'd readied himself for the worst, but had no idea until meeting Odie Shanks just how Odie could benefit him. The kid was smart. The kid was capable. But most of all, the kid had that quality about him that so many people did, especially in Eyeball's line of work: The kid was angry. Shady. Odie Shanks searched for meaning in a world that rarely served it. Eyeball, being a betting man, reckoned he could get Odie to jump ship.

And that afternoon in Tunica, Eyeball reckoned if he couldn't, he'd steal a page from Jake Armstrong's playbook. The one he'd employed since walking out the doors of the correctional facility.

The only way to know for sure who wasn't about to stab you in the back was to kill them all.

13

About a quarter to nine, after things had been slow for more than an hour, Jake moved in on the security guard, a mid-sized fella sitting in a van outside the Office Supply store in Wolfchase. The played word games with his phone and had no time to react when Jake stuck a gun in his face and told him take it real easy now, take it easy.

Eyeball came in through the sliding door in the back and told the guard to put together his wrists. He used a black, plastic zip tie to bind them together, then jammed the gun once to the guard's head. He opened a wound, but the guard remained conscious. Frustrated, Eyeball jammed him again and this time the guy's head slumped forward as blood ran free to his lap.

"You didn't have to hit him," hissed Jake.

Eyeball disagreed. He slid shut the sliding door and led the way toward the front doors of the Office Supply.

Odie hung back a brief moment. He took time to look over the top of the outlet store at the gathering clouds. Caught himself trying to remember when was the last time he'd seen it rain.

"It's flatter out here than where you come from," said Jake from behind him.

"I reckon that's true."

"Sometimes," said Jake, "it's so flat you can see into forever. You lose that behind those tall pines of yours back East or the skyscrapers in some of the cities. But this part of the world is flat and full of treeless stretches, and you can see storms brewing or the last breaths of a fiery sunset."

"And that's a good thing?"

"It can be," he answered, "but only if you prefer to see what's coming."

Up ahead, Eyeball hollered at them to get a move on. They did, and Stuart held open the door as Jake entered, his .38 already hoisted high.

"None of y'all move," he shouted to the room. "This here is a stick up!"

They had it timed. Somewhere in the night previous, Eyeball thought it funny how long it took Odie to smoke a cigarette.

"It's because I smoke a one-hundred," Odie had explained.

But still it tickled Eyeball something fierce until he rose a finger to the air and an idea struck his face. "I think old Odie here can be our stopwatch."

No sooner had Odie entered the Office Supply than did he light one of his one-hundreds with one hand while yanking free his brand new 9mm with the other.

Three people in the store and not a one of them moved, except to look at the others. Jake no longer pointed his gun at the ceiling, pointed it instead into the face of the manager.

"There going to be any trouble?" Jake asked him.

"No, sir," said the manager.

"Nobody act like an asshole, and this whole thing will be over in a couple minutes."

Odie kept near the door, cigarette hanging from his mouth. Gun hanging at about his waist. Finger off the trigger, like he'd been taught.

Eyeball and Stuart got right to it. They made a bee line for the back office. Stuart carried with him a small leather satchel and an unsettling determination. He tried the door knob, and it wouldn't turn. He tried again. He stared at it with his mouth hung open.

"You!" Eyeball shouted at the manager. "Give him the keys to that door!"

The manager's keys were attached to his hip by a neon yellow keychain. He couldn't for the life of him get it off quick enough. Eyeball nudged him hard with the barrel of his scattergun, which got him moving. The manager fumbled the door unlocked, then Stuart disappeared inside the office.

Jake stared at the cash register's many buttons. He pressed down one button, then another. The machine didn't like it none and let fly a high-pitched squeal. Jake grew tired of it and brought down the butt of his .38 against the top of the machine. It liked that even less, and suddenly the computer went nuts.

"Open this fucking thing!" he barked at the cashier.

She could do nothing. "You broke it," she said, "when you punched it with your gun."

She had a bit of sass, and Jake didn't like it. He told her to get down on the floor and don't open her mouth again. Told them all to get down on the floor.

"How are we on that cigarette, kid?" Jake called over his shoulder.

"Nearly half the way to the filter," Odie called back. "Let's get a move on!"

Odie looked away from the room, out through the front window. Far off, over a few lots, he could see a police car. Not one, not two, but three. Their lights rotating. Far enough away that there shouldn't be any concern, he told himself.

And the cigarette burned further . . .

Then, in the middle of all this, Eyeball said to the room: "Ain't this just like old times?" When nobody said anything in return, he said, "Did you hear me, Jake? I said, ain't this just like old times?"

"I seem to remember things different," Jake said. He didn't take his eyes from the panel of buttons on the register.

"You know what I remember?" Eyeball laughed. "You want to hear one of my favorite memories of all time?"

"Not right now, I don't." At Jake's feet, the cashier squirmed.

"This one time, I was up late with Danny Yeager." Eyeball took his time getting out the words. "Making a weekend of it. Remember those? Benders, I think the alcoholics call them. Parties that start on Thursday and could very well end on Wednesday."

"He was an asshole," Jake said.

"Among other things," nodded Eyeball.

Eyeball adjusted the scattergun on his shoulder before continuing. "But one night, he realizes I ain't come back from the bathroom in quite a while, and he finds me on the floor. He told me I wasn't breathing, so he climbed on top of me, and that's where I found him when I woke up. Him, beating on my chest and telling me don't you die, motherfucker. Wake up, don't you die."

"You were too valuable a customer for him to let go of," said Jake.

"You know what I always wondered?"

"What's that?"

"I've always wondered if you'd have done the same, if it was you who found me on that bathroom floor."

"You all came at me with guns." Jake no longer concerned himself with the cash register. "You all had designs to put me in the ground."

"What do you reckon we should do right now?"

"That's an awful big bag to carry around with you," said Jake. "Believe me, I know. I've grown mighty tired of carrying it."

"You going to be able to lay it down?"

Odie took a step closer to them. He carried the steadily smoking cigarette in front of him, between his thumb and forefinger.

"Gentlemen," he called, "I bet there's better times to have this conversation."

Odie's eyes were off the door for no more than a second, but that second was long enough, for somehow that security guard had loosed himself from the black plastic zip tie and found himself a gun. He charged into the Office Supply with a bleeding face and an anger unrivaled and pointed his own gun at Odie's head and soon an explosion swallowed him whole, an explosion and a loud, piercing scream that took Odie longer than imagined to realize was his own.

Odie fell to the ground. He dropped the gun and threw up his hands to his face, where he found a hot syrup blossomed. Chunks of ear stuck to his fingers, yet still he screamed. Standing over him was the security guard who brought around that gun, lowered it, pointed it square at Odie's chest and then again the explosion.

Above him, the security guard jerked first one way, then the other, as bullets ripped into him. One in the shoulder. One in the chassis. Then one from Eyeball's scattergun for good measure, which sent most or all of that security guard raining down upon Odie in a hot stew.

But Eyeball didn't reckon himself done just yet, and he let another shot rip, this time going wild and taking out the plate glass windows. The safety glass held all the world at bay with a spiderweb of impossible white strands, shot, and pellet. Jake dropped to a crouch, aware of just how close that shot had been at his own head and, seeing Odie down on the ground and bleeding, did not care to join him. He popped up from behind the cashier's partition and fired two in Eyeball's direction.

"I guess that about does it for bygones," shouted Jake.

"That shot weren't meant for you, Armstrong," shouted Eyeball. "My trigger finger moved quicker than the rest of me, I reckon."

"Step on out in the open, and let's you and me settle this."

Odie couldn't get a look at Jake's position, and neither could Eyeball. Nobody could except for the cashier at his feet and the soft-brain Stuart, who, upon exiting the manager's office with that satchel in one hand and his own 357 in the other, drew a bead on Jake. He fired two, the first splintering the cash register, and the second catching him in his gun arm. Jake wheeled around and opened fire, taking out the right side of the soft-brain's head. A big flap of skin and scalp, popping open like a can of something good, and all the stuff inside shooting out like a jack-in-the-box.

The room erupted in screams, not just Odie's. The stockboy covered his head with his arms and writhed, as if shot. The manager curled into the fetal and wept loudly. The soft-brain took his lumps like a champ, backed against the wall and bleeding out, his face somewhat serene and turned toward the back wall. In the distance: sirens.

"Jake?"

The call came from Eyeball, somewhere yonder.

"Jake?"

"I'm still here."

"I ain't letting you walk out that door."

Glass crunched somewhere Odie couldn't see. He scooped a mess of blood into the palm of his hand, then wiped it on his jeans as he rose unsteadily to his knees.

"Cops are coming, McBreen," said Jake.

"We only ever had one outcome."

"Oh, I don't know . . ." Jake sounded sick. Uneasy. "I think this could still go either way."

Odie heard Eyeball chuckle. Just arm's reach away, the cigarette floated in a creek of deep scarlet blood, smoked down to the filter.

"Odie?"

It was Eyeball.

"Odie, you hear me?"

Odie held his breath.

"You got anything to say about these goings on?"

Odie put his hand to the side of his head again. Pulled it away and looked sadly at the gore.

"Leave him out of this," said Jake.

"Oh, he's knee deep in it, don't you think?"

"This is between you and me, Eyeball."

Eyeball didn't say anything for a minute, the only sounds in all the world being whimpers, gasps for breath, and faraway sirens.

Then, finally, Eyeball called from somewhere unseen, "Odie . . . If you want to leave well, I guess I got no choice but to let you leave."

Odie didn't move.

"You hear me, kid?" The sound of the shotgun racking. "Go on and make for the door."

Odie took a breath and held it. The right side of his face, which had burned hot since the shooting started, now felt ice cold.

"Odie?"

That time, it was Jake.

"Odie, listen to me now."

It sounded like all of outside was one giant police siren punctuated with screeching tires and revving motors.

"Odie, when I come up over this counter, I'm going to come up shooting. You hear me?"

"Yeah, I hear you."

"When I do, I want you to break for the door."

"Jake, I—"

"I'll have you covered, kid." Jake took a deep breath. "Get your ass to Hollywood."

Odie wiped blood from his eyes and had every intention of telling Jake to wait just a minute, but never got the chance.

The shooting had already started.

#DEPUTY ROY RAINS

1

Deputy Roy Rains did not beg off early that night. He sat amongst the regulars at the All-Niter Café, jawing it up and sipping coffee. Talking politics and telling stories, as he was wont to do on a Saturday night, just as he was wont to do on any night of the week. As if Roy had lined the interior of the little highway diner with straw and kindling and built a nest. If not there, he could usually be found manning the speed trap out on the 809. Or sneaking a quick nap out behind the old mill. Life, to Roy, was that simple. All because he was the sole lawman in Lake Castor.

And sole lawman or not, that particular Saturday had been a slow one. Commissioner Stanley Rodenhizer's ribbon-cutting at the new Walmart out on the highway drew a crowd from three cities, but the Sheriff insisted some of the other boys from the county keep an eye on things. The deaths of the two joyriders still rankled the old man and he thought it far from wise to parade the deputy among other folks at the Walmart, eating turkey legs or corn dogs or whatnot. Instead, Roy stayed around Lake Castor and got two speeders early enough in the afternoon to justify heading in for coffee. Nothing ever came on the radio, so essentially, he'd spent the evening biding his time, shooting the shit.

"What do you think about what your favorite Senator said the other day?" asked Captain Dick Munson, blowing on his coffee. Little pools of nicotine slavers gathered in the many creases surrounding his mouth.

Able Riggs wiped his hands on the front of his overalls. "Well, Dickie, you know I'm a Republican. But honest to God, I don't think a damn one of them on our team is running with their elevators all the way up. I mean, what the hell is wrong with asking the richest two or three percent to pay their way? Just pay their share is all, same as you and me. You know how much I paid on that little place I got up on Bleak Mill Road? With social security and disability and pension and all that, I paid three hundred sixty-four dollars."

"You're kidding me," said Roy.

"No, I ain't. That's exactly what I paid. And if they asked me for twice that, I could have paid it and afforded it."

"Praise Jesus," said Pete Garrison. "You know how much I paid?"

"Point is," continued Able, "if they ask somebody making millions of dollars or so to throw a little more in the kitty, it ain't right if they don't pony up."

"It sure ain't," said Gil Tanner, wiping the last of his Boston cream pie from his mouth with a napkin, then wadding it up and tossing it down on the table. It fell to the floor, and nobody minded it until Frances, the night waitress, came up alongside and stood there staring. She didn't let up and finally Gil reached down to pick it up. "Real sorry, Frannie. It just dropped is all."

"I ain't here to pick up after you men, you hear?" she said and went about her business.

"So that's why I'm going to vote for Red Mason come November," said Able. The other fellas sucked the air from the room in one collective gasp. He met each and every one of their stares, daring them to challenge him, daring them to call bullshit. "I'm a Republican through and through, but I'll vote for Mason, and I think he'll do a lot better job if the Republicans just get out the damned way. Hell, he's practically GOP himself."

"You really ain't going to vote for Bobby Lufkin?" asked Captain Munson.

"And that don't make you Democrat?" asked Roy.

"I told Sonny the other day, I can't never be a Democrat no matter how much sense they make, not as long as they keep pissing away our tax dollars on bullshit." Able fussed with the tip of his nose and looked up and down the rows of booths in the All-Niter, some occupied, others not. Not that he ever would edit himself on account of other folk.

"Every time I see a homeless woman with a bunch of little homeless children, all asking the government for money because she can't afford to pay for all the kids she done shit out, it ain't going to be the Democrats doing what needs to be done."

"And what's that?" asked Tanner.

"Sterilizing them," answered Able. "Sterilizing every damn one of them to make sure they don't have more little ones to eat up all our tax dollars."

Each of the men stifled laughter best they could, for they knew Able would sometimes run at the mouth to try and fetch out a laugh, if there was one to be fetched. But at the same time, they could never tell when Able turned serious. Older folk from town could remember a time when Able and a few other men patrolled the polling place with guns to keep out the blacks, or met the voting officials on the town limits and replaced their ballots with the ones they wanted. There was no Klan in Lake Castor—not no more—but only because nobody wanted a ruckus. Everyone knew the score. Things changed, just as they did all over the rest of the country after 1965, but Able and a lot of other fellas thought it just fine that the blacks came over to this side of town to work and buy things, then went on home to yonder side amongst their own.

Roy checked his watch. Officially off-duty. He fished a couple singles from his pocket and set them on the table.

"That does it for me, boys," he said. He squeezed himself from the booth and jostled the table with his gut. Coffee sloshed from cups, the salt shaker tumped over. He harrumphed something like an apology, then tightened his utility belt around his waist, which only made him feel larger.

Frances came by and filled the others' coffee. "You leaving, Roy?" she asked.

"Yes ma'am," he answered. "I left you some money on the table right there."

"Well, ain't you something?" She smiled. "You have a good one. Rest of y'all need to hurry up and settle with me. Phyllis is coming on, and I'm going to need to check out."

The men grumbled, shuffled stuff around, fetched dollars from their billfolds and tossed them to the tabletop.

"Hey Roy," said Able, "you ain't got to go home yet, do you? You and me can head over to the Lucky Strike and hit a few pins, bowl a frame or two."

"I don't know . . ." Roy let it hang. He didn't want to go home, but he didn't have any extra clothes with him, and he damn sure didn't want to go out in his khakis. All day long he'd been tucked into this get-up and the last thing he wanted was a couple beers and hurling twelve-pounders down the planks while wearing gear an obvious size too small. *When did it get to be a size too small?* He'd gotten an earful from the Sheriff only a couple days previous and hadn't had time to sort it all out yet. Beers and bowling would only put that off some.

Sheriff wanted him to know: "Kids got killed, and that puts you on the map. They had some drinks from somewhere in town and were driving way too fast, and now they're dead. I got people from Richmond and Winston-Salem telling me about two boys running into that wall, but I can't get nobody from this here itty-bitty town to tell me where a pair of twenty-two-year-olds got enough booze to send them into the concrete at sixty miles an hour."

"I can't be everywhere at once," Roy had tried to tell him.

"But you're pretty damn good at being nowheres at once," the Sheriff barked back, "especially when you're on the clock. I got kids down at the water tower lighting bottle rockets at Braulio Ramirez. Why do I have kids throwing firecrackers at a high school janitor?"

Roy chortled. "How am I supposed to know?"

Sheriff didn't care for that answer. Roy wasn't cutting it, in his opinion. He'd kill to have another guy in his spot, but what options did he have? If a guy was worth his salt, he was needed somewhere else. It was rare for issue to come out of Lake Castor. Either nothing ever happened or they managed a way to take care of their own. He knew Roy wasn't the most active of his men, but Lake Castor seemed a speed even he could handle.

So Roy knew he needed to keep his composure. To run down to the Lucky Strike in uniform smacked of *irresponsibility*. They'd all be looking at him. Town was small enough; they'd know him no matter what he wore, probably even send over a beer or so, shake some hands. But in his uniform . . . That would be pushing it, a slap in the face. With those boys dead and all.

"I don't reckon it to be a good idea," Roy said. "I'll take a raincheck, though."

Able scrunched his face and scratched his head. He looked to Frances, adding up her checks and writing in a pad and said, "Hey, Frannie, you're still going bowling with me, ain't you?"

She looked over her wire-rimmed glasses. "I reckon so," she said. "You're going to be embarrassed that your little sister beats you at bowling in front of your buddies."

"Sounds like a challenge to me," said Able. He rose from the table and squared himself at her. "It's my name they got stenciled on the wall up there, my scores in the trophy case. I reckon I can take care of myself."

Roy put a hand to his belly. His juices riled. "Frances goes bowling?"

"Sure does," said Able. "Since we was kids."

Roy grimaced. An empty trailer waited for him back at his place. Two beers in the fridge with some milk and week-old biscuits. Nothing on TV and the VCR on the fritz. He fast-forwarded to the end of the evening and saw himself sitting in his skivvies, watching news from Richmond and wishing he'd gone out bowling.

The other fellas said their goodbyes and meandered out the door, leaving Able and Frances and Roy who had yet to move. He stood dumbfounded, as if trying to figure free a math problem that had yet to budge. Able smiled at his old friend, the fella he'd known since they was small.

"You should come out with us," said Able. "Won't nobody give you no guff about them two boys. They're just as torn up about it as you, I reckon."

Mostly, for Roy, that's where he took issue: It didn't tear him up. He could have cared less, had the Sheriff not raised hell. He knew Gideon Churchhill pretty well and felt bad for him losing his boy Ollie, but reckoned it the second time he'd lost him, all the same.

Gideon moaned on and on about his boy coming home, listening to that rap music and wearing his pants off his ass—smoking and drinking—and figured this was the best anyone could ever hope for the kid. The Hergenrader boy, well, that was a tragedy. He knew his mother from back when he'd gone to First Baptist and hated it for her. There weren't nicer people than the Hergenraders and, best he could tell, they didn't deserve to have their boy killed in a car wreck.

But they had no right ruffling feathers either, and that's exactly what they did when they went rip-roaring down Creechville Road and ran their pickup truck into the concrete wall on Old Man McCarthy's front lawn. Ruffled feathers and landed Roy in a world of shit with his boss and from that he saw no respite, not anytime soon. He took his hand from his belly and rubbed his fleshy cheek.

No, he was in a world of shit and bowling or no bowling, he'd stay in a world of shit unless something changed and he knew that change wasn't happening overnight. He looked at Frances, at Able, then at the clock.

"On second thought, Abe, count me in," Roy told Able. Then added, "Got an extra shirt in your truck?"

2

For years, Deputy Roy Rains seemed poised on the heels of a comeback. Over time, his image had taken quite the hit. But that was then. The deputy felt different Sunday morning. Hell, he felt different when he lay down to sleep only hours earlier. He was a new man. It was a new day.

He'd pulled his old hat out of the closet, a Stetson he couldn't remember the last time he'd worn. Mel Pritchett'd reshaped it a few years back, and Roy hadn't found the occasion to pull it out ever since. Why not today? He slapped aftershave onto freshly shaved cheeks and enjoyed the hell out of the brace. It felt good. Smacked some new creases into his uniform shirt with an iron he didn't even know worked. He pulled dusty dumbbells from beneath his bed and pumped at them for ten minutes before he polished his boots for maybe only the second time since he'd bought them over in Deeton. On his way into Lake Castor, he played a Bob Wills cassette he hadn't heard in forever.

He drove past his usual turn-off and straight into downtown. He wanted to make sure he was seen. Past the old tobacco buildings and forgotten chutes and smokestacks, he steered into the cobblestoned section of town and found himself surprised at all the open parking spaces. He slipped into one and stepped out of the car, ready to walk the streets of Lake Castor.

Any other man would probably still be in bed after the night he'd had. Most others would cower behind throbbing heads and worrisome shame. Not Roy Rains. He awoke with a vigor most unexpected after tying one on as he did at the bowling alley. Had he only known how much fun he would have, he would never have initially resisted.

He'd known most everyone there after eleven. Ricky Hensley from Ricky's Tires had a few fellas holding the first three lanes, seven guys playing three lanes at once. Ricky waved him over, and they shook hands and swapped sad stories about business and home and tried to outdo each other on how bad off things were, but that turned into a round of dirty jokes, and in no time, he was in on a pitcher of beer. Able Riggs and Frances Mabley got a lane just down the way, next to Charlie Whittleman and Keith Bolanger, and they had plenty to say about the football team and the coming season, and how they sure enjoyed Roy keeping an eye on the riff-raff in the parking lot during Friday games. Soon, they'd bought him a beer as well.

And then someone brought over a whiskey. Roy never touched the stuff. His daddy had a brother who'd gone crazy drinking it, and Roy half-thought even after the old man'd gone to his Kingdom that he'd return quicker than sin if the deputy so much as smelled the stuff. But one of the fellas from the tire shop brought it over and wanted them to all swallow it at once, so he did, and a little while later, he'd gotten another in him and in no time, found himself chatting up the entire bowling alley.

Frances noticed the change in his spirits. He reckoned no other woman had seen more of him over the past fifteen years or so, due to the amount of time each of them spent in that diner. She sucked on her cigarette and watched him bemusedly between tossing her turns.

"You got a little spring in your step, Roy." She smiled. "What's got into you this evening?"

"I reckon I best turn a new leaf," he told her.

"Seeing you out there back-slapping with these good old boys suits you," she said. "Makes you look ten years younger."

Roy stopped for a minute, unsure of what he'd just heard. *Ten years younger?* He tried to think of himself ten years ago. *Ten years?* Was he slimmer then? Younger in the face?

And he looked at her. He'd known her since high school. Frances, Able's tow-headed little sister, tagging behind them after school, threatening to tell on them if they were up to no good. She'd come into herself by her senior year, filling out nice and pretty and then up and marrying Jim Mabley without so much as giving another fella a chance. She was from another time. A time long before the All-Niter Café, a time before the mill closed, before everything went to shit. It struck him funny, how he could see someone every day for decades, then suddenly see them for the first time all over again. Frances Mabley, widowed waitress of the All-Niter, sister to his best friend, looking beat and pretty and waiting her turn to bowl.

Roy's chest felt tight. His head flushed, cheeks heated up. The damned devil whiskey'd gotten to him. A funny feeling rumbled from the back of his mind or the pit of his stomach or somewhere just as confusing. His daddy had been right: corn liquor ain't nothing but trouble. He'd never felt this way and never would have, had he not taken that swaller.

So he asked for another.

He knew so many fellas taken to whiskey that fell to shadows of themselves the very next morning, had run more than a few home to their wives under the threat of jail if they didn't straighten up quick. But Roy felt *great*. He took to the streets of Lake Castor that morning, but they were empty. No one was to be found. Maybe three cars in parking slots in all of Main Street. He scratched his head and headed on down the sidewalk.

Where was everyone? Sure, most of the stores and shops were gone, but the ones that stayed usually got a handful of people milling about during the day. The abandoned old courthouse stayed silent, but the post office annex usually had folks going in and out. Not today. Today, there wasn't a soul to be found. Gooseflesh pimpled Roy's arms.

Up ahead, a couple about thirty peered inside the dusty windows of the antique mall. Roy was on them like a cat on a June bug, rushing a bit before they got away but trying like hell not to seem too hurried, coming upon them and tipping his hat just so, smiling and saying:

"How-do, y'all. Nice morning, ain't it?"

Roy recognized neither of them, figured them for out-of-towners. The younger man seemed put out, his woman anxious to be let inside the store. "Do you know what time the store opens, Officer?"

Roy scratched his head. "That's odd. Taylor usually opens her up by now except on Monday when she's closed and Sunday when she—"

Sunday. No wonder. It was Sunday morning. There would be no hustle and bustle at the post office, no fighting for a parking space, no throngs of citizens out to shake his hand. If he wanted to get decked out to meet and greet, he should have headed toward the First Methodist. There'd be lines of them snaking out from the aisles any minute now after getting their Sunday message delivered.

"I can't imagine anybody closing an antique store on Sunday," said the man.

"Taylor'll open it up as soon as church lets out." Roy forced a thin smile. *Church . . . who knew?*

"That's too bad," said the woman. "We're passing through town on our way back from DC. Looks like everything's closed up."

The man took her hand. "We got to get back on the road. Maybe next time we're through."

"Maybe," said Roy. All three knew they'd never be back. They shuffled off to their car, and Roy figured he'd walk on up the road anyway. No reason to let something as simple as Sunday services take the wind out of his sails. His polished boots clip-clopped the cobblestones as he headed up, passing the donut shop, which Koreans owned now. Folks hemmed and hawed about buying donuts from Koreans rather than townfolk, but in the end, where else were they going to buy them? So the Koreans did just fine as some of the unholiest people in Lake Castor, working on a Sunday. He tipped his hat and went on.

***

The little café next to the donut shop had been there for years, once serving nice, home-cooked dishes, the hottest ticket in town. As time ticked on, the menu dwindled to its current state of cold sandwiches, coffee, and bottled drinks, and being open only during weekday lunch hours. The bookstore next to it only housed used, tattered titles at discount prices. The few city council folk left fought the addition of a Salvation Army storefront to peddle goods, afraid that would ring in the poor and colored, but there wasn't much fight left in them, so Roy figured it only a matter of time before they took the spot formerly vacated by Mr. Jacobson's hat shop.

Quiet as the visitor's center, normally staffed by little old ladies and retirees who gave directions to the marker commemorating the Civil War skirmish or a place to eat or, more than likely, the quickest route out of town. The stubborn antique malls where folks sold off what once was sacred, now was junked. Tobacco buildings tall and useless, leading folks down corridors of nothing, past nothing, and into more nothing.

The old abandoned mill looming over downtown like a reminder of the damage that can come overnight, left up as a warning to them all.

Roy couldn't take any more. Needing to lift his mood, he reckoned he needed to get the hell out of downtown. He walked briskly back to his cruiser, more brisk than he was known to walk. He started the car and tried like hell to focus on the good stuff, or something other than rot and decay, on something that would rejuvenate his revival. He thought again of Frances Mabley.

"What do you think happened, Roy?" she'd asked him the night before at the bowling alley.

"Happened to what?"

"I don't know." Years shed from her. All that tired, graying, wrinkled skin tightened. Her eyes lost their sadness. Her hair lightened. He felt a hundred pounds lighter. Her, so insecure, out of place, wistful. "Something happened. My daddy worked at that mill his whole life, and now it's just a building sitting there, like a gravestone. I'm glad he didn't live to see it go. It seems sometimes, everybody's just so sad. You worn that badge since as long as I can remember. I see you up and smiling and shaking hands like nothing happened, and now everybody's standing around you smiling like nothing happened either."

"I don't follow, Frannie," he said. He'd seen her near everyday at the All-Niter, but was this really the first conversation they'd had since the Seventies?

"It's a good thing. Sometimes people need to forget and be people again. Like they was before. You know, bowling and smiling and having a good time. And having the Deputy in here showing them it's okay to do it is a good thing. A real good thing."

"I'm pretty sure they'd be having a good time even if I weren't here."

"Maybe. But whether you like it or not, you're a leader, Roy. People look to you. That badge means something, you know. And when they see you out among them, they appreciate it."

And here he was, trying to get out among them, and they were in a goddamned church. He passed First Methodist and again cursed himself. Could he have attended this morning? Stood and sat and sang hymns in an aisle while in uniform? Shook hands alongside the parson as folks quit the building? He told himself he should drive out to the buffet lines at the Jefferson or the Silver Steeple, both restaurants soon to be packed beyond capacity with well-dressed families fresh from services, but his squad car found its way to his slot at the All-Niter.

He needed a cup of coffee first. He needed the fellas to lift his spirits again. He would practice being a great citizen on them.

"Afternoon, citizens of Lake Castor," said Roy as he walked in, cowbell clanging behind him. A handful of old-timers ate their breakfast, sipped their coffees. They looked up from their plates at Roy, kept their eyes on him, watched him as if he were some type of zoo creature recently escaped. No one returned his greeting. Roy reckoned it to be the hat. He removed it and placed it atop the cigarette machine.

Gil Tanner sat at the counter. Roy took the empty seat next to him.

"How-do, Gil," Roy said. Gil grunted a response, didn't look up from his food, kept eating. Roy watched him a moment. Waited for some acknowledgment suitable for the lawman of Lake Castor. He raised a finger to Beverly, the day waitress, and she brought him a cup of coffee.

"Didn't think we'd see you here this morning, Roy," she said carefully.

"Is that a fact?" he smiled. "Crime don't take a day off here in Lake Castor, so neither do I. What's Dave cooking that smells so good?"

"He's cooking a hamburger," she said, not willing to play her part. She noticed everyone in the room looking at them. Hell, Roy'd noticed it too. He started to feel strange in ironed clothes. He damned that hat. "We figured you'd be up in Tucker after what happened last night."

Roy chuckled. "Last night? What do you mean what happened last night?" His mind raced. Who in the hell would have told on him? Not Bolanger, for sure. Definitely not Ricky Hensley.

She leaned across the counter and whispered. "It's all anyone's talking about."

Roy looked around the room. Some of the farmers had quit shoveling eggs and grits and stared at him.

"It's hardly the end of the world, Beverly," he said. He tried to remember every detail about who had been at the bowling alley, who could have seen him drinking that whiskey. "Who's been running their mouth about—"

"Maggie Hornbecker's been all up in fits," Beverly said. "She wants your badge. Something tells me Lorne just might give it to her."

"Maggie Hornbecker? From the Pizza Pick-Up? What the hell does she have to do with anything? She wasn't there." He was pretty sure she wasn't. She had great tits and a big mouth to boot, so she never would have slipped past Roy's radar, no matter how much whiskey had been introduced.

"What do you mean she wasn't there?" Gil Tanner piped in, mouth full of ham and biscuit. "She spent the whole damned night in the walk-in freezer."

"She'd have caught pneumonia if she weren't so damned hot and angry," Beverly said.

Roy laughed. He looked around the diner. *Where's Able?* This had to be some kind of joke, and he figured that old coot was in on it. Able weren't around, and no one threatened so much as a smile.

"What are you two talking about?" he asked.

Their faces fell. "You ain't heard?" Beverly's mouth gaped. The corners threatened a sick, crooked grin. "Oh shit, Roy. You better get the Sheriff on the horn, pronto. I think you're about to catch hell."

3

When Sheriff Lorne Axel opened the door to the All-Niter Café that Sunday morning, he liked to have sucked the air from the entire building. Some folks who'd come in for breakfast nearly a whole hour earlier kept still in their seats, unwilling to leave before things got started. A small crowd gathered near the cigarette machine, and folks fidgeted restlessly in their stools at the counter. So when he stepped into the diner, he had everyone's undivided attention.

Not only did he feel he needed to see Deputy Roy in person, and not only did he need to see him at the All-Niter in front of God and everyone, but he felt he needed to see him with Maggie Hornbecker herself. And in the end, Roy couldn't tell which of the two raised more of a ruckus.

"I want this son of a bitch caught," she demanded, "and I want this here bastard to be the one to catch him. And if it ain't done quick, I want his badge. And you're going to give it to me, you hear me, Lorne?"

"Ms. Hornbecker, please calm down," Sheriff Axel said, but it wasn't working. Maggie had gotten in a lather and nothing could stop her.

"Calm down? Calm down?" Maggie slammed her hand to the formica, and a fork clattered to the floor. No one bothered to fetch it.

"I spent the night in a goddamned pizza cooler, Lorne. Calming down ain't high on my shit-to-do list today. Right now, I got other things higher in priority. One would be climbing inside this lazy bastard's ass and building a condominium, because I plan to stay there so long, I'm going to need somewhere to sleep. Do you hear me?"

"Maybe we should step—"

Maggie continued: "Second would be finding that white-trash, inbred trailer park motherfucker that stuck up my restaurant and kidnapped my manager. I want him, Lorne. I want you two hicks to find him and bring him to me, dead or alive."

She looked up to make sure everyone could hear her. By now, Able Riggs and Captain Munson had taken seats alongside Gil Tanner at the counter and watched the pizza lady make hamburger of their buddy.

"Maggie, I swear we're going to get to the bottom of this," Axel told her. "Deputy Rains here isn't going to sleep until he figures out what's going on. Are you, Deputy?" When Roy didn't answer quick enough, Axel turned on him and glared, caught him looking over at his buddies at the counter. "Are you, *Deputy?*"

Roy snapped to attention. "Yes, sir, I'll get in there and get it done,."

Maggie looked at the Sheriff as if he'd wet his pants.

"And to make sure the Deputy stays focused, I'll be sending another man down here," Axel said. "I'll bring over Deputy Harris to help out. How's that sound, Maggie?"

Roy winced. *Please, not 'Harmless' Harris.* His day only worsened. Roy enjoyed an autonomy not shared by others under Sheriff Axel's supervision. That ended the second another badge ventured over the county line. And Deputy Zeke 'Harmless' Harris wasn't just another badge. If a ruckus was to be raised, Harris certainly had no qualms seeing to it.

"Make sure this gets handled, Lorne," Maggie said. "I know how to make trouble for people, and it's more than a passing hobby of mine. Don't give me an excuse goddammit."

"Easy, Maggie," urged the Sheriff. "It's Sunday."

"I know what day it is, Lorne," she hissed. "I spent most of it in a freezer. I ain't been to bed yet. And don't give me this *It's Sunday* shit, neither. I've got God on my side here. You understand? And if I don't, then I don't give a flip, because I've got no use in a God that does not smite."

She stood to leave, but gave Roy one long, vehement look. Roy ducked his head. She turned in a huff and threw open the door on her way out, nearly breaking the little cowbell.

"Y'all want some more coffee?" Beverly asked. She'd known their cups were empty for some time now, but she wasn't coming anywhere near the table as long as Maggie'd been there. Lorne Axel shook her off and turned back to Roy.

"You think that's bad?" he asked. "Oh, it's just the beginning for you. I'm serious about putting Harris over here. The two of you ain't off-duty until we're at the bottom of this thing."

Roy didn't say a thing.

Axel continued: "It means you got the Shanks boy, dead or alive. I want to see him with my own two eyes right away. The quicker, the better. Because this could get seen as a kidnapping. And if this fella crossed the state line, then the problem goes Federal. As it is, you'll be spending the last remaining days you have at this job working with Zeke Harris. If you think that's bad, imagine spending it with a couple of FBI guys. Because they'll be turning over a few rocks, and I can only imagine whatever they uncover will send you straight into retirement. You get me?"

Roy didn't say a thing.

"You better tell me right away if any of this stuff is registering, Deputy Rains. I can never tell with you if you're just late to the picnic or if you're even coming at all. Please, give me some kind of signal that what I'm telling you is penetrating that fat skull of yours."

He took a breath and continued his tirade in a tone more hushed. "Look, Lake Castor is changing. Things can be real nice here. We don't need shit like this mucking up the works. That new Walmart is just the beginning. Think of all the jobs it will bring and people right along with it."

"If you ask me, there's a perfectly good Walmart already in Tucker, Lorne, and I—"

The Sheriff no longer concerned himself with remaining calm. The time for familiarity passed long ago. Axel wanted to reach across the table and slap Roy as if he were a school kid caught Frenching behind the gym. They were separated in age by only four years, but Axel found the schism astonishing. "I need you on this, Rains. I need you and Harris to put this away before I catch wind of any Federals. Bring me that Shanks boy, and give me somebody to arrest for that robbery. You do those two things, and I may let you retire with a county pension."

"Yes, sir," Roy said.

Axel had nothing more to say. He stood and put a five dollar bill down on the table. He tipped his hat to Beverly and started to the door. Folks watched him stop at the cigarette machine. He looked once at Roy's hat perched there, then back at Roy. He shook his head and was out the door, bell clanging behind him.

Roy sat in his booth a long while, left to soak everything in. Over at the counter, Able Riggs looked at the other men, wondered what they were supposed to do next. Never one to leave behind a fallen brother, he decided it should be he to try and cheer their crony. He slid into the booth next to a despondent Roy Rains.

"There weren't no way you could know that Shanks boy was going to get robbed, Roy," Able said. "No way at all."

"I should have never gone bowling," Roy muttered.

"Now, Roy, you ain't got to be like that," Able said. "There ain't no point in it. What's done is done. We had us a time and there ain't no going back."

Roy glared at him across the table, figured Able had to be one of the worst or best friends a guy could ever ask for. He had a point, but a point was not what Roy needed. *Not right now.*

Able went on: "Having old Harmless over here sure will be a mess, all right. He's a handful all on his own, and I don't think he'll take to the way things get done over here."

Roy said nothing. His wheels turned.

"What do you figure to do, Roy?"

Roy licked his lips and stared into his coffee cup. With a quick motion, he killed what was left of it and wiped his mouth, then looked into Able's eyes.

"I reckon there's only one thing we can do. We got to find Odie Shanks and the fella that took him. And we got to do it pronto."

4

Roy stepped into the All-Niter Café for the second time that day, only hours after Sheriff Axel and Maggie chewed him out for all the world to see. He never wanted to come back, but this time it wasn't his choice. He was no longer a solitary animal.

The fellas in the booth jacked their jaws. Frances sat over in a corner by herself smoking a cigarette, as there wasn't but one other table besides the fellas. She waved at Roy and he wanted to tell her about his morning, how much everything she'd said to him the night before had meant to him, how he wanted to change it all on account of what she'd said, but goddamn Odie Shanks and Maggie Hornbecker had dropped a fly in that ointment. He wanted to ask her when her shift let out. He wanted to say and do quite a few things but instead just waved and took a booth across from his buddies.

Able Riggs interrupted his tirade to address Roy. "What're you doing way over there, Roy? You too good to sit with us today?"

Roy's face darkened. "I ain't alone today, dammit. I got Zeke Harris riding with me. He's in the pisser right now, because he drank a bunch of sodas, and I seriously don't think the kid's got a bladder bigger than a plug nickel."

The men looked at each other. "They partnered you up with Harmless?" asked Gil Tanner. "How long's that for?"

Roy shrugged. "I reckon it will be for a spell. Lorne wants us to figure out this mess with the Pizza Pick-Up, and he says he needs his two best men on it."

Able laughed into his hand. "So he's sending a different pair of county boys over?" The men all shared a chuckle, and Roy stung when he saw Frances heard it too while bringing over his coffee. She smiled at him, but thankfully didn't laugh. He reckoned he couldn't blame her if she did.

"So Roy," said Able, "we been talking about that chicken and fish joint they put in over in Turlington. You heard of that?"

"I believe I heard tell of it somewhere or another," he answered. "What of it?"

"Able said he ain't going to eat there," said Captain Munson. "Me and Gil went out the other day, and it's pretty good."

Roy smiled. "I don't reckon Able's going to get much pleasure spending his money at a chicken and fish joint."

"No, I ain't eat there," said Able. "And I'd tell you why, but I don't care to because apparently my politics is unpopular." He shot a glance at his sister filling up their coffees. She had nothing to say.

"What do politics have to do with a fish and chicken joint?" asked Pete Garrison.

"I don't like to support black-owned businesses," said Able.

"And you don't figure that to be racist?" asked Gil Tanner.

"I don't care if it's racist or not," said Able. "If it's racist, then sign me up as a racist. Tell me where I have to enlist. But I ain't walking into a restaurant that announces itself as being *black-owned*, as if that's supposed to send a different message than when we walk into a restaurant advertised as *white-owned*. You remember old Clarence Bossey, and how he nearly got run plum out of town on account of him putting those Rebel flags on his sauce labels? The same flag that many people fought and died for over a hundred-fifty years ago."

"Yeah, I remember," said Garrison. "He said since he made the sauce, he could put whatever he wanted on the label."

"You'd think so. But not according to public opinion. Hell, he could have pasted on a goddamn Muslim flag and caused less a stink."

"Watch the language, Able," Frances called from across the room. The couple in the other booth near the door probably hadn't heard, but she liked to keep order, especially when her brother grew rambunctious.

He continued: "They took his sauces off the shelf. They went into each and every grocery store across the area and pulled them off. Remember when you could go in and get a bottle of Clarence's Tangy? I used to put it on everything, but I can't no more. They plum got rid of all of them."

"Can you blame them?" asked Tanner. "You ask me, he didn't get sick the other day at the Wal-Mart. They probably asked him not to serve up hog, because they didn't want to rankle nobody."

"I blame them pretty good when you figure in what replaced them."

"Now Able, you don't know that's what replaced them," said Roy, not really wanting to throw his hat into this one.

"The hell I don't," spat Able. "They take Bossey's Tangy and Bossey's Hot off the shelves, and a week later, they've got a vinegar and pepper sauce from Tee Bone B Q on the same damn shelves. Almost like *reparations* for serving Bossey's the past thirty years or so."

"He raises a good point," said Garrison.

"Damn right I do. So this man is sent under, sent down to fail by our society, because he respects his own heritage, but at the same time you can get people advertising themselves as *black-owned*, and it gets far less vitriol and hate than if they mention the color of the alleged majority. Where's the God in that?"

"There ain't none," muttered Gil Tanner, shaking his head.

"No there ain't," said Able. "Not a goddamn bit. And another thing—"

That cowbell rang and stopped him short. Those with their backs to the door turned in their seats to get a good look at the fella walking in: Sheriff's Deputy Zeke 'Harmless' Harris, a mean-spirited cuss if there ever was one. Only in his late-twenties, Harris garnered himself quite the reputation around the county for bad behavior when off-duty. He had a pretty good habit of limiting his hi-jinks while in uniform, but even had he committed them, it would have been done under the guise of law and therefore hushed. But most of his troubles happened out at the 809 where maybe he got to drinking and even a little grabby or felt someone talked up a girl he fancied too much, so he had to defend the honor of a stripper. At any rate, Sheriff Axel spent an inordinate amount of time cleaning up Harris' messes, mostly with the addendum folk had taken to describing the man: "Oh Deputy Harris, he's *harmless.*"

Harmless considered the folk in the room but didn't consider them much as he stepped, dusty boots rapping the tile, to Roy's booth. He removed his hat and sat, looking around the room as if he were afraid it was haunted or worse, teeming with deer ticks.

Frances appeared tableside. "Y'all want a minute to look things over?" She brought coffee for Roy and a glass of water to Harmless, held her pen and paper at the ready. Like most folks, she'd heard of Harmless, had her own run-in a while back when he'd caught her for speeding and had been more than a jerk about it. "Special today is pot roast with two sides."

Harmless rubbed his shaved head, looked over the menu with de-tachment. "There ain't much on here I care for," he said, "but I'll have that cheeseburger plate with some fries and a soda."

Roy looked at the kid when he ordered his coke, but said nothing. At some point, he planned to try and get him to piss his pants, if possible. Roy ordered the special and looked to his buddies. Their conversation continued, their world still turned. Roy felt like a for-eigner in his own country, exiled to yonder booth with Harmless Harris, while his companions enjoyed the spoils of war. Or something like that.

"Be nice," Roy growled. "I still got to eat here after you've run back to Tucker or wherever."

"Maybe," said Harmless. "But for all we know, you ain't going to be here after I'm gone. Trust me, I ain't out for your job, old man. I liked things just fine over yonder in Tucker, where there's a few more heads to crack. The last thing I need is to take things slower. I mean, a dude like me could really get lost out here. Writing tickets? No, thank you. First thing I want to do is get back where I belong. But why do you really think they moved me out here?"

"I hear it's because the blacks over in Tucker say you harass them," said Roy. "Some whites too."

"Hear what you want. But maybe you better hear this: you're on your way out, old man. They put me over here to see how exactly you spend your time, and why things ain't getting done. I mean, a kid got kidnapped, and what have you done since it happened? You been to eat twice, and you wrote up three speeders on the highway. You're your own worst enemy, partner."

He continued: "Believe me, I want to catch this fucker. I want to catch him so they put my name in the paper and move me back to Tucker. If that means you keep your job in order for me to get what I want, so be it. In fact, you could call me the biggest proponent of you staying employed. But we both know that ain't happening. I mean, you're going to have to do Superman-type shit to keep your ass in this seat and I don't believe in miracles. Nope, it'll be me bringing this home and everyone's going to know it, and they won't waste my talents in Lake Castor."

Harmless tapped his finger on his wristwatch. "Time's ticking, Rains. Ticking on your career."

Roy seethed. He was in a pickle. He needed the Shanks boy, but he needed to find him without Harmless. If they solved it together, Harmless would get all the credit. But it'd be a trick-and-a-half to get out of his sight long enough to do anything. If they didn't solve it at all, Roy would be finished.

"What do you reckon we do?" asked Roy. "What's your plan?"

The food arrived, and they set upon it. Not the type to wait until he was finished chewing before speaking, Harmless plunged into it. "Every one of these shit towns has a little crowd of assholes who like to mix it up a little. Whites and blacks both. You know who they are."

"I know there's a card game out behind Mel Holliday's shop every—"

"No, sir," Harmless said sternly. "I'm talking about *mixing it up*, not folks staying up after lights out."

"Well, Harmless, Lake Castor is a pretty quiet little town."

"Not lately," said Harmless. "It's quiet until it ain't. It's quiet until some tweaker gets loose and starts sticking up pizza joints and kidnapping people. They struck first, so we got to strike back."

"Strike back at who?"

"Don't really matter," he said, wolfing down the cheeseburger. "We find some troublemakers, go in hard and make a stink. Get people to talking down at the 809, and that will rattle who the real assholes are.

Get them scared enough to do something stupid. And that's when we move."

Roy would have none of it. "That's insane. You're suggesting we cause trouble for someone we don't believe had nothing to do with it? All in the name of finding the Shanks boy? And this is supposed to help us how?"

"It'll help a lot more than sitting on your fat ass in this here diner," said Harmless. "At least it's doing something. And it's doing it out loud. Lorne'll hear and feel better about what's going on out here. Won't feel like sending nobody else or, god forbid, the Federals."

"I think we need to discuss this a little—"

"The only thing we got time to discuss, old man, is who we're going to hit. Now there's got to be someone you know of that you'd like to play a little chin music for. Somebody that's just been *pushing it* for some time now. Somebody who's feathers you'd like ruffled."

Roy thought about it. Sure there were a few names he could throw out there, but nothing along the lines of what Harris wanted. If Roy heard him right, he could be getting into some shit best left forgotten or ignored or never known about. Lake Castor wasn't the type of community that liked getting ink in the papers. Whatever folks did around town or outside town, they'd been doing it for a while and liked it best that way. Roy knew that if Harmless got to digging, he'd find some likely candidates and probably not the ones they ought to be messing with. Roy needed to find a distraction.

"I want you to think on this," Harmless said. He polished off the food in record time and tossed his napkin to the plate. "Ask around if you have to, although I doubt very seriously you do. And if you don't, then I will. I know a few guys down at the 809 who could have me pointed in the right direction. But right now, I got to piss. That soda's going right through me."

He got up and clopped across the tile, and the bell rang on his way out. Roy sat there, staring at his plate, appetite dashed. Frances stopped by, refilled his coffee.

"I don't like that one there," she said. "I don't like him one bit."

"A necessary evil at the moment, Fran," Roy muttered. "Thanks for the coffee."

"You know, he may be a necessary evil for you," she said, "but he ain't for me. I think you're an all right guy, Roy. But if it's all the same, I don't really care to have him in here no more. Do you follow me?"

"Ten-four, Frannie," he said. Roy's shoulders slumped. *What a bad day.* He sipped at his coffee. The fellas chatted each other up, off in their own world. He thought about what Harmless planned to have them do, and how he would probably be having them do it until he was gone or Roy was, whichever happened first, and thought: *This just ain't going to work.*

It ain't going to work one bit.

5

The sun finally began to set on what turned out to be a very long day, but the heat went nowhere. The air was no less still. Roy told Harmless to turn off the gravel road and onto the dirt road, but Harmless already knew the way. Besides, he quit listening to anything coming out of Roy's mouth a long time ago.

"Look, these here boys are a touch skittery," Roy said. "They tend to get nervous. When we get up here, why don't you just park the car and let me go in and do the talking? These boys know me a little better and probably won't be as twitchy if they see it's just me."

"That's exactly what we don't want," Harmless said. He could see the doublewide trailer up ahead, sun going down behind it, casting it against a mess of pinks, oranges and purples. "I want them nervous, I want them scared. I want them likely to do something stupid. And I'm well aware that sending you in first is precisely how to muck up getting what I want."

Rocks and sticks and pinecones crunched beneath the cruiser's tires. Angry, pulsing music screamed from inside the trailer—*rap music*, Roy figured—and screamed it loud, so no one heard the police car pull up. The shades were drawn. Two souped-up motorcycles sat outside the front door, as well as two pickup trucks, a shitty coupe on blocks and a nicer four-door. Roy could match every vehicle except the coupe to a driver and it comforted him none.

This is going to be painful, he thought.

Had his life not been interrupted, he'd be settled in at the All-Niter, where it was air conditioned, listening to whatever crap Able spewed. Instead, he rolled with Harmless Harris into what was probably Lake Castor's biggest drug den for white boys. Harmless killed the headlights, pulled up right behind the bikes, so they were blocked in, then killed the engine. He checked his service revolver, made sure it was ready for action, then holstered it.

"Let's make this Sunday night memorable for these bandersnatches," he said, then leapt from the car.

Roy banged on the door hard, like they'd discussed. Not hard enough. Harmless told him to do it again—"*Louder!*"—but still no one inside heard it over the stereo. Harmless had enough and left his position beside the door and banged on it himself, this time much, much more forceful. Immediately the music stifled, and Harris jumped away from the doorway. Footsteps raced to and fro inside the trailer, shit was moved around.

"Who is it?" asked a woman's voice.

"Police," called Roy. "Open the door, please."

"What's the problem, Roy?" called a voice. Roy knew it to belonged to Eddie Mercer. Worked at the auto parts shop. Drove the blue pickup.

"Just open up, y'all," he called back. "We just want to have a word, that's all."

"What do you mean *we*?" Eddie called back through the door.

"This is ridiculous," Harmless grunted. He left his position and faced the door. He took a breath then drove forth his foot, striking the wood next to the door knob. Nothing happened. He kicked it again, which still did nothing.

"What the hell are you doing, Roy?" called Eddie through the door.

Harmless threw another kick, and this time it worked. The door flew open but hit something on the other side, something that wasn't ready for it and went flying into the entryway along with the door. Roy figured it to be Eddie Mercer, auto parts employee. Harmless rushed in, service revolver drawn, waving it here and there.

"Everybody get on the floor and lock your hands behind your head!" he shouted. There were about eight people lounging in the tiny trailer's living room, and all eight of them hit the deck, did as they were told. "Nobody move because my trigger finger's real itchy. Maybe y'all heard of me!" He called back to the doorway: "Get in here, Roy. Come have a look-see at what happens when you make people pay attention."

Roy stepped into the trailer and looked around. Folks on the floor, Harmless with a gun at the ready. Eddie Mercer rolling on the linoleum entryway floor, blood spurting from his nose. A bathroom mirror had been removed from the wall and now sat atop a ratty coffee table in the middle of the living room. Roy didn't need a criminology degree to know that if he licked the glass, he'd get no sleep before Tuesday.

In the back of the trailer, a toilet flushed.

"Dammit!" cried Harmless. "They're getting rid of the shit! Watch them, Rains!"

He raced through the trailer, hitting nearly every wall on the way back to the johnny. From there, Roy heard shouting and a scuffle. Roy kept his revolver drawn but didn't bother pointing it at anyone. The folks in the living room stayed put, except for the older one, Tank Tillotson. Tank graduated two years behind Roy and ran a garage near town. Tank lifted up his head and looked Roy dead in the eyes.

"What's your damn problem, Rains?" Tank wanted to know.

"Zip it, Tank," said Roy. "This will all be over with in just a bit. Deputy Harris has a couple questions he wants to ask y'all. This is only as painful as you want it to be."

"I want you to hear something, Roy," Tank said. "I want this to be pretty painful. I'm fine with it. I thought we had an understanding, and here you go mucking things up."

"We didn't have no understanding, Tank. I've known for years what you fellas have been up to out here, and I ain't said or did nothing about it. I've let it slide, because you boys keep your troubles out here in the woods. You ain't never started no problems, so I didn't start none."

"Like I said: *an understanding.*" Tank stared at him until Roy found something more interesting to look at. "I can cause problems too, you hear me, Rains?"

"Is this piece of shit threatening you, Roy?" Harmless stomped into the living room, dragging a skinny kid of about eighteen, kid knew to work at Tillotson's Garage. Harmless dropped him to the ground and stepped over two men to get to Tank, give him a swift, hard kick in the side with his boot. Tank crumpled and rolled over, clutching his ribs. The other folks in the trailer, including Roy, shouted in protest.

"What the hell are you doing?" Roy called.

"This man was talking sass," Harmless said. He backed away and pointed the gun at the entire room, in case anyone felt like doing more than just bitching. "We don't talk sass to law, you all hear me?"

"Zeke, can I talk to you outside?" Roy asked.

"Right now?" Harmless asked. The smile plastered across his face scared the hell out of Roy. "This moment here is what they call *inopportune.* We got a couple questions to ask these here fine, upstanding citizens of Lake Castor. Are you folks ready to answer some questions?"

Tank grunted, clutching his ribs. He writhed in pain. Roy wouldn't be surprised if one or more of them were broken. The others said nothing, kept their faces in the shag carpet. Eddie Mercer didn't move from the doorway.

Harmless got down to brass tacks: "All right, we got us a little situation in town. I'm sure you heard tell of it. Somebody up and robbed the Pizza Pick-Up last night. Took the cashier hostage."

"That ain't us," called the skinny kid, who Harmless found in the bathroom. "Why don't you go roust some blacks or somebody on the other side of Jefferson Street?"

"We thought of that, trust me," said Harmless. "But we had witnesses, and witnesses said it was a white fella done it. There ain't many white fellas around town that would or could pull something like that, so we had us a short list to work from." Harmless stepped over a couple of folks to get to the skinny kid and put his boot to his back. The fella squirmed. "Don't interrupt while I'm talking please."

"Deputy Harm— er, *Harris*," grunted Tillotson, "I promise you none of my boys would have anything to do with that. We don't go waving guns at folks. We're peaceable. When we're left alone, don't nobody get hurt."

Harmless applied more weight to his boot, and the skinny kid cried out. "Please, old man, if you can't say something that don't sound threatening, then maybe you shouldn't say nothing at all."

Roy kept his gun drawn but would rather have holstered it and walked out the door. Just walked away, got in the cruiser and drove on. On past the All-Niter, on past the edge of town, on out of all of Virginia if he could. Harmless could act like this, because he knew he could get away with it. He could keep up the tough guy routine longer than most, keep it up and never have to worry about letting his guard down. He was young and had a stronger stamina for being an asshole.

But most likely, Harmless would get shipped back to another corner of the county and Roy didn't much care to clean up after him. No, he'd rather just run for it.

But Roy could not run. He couldn't leave the trailer, nor could he leave town. He had nowhere else to go. Not enough money to relocate and honestly, not enough drive. Lake Castor was his home. This was his job. And dammit, he felt he had to do a little more to keep it. He had to contain the fallout.

Harmless kept at it, asking the same question in different ways, switching up the words some, asking the people one by one, trying to rattle a cage or two. They gave him nothing. Roy reckoned they were either great at keeping mum or they were telling the truth. Nothing about Tillotson or his boys suggested anything like the magnitude of the Pizza Pick-Up robbery, but Harmless wouldn't listen to reason. Not reason that didn't have his boot print all over some poor fella.

Harmless lined them all up against the living room wall. There were ten of them all together, and the wall wasn't near long enough, but this struck Harmless funny, and he made them all squish in tight, so tight that it would only be funny to someone like Harmless.

"Y'all listen up," Harmless said, once he had them all hushed. "We're going to find the Shanks boy. Now we got all kinds of leads to run down and some rocks to turn over, so we're going to be busy and need all the help we can get. That's why we're counting on the likes of you. We're stopping by here every night. Every damn night until we find the Shanks that boy alive or dead and the fella that took him. So if I was you, I'd get to looking for that Shanks boy him as well. Ask your buddies. Ask the scumsuckers coming by to buy whatever shit you're cooking in your bathtubs. Ask everyone coming through for an oil change or a lube job. Point is: quicker we get our job done, quicker we're out of your hair. You hear?"

No one said a word, but Roy felt they'd made their point. *Alive or dead.* Roy shuddered. It was the first time he'd considered the possibility of the robber killing the Shanks boy. And once he'd thought about it, he found it hard to shake. Although he had other concerns at the moment, he knew he needed to keep Harmless from wanting to return to that trailer ever again.

The way Tank kept eyeballing him, he figured he already had some ideas on how to go about that.

Roy didn't want that either.

Alive or dead. It wouldn't leave his mind. All night long. After he dropped Harmless off at the old police station, it was still there. The possibility the Shanks boy had been murdered. He started to wonder if things would ever get back to normal. If things could return to how they were only twenty-four hours ago. He wondered again if the Shanks boy would be found alive.

And in no time, he began to formulate a plan.

6

Able Riggs took a big swig of iced tea and kept right on talking, never minding anyone who didn't care to hear it.

"I say if they're going to live in our country," he said, "they need to learn the damn language. It's going to cost too frigging much to reprint all those government forms, so they have both English and Spanish on them, just because some immigrants don't want to learn the language."

"You reckon so?" asked Gil Tanner. He kept in mind the Mexican couple in the back booth, wanted to make sure they continued chattering away at each other and paid no mind to what the *gringos* were saying.

"I more than reckon it," said Able. "I guarantee it. Then what do you think will happen next? They might as well start putting Arabic on them too."

"Or Ebonics," said Captain Munson. He frowned and rubbed at his stubbly jowl with a liver-spotted hand. "Y'all heard about that one, right?"

"On *Sixty Minutes* a while back, I did," answered Tanner. "That's the black folk language, right?"

"It sure is," said Munson. "I been working around colored folk as far back as I can remember, and I never got to where I could understand ninety percent of what they were saying. I had no earthly idea it was because they was talking a whole another language."

"You hush, Abe," hissed Frances. "Don't you get all these boys to going neither."

"Aw Frannie, them folks over there can't understand nothing we're saying." Able looked in the direction of the Mexicans and waved his hat. "Hey there, you two! We ain't bothering the two of y'all with our old folk talk, are we?"

The Mexican man smiled big and toothy, then waved back. His woman turned in her seat and nodded.

Able turned back to Frances. "See? No harm, no foul." Frances had more to say but never got the chance. The front door swung open, the bell making a racket and in came Roy like a tropical storm, his arms flailing wildly and sweat sticking his shirt to him. He came, panting and gasping to the booth where the old men kept and grabbed his seat.

"Abe, I got to talk to you," he said.

"To me?" Able smiled. "What's the pride of the county want to talk with me about? Where's your new buddy Harmless? Ever since you took up with him, you haven't come around to see your old friends."

"I'm serious, Able," he hissed.

"Where's Harmless?" Able asked.

"He went down to that spot out near Blood Holler where kids go to smoke cigarettes and whatnot when they skip school. He said he was going to put a little scare into them and see if they give him any good leads."

"Good Lord," breathed Tanner. "Leads to what?"

"That Pizza Pick-Up thing."

"You've got to be kidding me," said Able. "What do high school dropouts have to do with the Shanks boy going missing?"

"Like I know?" said Roy. "And it ain't a kidnapping yet. Don't say that." He winced at the coffee. He wiped at the sweat on his forehead with a napkin. "Last thing I needed today was to go about rousting high school kids, so I gave Harmless the slip."

"How'd you do that?" asked Captain Munson.

"Well, he made us take lunch over at some burrito joint by the river, on account of neither him nor Frances wants him taking lunch in here anymore. So I told him that crap upset my stomach." He put a hand to his belly and bit his lip. "Not exactly an untruth."

"I can remember when Al and Faye McBriar used to sell hot dogs out of that building," said Able. "Then they go and put a burrito stand in there."

"We don't have time for that right now," Roy said. "I need to talk to you, Able." He looked to the other men, then said, "In *private*."

Munson and Tanner nodded then went back to their coffees. They looked anywhere except at Able and the lawman.

"Captain . . . Gil," said Roy, "if you don't mind . . ."

Realization hit Munson's face. "Oh, are you wanting *us* to leave the table, Deputy? I ain't going nowhere. I got my coffee to drink. If you want to talk to Able in private—"

"Fine," spat Roy. "Come on outside, Able. This is important."

Able grumbled a bit, then got up and followed Roy out the door, jingling the bell as they exited. It was still hot outside and never felt more so than when a person stepped from the sanctuary of the hardest working air conditioner in Lake Castor. It felt like stepping out from a refrigerator into a steam bath. Able'd put his hat on after reaching the parking lot, but almost immediately removed it and began to fan with it.

"Where's the fire, Roy?" asked Able.

Roy looked around the parking lot. The heat emanated from the cracked asphalt in waves.

"I can't talk about it all right now, Able, so you'll have to bear with me." Roy glanced over his shoulder at the door, made sure the coast was clear. "All I can say is that I'm bound to be in a real fix, and I can't see but one clear way out of it. We been friends a long time, right?"

"Of course we have," said Able.

"So if I was up a tree, you reckon you'd be there to get me out?"

"Sure. I guess so." Able grinned. "Not like it'd be the first time. Not like you ain't done it for me once or twice."

Roy patted him on the shoulder. "You're a good man, Able. Ain't many like you."

"If you try and kiss me, I'll pop you one," Able growled. "I don't care how long we been friends."

Roy wiped his hands on his khakis. "Listen, tonight Harmless is going to want to ride up to the 809."

"Oh hell. Hasn't he had enough of that place?"

"I think he's got old scores to settle." Roy grimaced. "And now he wants to ride up there, while he's wearing the badge to settle them. Say he's doing it in the name of the Shanks boy. I can't have that. I especially can't have him doing it with me standing there. That's a good way to get me lynched."

"I understand the man has a need to poke sticks in every hornet's nest he hears tell of, but I can't for the life of me figure why he's got to keep messing with that one."

"Me neither," said Roy. "Listen, I'm going to stall him. I'm going to force him to put that little trip up to the 809 off until tomorrow. But I won't be able to put it off longer than that. He's got an itch and there won't be nothing in this world short of a hand grenade to get him not to scratch after it. So we got no choice but to act fast."

"What do you need me to do?" Roy looked about again. Clear. He scratched at his head and leaned into Able. "I need you to grab a couple of shovels," he said. "Then meet me out on Nokomis Road tonight about nine. Don't worry yourself if I'm late. I'll be there, I just got to shake Harmless."

"Gotcha," said Able. A small fire lit behind his eyes. The man's heart normally pumped propane, but it hadn't caught flame in years. Able was raring to go.

"And Able," said Roy as he high-tailed it back to his cruiser, "be ready to get your hands dirty."

7

Deputy Harmless Harris perched at the edge of the cornfield and watched the road leading up to the house. He was at full alert. He kept his sidearm holstered but the safety switched off. Instead, he carried his scattergun. He loved the feel of the artillery in his hands and relished any opportunity to bring it out.

"Where is that son of a bitch?" he growled.

A few corn rows over, Roy and Able bent just below the tops of the stalks. Their crouching days were well in the rearview. Able didn't have the knees anymore, and Roy'd just flat-out gotten too fat. They kept an eye on both the road and the house. A good fifty yards separated the cornfield from the home, a fallow field splitting the two.

"He'd have just got off work at the plant a half-hour ago, Harmless," Roy called back, just above a whisper. "He'll be here. Hold your horses."

Harmless spat at the ground. "I don't see why we're sitting out here waiting. We should just charge in and see if the Shanks boy really is kept in there. When he comes home, we pop him then."

"I thought you liked to take them by surprise," Roy said.

"We'll surprise him sure enough when he opens the door and sees us sitting there with the Shanks boy, don't you think?"

"We don't technically have cause to be in that house," Roy reasoned. "Remember, it was an anonymous tip that got us here. We go in there without a warrant, and we won't be able to hold nothing up in court. And if he sees us before he gets in the house and rabbits, he'll be in the wind and we'll never catch him."

Harmless hated it, but he knew Roy had a point. Yet Harmless really hoped for a reason to use his precious shotgun and that Joseph Two Trees would never see the inside of a courtroom. He prayed the oily old Injun would be armed and, when he saw the law move in on him, he'd realize the jig was up and come out shooting. Harmless was ready. He wanted a piece of him.

When Roy approached him earlier that evening, Harmless' sights were set on the old 809, the converted doublewide trailer turned nightclub that got its name from its location out Highway 809. He'd had run-ins with the notorious watering hole and had been jettisoned several times as a customer, sometimes so abruptly that he felt need to express his frustrations in the parking lot and on as many people as possible. But Roy's news derailed his plans, and he figured he could take on the crew at the 809 another night.

"I got us a lead," Roy had told him. Harmless could only wonder what kind of rocks Roy would have turned to get anything resembling what could be called *a lead*. "You ever heard tell of an Injun in town by name of Joseph Two Trees?"

Indeed, Harmless had. Joseph Two Trees was a Catawba fella, a loner who worked out at the dog food plant on the edge of town. For most folks growing up in the area, Two Trees served as a bit of a curiosity, a man well assimilated, but still ingrained with his mother culture. No other Catawba remained in the area, and to anyone's memory, he never married. Occasionally he would show up in town drunk and punch out a car window or some other act of mischief, but his main crime up to that point had been coming off a touch weird.

So when Roy told Harmless that he and Able had run down some awful reliable information that led them to Two Trees' house in search of the Shanks boy, it sounded good enough. Sure, he wanted to know a few things, but Roy insisted on keeping his trap shut and, after a bit, Harmless decided he didn't care as long as he could bring his shotgun.

Bringing Able along had been Roy's idea. Harmless couldn't stand the guy. He'd known them all his life. Growing up in the county, he'd heard both the loud crowings of old men clinging steadfast to their fading power and influence, knew to fear more their hushed whispers. His father had been one, over in Tucker. They refused to cede authority, clutching it tight with both hands until lowered to the grave. All the while, spewing toxic shit from both ends. Roy said it wasn't happening without Able, no way was he going into the den of Joseph Two Trees without backup. Harmless consented, because the last thing he wanted to do was call for assistance.

"No way one of those assholes from the county are getting any of this," Harmless had growled. "This is all mine."

And so Able Riggs joined them, dressed in a faded pair of overalls and hefting a hunting rifle from a bygone era.

The three men ducked a little lower below the cornstalks as twin headlight beams slowly wound the bends of the road heading up to Two Trees' house. Harmless' grip tightened around the stock of the shotgun, waiting to hear the telltale rattle of the recluse's motor. As it came through a stand of pin oaks, he heard it.

"It's him," he said.

The headlights swept past the cornfield, lit them up for a second, but kept on moving as the truck pulled into the gravel lot next to the house. The men froze. *Had he seen them?* No one moved, Harmless ready in an instant to attack should the truck back out again. But it didn't. The engine shut off, killing the old pickup's rattle. The night plunged into silence, save for the siren of crickets and the faraway *harrumph* of bullfrogs. The driver door creaked open and out came Two Trees, carrying a sack of groceries. Harmless figured if Injuns had some sort of third eye or sixth sense, Two Trees would turn tail and run, but his myriad of pagan gods must have all been asleep at the wheel, because the old hermit wandered across his gravel lot to the house like it was any other night.

"Let's move," Harmless whispered the second Two Trees had gone inside. The three men, clutching their weapons, crept closer to the house. "And remember to be careful in there. The Shanks boy may still be alive."

But Roy knew that would not be the case, for he and Able had seen to it that the Shanks boy would not be telling any tales that evening, nor any others.

The living room light clicked on. Roy and Able took both sides of the door, backs pressed flat against the walls of the porch, weapons ready. A light came on in the kitchen. Two Trees was moving through his house. Harmless stood at the door, poised for action. He looked to the other two, made sure they were ready. A light clicked on in the back bedroom.

This is it, thought Roy.

Harmless nodded, then moved to the door, gave it a pounding the likes of which it had never seen.

"Joseph Two Trees," he shouted into the door, banging away. "This is Deputy Zeke Harris from the County Sheriff's. I need you to open this door right away, you hear?"

Something broke inside the house. A few things slammed against the wall. Two Trees made a sound, and it was difficult to tell what it could have been.

"Two Trees, you open up now. There's a whole mess of us out here with guns, and you're coming out of that house one way or another!" Harmless bared teeth. "I'm giving you to the count of three, Two Trees!"

Inside, they heard glass shatter in the bedroom. Then the sound of wood splintering.

"Sounds like he's running for it," barked Able. He bounded off the porch and rounded the house.

"What the hell is he doing?" demanded Harmless, but he had no time to bother with it. If anyone was shooting the Injun, it was him, so he started kicking at the door, two or three times with his dusty old boots until the jamb cracked, and he could go at the rest with his shoulder. After a messy affair, they were in, and Harmless scattered through the living room, the kitchen, following the trail of house lights until he stormed all fevered into the bedroom.

Harmless never lost a step. Rushing through the house, he had but one focus: Get that Injun before Able did. Normally there were all sorts of procedures and protocols. His mind switched to autopilot. For all he cared, there could have been cigar-smoking monkeys hanging from the wallpaper throughout the house, it would not have stopped him in the slightest as he barreled straight for Joseph Two Trees, shotgun ready to fire.

So the dead kid on the bed in the back room deterred him none as he shouldered his way through the door. The sight of his face smashed in and discolored didn't faze him at all. The rifle-toting Injun stuck half-in, half-out of the bedroom window held Harmless Harris' full attention hostage as he exploded into the room. The expression on

Two Trees' face said it all. His eyes bugged. His mouth opened to speak, but given the situation, had no earthly idea what to say.

"Get out of that window, Two Trees," barked Harmless. He planted his feet and pointed the scattergun at his quarry. "And you'll want to drop that rifle."

Two Trees froze, seemed to weigh all his options. Found there weren't near as many as he'd hoped. But he wouldn't drop the rifle. In fact, his knuckles whitened around the breech.

"Deputy Harris," he stammered, "I don't know nothing about—"

"Drop the rifle!" Harmless shouted. He didn't like what he saw in Two Trees' eyes. "I ain't telling you again."

Two Trees didn't move. "You listen! This isn't what it looks like. I'm telling you that—"

He didn't finish speaking. Harmless heard a gunshot, a solitary rifle crack, and Harmless fired his shotgun into Two Trees, buckshot ripping through him and launching him through the window and out into the yard. Able stood on the opposite side of the window, grinning like a maniac, his rifle smoking at the barrel.

"Holy hell, Harmless," Able shouted, "you killed the bastard."

"I heard a gunshot," Harmless sputtered. "I swear I heard a gunshot."

"That was me," said Able. He inspected Two Trees' body out on the lawn, pried the rifle from his hands. "I was giving him a warning shot is all."

Roy eased into the room, surveyed the scene. He looked at the dead kid on the bed, the gunsmoke filling the room, the wall where the window used to be. He whistled real low.

"This is a pickle," he said.

"No shit it's a pickle," spat Harmless. "I think of all the things you could say right now, that's got to be one of the most useless." He turned from the window, sick of looking at the body of Two Trees. For the first time, he looked at the corpse on the bed. Even without the face, you could clearly tell it was a kid. Discolored and bruised and a pallor quite deathly. Dead a while now. He'd been dressed in a nice, black suit for some sick reason or another. Harmless didn't pretend to understand the machinations of a depraved Injun. He walked over to the body and felt its leg. His hand shirked away almost immediately.

"What the hell?" he snapped. "Did that sick fuck embalm the Shanks boy?"

Roy watched him steady. Harmless, for as stupid as he was, wasn't dumb. Roy gave him a matter of a minute before he started putting things together. Probably less time, if he kept poking around the dead kid like that.

***

The idea to smash the body in the face had been Able's. He figured it would initially be more shocking and serve to distract both Harmless and Two Trees, keep them from nosing around until everything played itself out. Roy found it a touch morbid, but since it had been his idea to dig up the Churchill boy in the first place, he reckoned he couldn't go pointing any fingers. The task at hand now was to wrap things up here, for their work was far from done. It had been a long day for Roy and Able, and they couldn't quite call it quits just yet.

Earlier, down on Nokomis Road, Able posed the only objections he'd had concerning the entire ordeal.

"If I'm going to be doing all this digging," he said, already knee-deep in the hole, "then I get to do the shooting."

"I'm fine with that," said Roy. He turned over loose dirt and went back for more. That was part of the genius of the plan of course, since Oliver Churchill had only been interred three days ago. The flesh had not gone to rot yet, and the dirt was considerably easier to manage than the grave of someone buried earlier.

"I'm serious, Roy," Able said. "I been wanting to crack a shot at that fella for some time now, and I want your word that I'm the one gets to do it."

"You have my word," Roy said. "Now we better hurry because Harmless will be expecting us in about an hour, and we can't look like we've been digging up a body."

So they got to digging faster, and soon enough got themselves deeper into the hole until they hit the top of the coffin, and Roy stopped for the first time to take a breath. He'd ruined his shirt. His fleshy chest heaved up and down. and if he fell over and died right there on top of the kid's grave, he figured he'd be just fine. Let Able clean this up. He scanned the horizon for something but knew he'd find nothing. It was just he and Able and the dead. Maybe nightingales or toads or some shit. He cleared away the dirt and stuck his spade into the side of the coffin to pry it open.

"It's like 1974 all over again, ain't it?" Able said, wiping his brow.

Not exactly what Roy wanted to hear, but it wasn't like he didn't already think it himself. He brushed away the thought and leaned on the end of the shovel until the coffin top popped open.

"Except this time it's an Injun that's going to come home to a body in his bed he's going to have to answer for," Able said. The grin stretching across his face was both wicked and sentimental.

Roy set aside the shovel and looked across the graveyard. Only twenty yards away sat the iron fence, mostly rusted out but still there and as long as the folks running the county still ran the county, it would always be there. Overgrown brush grew through it in places, spaces where bars now missing once separated the two halves of the cemetery. Folks at the church paid a colored fella to come round and keep the graves clean and, even though no one bothered to have him or anyone else maintain that fence any more, it would never be taken down. Not in this lifetime. Not until someone sent down the National Guard or some edict from God to tell them that blacks and whites had to be buried alongside each other like in counties up North.

"No," Roy had said, "this time it's different, I suppose."

He peered down at the top of the coffin and figured him and Able had gone back quite a ways, been in a scrape or two together over the course of fifty some-odd years. Things passed between them that many folks would never know about. The entire community of Lake Castor had been built and preserved on the backs and actions of men like Able Riggs and Roy Rains, but there would never be any statues built to commemorate them, never any roads named after them. Folks weren't going to stop on the square and say thank you for keeping our streets safe or at least making us think our streets are safe, and thank you for all you've done to protect the ways and traditions of the very same folks that populate this here boneyard, and one day Roy knew that all those dirty secrets would join him and Able six feet down, no one ever knowing and, quite honestly, he was okay with that. In fact, he wanted it no other way.

"And you feel pretty sure Harmless will bite?" Able had asked.

"It's about the only thing I'm pretty sure of," said Roy. "If he walks into the 809 tonight, he'll have to work at it pretty hard just to put the cuffs on some guy he fancies an asshole. But come hell or high water, he knows he'd have a chance of squeezing off a shot if we get him alone with Two Trees and no other witnesses."

"What if he wants to take it to the Sheriff?"

Roy looked sideways at him. "You think Harmless is going to want to take this to the Sheriff? He wants this just as bad as I do. He ain't going to want any backup or any witnesses or nobody else to see his moment of glory."

Roy knew that getting Harmless to go along with riding out to Two Trees based on some half-baked story about insider tips would be relatively easy. The hard part had been finding the scapegoat. If Maggie Hornbecker hadn't already identified her assailant as white, it'd been much easier. They'd simply have to ride over to the other side of Jefferson Avenue and roust a colored kid, then put the body at his house. And since some sick code of Able's prevented him from setting up an actual white man, they had to make allowances. Lord knew neither of them raised any issue with Catawbas or any other red man's race, but circumstances dictated compromise.

Two Trees worked a good eleven hour shift at the dog food plant which gave Able plenty of time to plant the corpse, while Roy went to whip Harmless into a lather. It was a lot of work sure, but Roy preferred it to another couple of months following Harmless in and out of every spiderhole in Lake Castor, getting folks worked up over the smallest things. So this, he figured, was the way it had to be. They opened the lid and peered inside. Roy covered his nose and mouth with his sleeve. Able winced but recovered, knowing he'd get used to it.

"Like I said," Able had muttered, "your word that I'm the one does the shooting."

***

And later that night, Roy knew as he watched Harmless inspecting the body of Oliver Churchill in the bedroom of Joseph Two Trees, that any minute he'd wise up and put two and two together. He picked at the suit jacket, felt the skin, wondered how Two Trees could go about embalming a body and beating in its face, kept thinking aloud how something wasn't right. Roy knew something needed to be done, but he remembered his promise, remembered that he'd given his word. He stepped aside, a few feet back from the deputy.

"Where do you think you're going, Rains?" Harmless wanted to know.

"Able," said Roy, "you waiting for a personalized invite or what?"

Harmless turned toward the window, wondering what Roy could be talking about and saw Able Riggs leaning over the sill holding Two Trees' hunting rifle and drawing a bead on him, started to say something, but it was lost to the ages as Able fired and caught Harmless Harris square in the chest, spinning him around and slamming him against the wall.

"Again?" Able shouted. "Do I need to hit him again?" Harmless didn't move. He stood, back to them, face pressed against the wall for what seemed like an awful long time. Then the hole in his back grew darker, stickier, and there was no doubt he'd been hit and hit good. His knees gave, and he slid to the floor, smearing blood against the wall all the way down.

"That ought to do it," said Roy. "Now let's get the gasoline."

Roy liked to nearly choke on the fumes as they doused the room, it got so thick in there. They made sure to get plenty on the body of the Churchill boy. Ever since the OJ Simpson ordeal out in California, folks got the scare that no bad deed could ever be left unsolved so long as DNA evidence was left intact. Roy poured a mite extra on Harmless too, just out of spite, and told Able to go ahead, drag Two Trees in as well so they could get him to burning. Able went out to round the house, pulled the Injun back in the door and was gone a spell, then wandered up to the windowsill from which he'd shot Harmless.

He said: "Roy, Two Trees is gone."

Roy didn't have a response to that, just stared at the window at Able, waiting for him to crack a smile and say he was only kidding but it didn't happen. Instead, they stared at one another.

"What do you mean he's gone, Able?"

"I mean he ain't here." Able turned to look again, but the result had not changed. "I mean, he was here when I left him, just as dead as could be but now he's gone."

Roy still could muster no more than an idiot's stare, mouth agape and eyes blank. His arms fell slack at his side. He was lost.

"We've got to find him," he said. "We've got to find him now."

Able looked back from the windowsill. "Where do you reckon we start looking, Roy? I mean, he was right here, and now he whoa—"

Able stopped short. Roy still hadn't got the juices flowing, so when he saw Two Trees pounce Able and grab his head and jam a blade into his throat, he watched it just as immobile as if it were on the television. Two Trees punched the knife right into Able and jostled it around, so Able choked and gargled on his own fluids.

Two Trees finished with him, extracted the blade and let him fall to the ground. He turned to Roy and, if looks could kill, well, the Injun's eyes were guillotines.

Roy hadn't moved since forever. He took the news of Two Trees' disappearance the same way he'd taken the assassination of his best friend. The blood stopped pumping in him. Thirty years ago, he probably would have had all the answers. He probably would have put together the proper arguments and assertions to reason with his would-be attacker before any further issue got raised, but instead the only issue he raised was his service revolver, and he put one right between the filthy animal's eyes.

Roy did not move. The gun stayed pointed at the broken window, through the sill, as if Two Trees would re-animate. But he wouldn't. Nor would he ever again.

"Able?" Roy whispered.

But Able wasn't coming to the window either. No prayers or juju anything short of the devil would bring him back, and Roy was left alone to clean this mess. He holstered his weapon and sat on the bed next to the Churchill kid.

"This is all your fault," he told him. And he believed it too. He put his head in his hands and knew that before he lit that match, he'd have to head round the house and drag in Two Trees all by himself, because this was a load all right and one he would have to shoulder alone.

8

It seemed everybody had something to say about this mess. The fire that ate Joseph Two Trees' home had yet to quit smoldering, and the urns to house of the remains of the dead hadn't been selected. The weekly paper had still another two days before it would be delivered, but everyone in town was abuzz. And funny, for as much as folks seemed to want to talk about it, no matter where Deputy Roy Rains went, people sure shut the hell up the second he arrived.

Well, not *everyone*. The folks that wanted to talk to Roy about the matter were of a different sort. And the usual how-do-you-dos and the man-it's-a-hot-one-todays just weren't going to cut it. Roy would need real answers for these folks.

For example, Sheriff Lorne Axel held an opinion. Folks believed Lake Castor to be the sleepy, quiet, depressed little corner of the county. Now it had a body count. Lorne felt it not good for business and wanted Roy to share his pain. He brought with him two new deputies—two men from Whitfill—and said Roy would be taking a few days off. He was on leave.

Lorne had more to say, a million questions to ask, but he would have to wait his turn. Two other people with interest in the case were the Federals who made it down to Lake Castor. Anywhere else, the Shanks ordeal wouldn't raise so much as an eyebrow with the Federals, but with Lake Castor being so close to the state line, the chances of it going interstate ticked a bit higher. Still, it rarely warranted more than a phone call, but these two already happened to be en route to an ordeal down in the Carolinas.

The first one spoke with a New York accent. "What led you to Mister Two Trees' house last night, Deputy Rains?"

"A tip Harmless picked up, sir," said Roy.

"Harmless?" asked the second one, a friendly fella with a bushy moustache.

"Deputy Ezekiel Harris," corrected Sheriff Axel. "Harmless is a nickname."

The New Yorker nodded. "Deputy?"

Roy continued: "Yeah, Harm—er, *Harris* and I spent the last two nights running around town, trying to figure who knew something about the robbery out on Pleasant Ridge Road. This issue was top priority for us, as you can imagine." He glanced toward the Sheriff, then quickly looked away. "We reckoned it had to be a local fella."

"Why's that?" the second Fed asked.

"A couple of things Mag—*Mrs. Hornbecker* said," answered Roy. "If a white boy done something like that around here, there are only a handful of doors you'd go knocking on. Deputy Harris and I were able to put two and two together from there."

"These people led you to Joseph Two Trees?" asked the second Fed.

"In a way," answered Roy. "They said things that led us to look in directions which brung us to Two Trees. Harmless got a phone call from someone that said Two Trees had been acting weirder than usual. We followed up on it, and Two Trees caught us sniffing around. That's when he started shooting."

The New Yorker consulted his notes. He looked over the top of his glasses. "One of the people killed was a gentleman named Able Riggs.

He was not, nor has he ever been in the employ of law enforcement out here, is that correct?"

"Correct," answered Roy.

"Then why did he accompany you and Deputy Harris last night?"

Lorne had spent the majority of the morning asking Roy the same question. Except he asked it with a bit more volume. Lorne found fifty different flavors of problems with the same question. He voiced them all upside his deputy's head only moments before the Feds arrived.

"One," he began, his index finger shaking and only a hair from Roy's nose, "Able Riggs was not a police officer. We do not have people that are not police officers or in the custody of a police officer in our unit. This is a big issue, and you understand this issue, because we've discussed it several times."

Roy nodded, and Lorne continued: "Two, we do not include people who are not police officers in active investigations. In particular, we do not involve them in investigations which lead us onto the property of folks who are known to be strange, reclusive, and armed."

Roy shook his head, and Lorne went on: "And most importantly, we do not include people the likes of Able Riggs. The Federal Bureau of Investigations will probably ask you these very same questions in less than five minutes. Rains, I didn't grow up in Lake Castor, but even I know the reputation of Able Riggs and how it stretches all the way back to Jim Crow and some shady undertakings in days gone by—far, far gone by. Do you hear me?"

Roy said nothing, only looked at his boss. Lorne licked his lips and said, "When these Federals get in here, you are to watch it when it comes to Able Riggs. Do you hear me? I want these pricks in and out of here and on their way. And that better happen, Roy. You're on leave until your papers are processed, and that's as good as it gets for you, you son of a bitch. But you better believe me it can get worse, and if you want to see how much worse, then make this an issue. You make the fact that a well-known civil rights violator and an all-around piece of shit like Able Riggs went out with two men under my command to deliver a what-for to a Native American. All this before everybody ended up shot to hell and burned to death."

Roy got the message loud and clear, so he told the Feds: "Able happened along the road when the shooting started. That was the kind of fella he was."

The two agents looked at each other, then down at their notes. "The gunfire started when, Deputy Rains?" asked the friendly one.

"We went knocking on Two Trees' door," said Roy. "Just to ask a couple questions. He wasn't home, but we figured if we peeked in the window it wouldn't do no harm."

"Did you see something in the window?"

"You bet we did."

"What did you see?"

"The dead body of Odie Shanks, sir."

"How did you know he was dead?"

"There was no question he was dead."

The New Yorker checked his notes. He said, "What did you do then?"

"No time to do nothing. That's when Two Trees showed up. He saw us and came at us with the rifle."

"And chased you into his house?"

Roy's toes curled. He rubbed at his cheek. He needed a shave. Hell, he needed to sleep. "No, sir, he ran into his house. He squeezed off a couple rounds at us as we covered behind the domicile. He ran inside. I guess to make his last stand."

"Last stand?"

"I reckon he wanted to burn down the whole place, himself, the Shanks boy's body, house, and all. Like I said, he was a weird one, that Injun. We chased him on in there and that's when the gunfire got to going. Next thing I know, he'd hit Harmless, and Able was alongside, shooting as well. I got him, but not quick enough. He'd already gotten Able, and the place caught fire. I tried to get Able out the front door, but I couldn't."

Actually, Roy had tried to drag Able back into the bedroom from outside but reckoned it easier to simply doctor the story. He ended up leaving him as far as the front door and got to work on setting the house on fire.

"You saw the body before it burnt up?" asked the New Yorker.

"Which body?"

"The Shanks boy's body."

"Yes, I did." Roy lowered his head. His eye twitched, and he feared it a tell. "He was laid out on the bed in the back room. The bedroom. I reckon the Injun had been doing some things to him, but I couldn't tell for sure. He had him decked out in a suit, lying on the bed."

"Indeed," said the friendly Fed. They gathered their papers. "I think that does it for us. It looks clean on our end." He rose and extended his hand to Roy. "Good job, Deputy. I'm real sorry about your friend."

Roy shook his hand and kept his head lowered. "Able was a real fine fella."

"I'm sure he was," said the New Yorker. They all shook on it and said goodbyes and soon enough, the Feds were long gone. Lorne had nothing more to say, and Roy found it best to get the hell out of there, drove to the All-Niter of all places. All things being equal, he'd rather go anywhere else, if he put any thought to it, but he didn't, and in no time, he found himself in the parking lot and the bell ringing as he walked in the door.

Only Gil Tanner sat in their booth. Quite a few people came in for the early dinner rush, but the place felt empty.

No Frances either. Phyllis waved at him and got to work on the coffee. He took the seat in the booth across from Gil. Gil half-looked up, half-smiled. The air had gone out of him. Since high school, they'd lost a few here and there, but this one had him licked.

"Roy," he said.

"How-do, Gil," said Roy. Phyllis brought his coffee and made small-talk. She was in pieces about Able and felt bad for his sister and would do what she could in the meantime to help out poor Frances. Roy exchanged what pleasantries he had and after a while, she went on her way. Gil never so much as looked up. "They say Able's a hero," Roy told him.

"Is that so?"

"That's what they're saying," said Roy. "I was there, Gil. It's true. Able did real good."

Gil said nothing. He sipped his coffee. After a minute, he lit a smoke. He sucked the blue tobacco into his lungs, let it linger, then blew it out.

"He was a good man," Roy said. "He died a good man."

Gil snorted. "You think so?"

"You bet I do," said Roy. "I knew him as well as anyone else. And I say he did."

"You're the law, I reckon."

Roy watched him a second. He sipped his coffee.

"I am," said Roy, slowly. "For the time being."

Gil stared into his cup. "I get it that we're all going into that hole one way or another," he said. "I just never thought it would be like that. Not to one of us."

No one had anything to say for a minute.

"What's happening to this town?" asked Gil. "I mean, what changed after all these years? It was the way it was, and now all of this."

Gil continued: "I mean, for the longest time, they told us it was the Coloreds. That all the black folk moving in would bring us down. Then it was the foreigners. They were going to eat up all of our jobs."

"Able used to talk about that all the time," smiled Roy.

"I don't think that's what it is. I don't think so at all. I think we can run this town into the ground just fine on our own. I don't think we need nobody else to do it." He fetched a couple bills from his pocket and set them down on the table. "I'm going home to be with my wife."

Roy sat there for a bit after he was gone. Folks came in and out. Phyllis dumped his cold coffee and started him fresh. Music played on the juke, other times it didn't. After a long while, he up and paid and headed off to the funeral home.

At the steps of Byrum's, a few old fellas smoked cigarettes, stepped on them as they saw Roy's cruiser pull up to the curb. Roy knew each and every one of them. They'd been around as long as anything else in Lake Castor.

"Deputy Rains," called Benjamin Forrester, fella owned the last bank left in town. "May we have a word with you?"

"How-do, gentlemen," said Roy. He ran his hand along his fleshy neck and chin. He needed to sleep. "I'm afraid there's probably little I can do for you this evening."

Forrester smiled. He looked to the other men. Ricky Hensley from Ricky's Tires stood in a suit jacket although the weather dismissed those long, long ago. Old Man McCarthy's boy stood a head taller than them all. Keith Bolanger was there, so was Amon Caldwell. Roy reckoned if an eighteen-wheeler took out the front of that building and everyone standing there, the town would crumble to ruin.

"I think the question is what can we do for *you*," said Forrester. "We're very sorry to hear about Able. He was a good man."

"A very good man," said Hensley.

"That he was," said Roy. "Is she inside?"

Forrester nodded. "She is. But would you have a minute for us to bend your ear?"

Roy knew better. Not a man among them needed permission for a thing. If they wanted Roy's attention, the last thing they'd have to do was ask for it. Able and these men'd been thick as thieves. He, like most folks in town, had shaken hands with them at one time or another, but he could never truly say they knew what these fellas were all about. All you needed to know about each and every one of them was they had *reach*.

"Not at all," said Roy.

Forrester offered Roy a sip from a pewter flask and pulled from it after Roy declined, returned it to his pocket. "If you don't mind, I'll get right down to it. We appreciate what you did for Able. And what you did for Lake Castor."

"Excuse me?"

"Keeping that little mess with the Native as clean as you could. I know that had to be challenging with ol' Abe, but we appreciate you doing it all the same."

"I don't get it."

Caldwell, a big-deal realtor over in Whitfill used to be a big-deal realtor in Lake Castor. He was a fella who knew when to make a move. He said, "Able'd been in a scrape or two, knew how to make a mess when a mess was called for. Sometimes made one even when it weren't. We know how tough it is to clean up after him. That takes a special kind of fella. And there ain't many of those."

"He was one of a kind," said Forrester. "A real good man and we took care of him."

Roy didn't say anything. He couldn't be sure what was happening. He looked to the sky and wished it would rain.

"And old Harmless." Bolanger spit on the sidewalk, smeared it with his leather loafer. "He's a messy fella himself."

Forrester watched Roy's face. "We don't need any more of them like Harmless coming over here, you know. Men like that don't know how to police a town like Lake Castor. Not like you do. You been doing it for a while, and I reckon you should be doing it for a while more. There's not any need in them sending over more of those boys from across the county."

"That's well and good, Mr. Forrester, but Lorne done told me that I'm pretty much finished out this way. Once I get off the desk, he'll have me out."

"Is that what he said?" asked Forrester.

"He told me so today." Roy told him about the Sheriff barking up his tree earlier and the two men from Whitfill being reassigned. They listened, or Roy figured that's what they were doing, and when he finished, they swapped glances like secret handshakes and got down to it.

"Let us handle Lorne," said Forrester. "We did some digging, and Sam McCarthy found some money in the coffers for a man over here. We saw what happens when someone we don't know tries to do policing over here. We prefer someone we know."

Bolanger piped in: "We want someone who'll make folks answer for things when things got to be answered for. Like you did with Two Trees."

"Someone who don't need long, messy trials and a media circus to help get things done."

"Someone quiet."

"Someone like you."

Roy chewed on his lower lip. He got the picture. He didn't need it spelled out. Without saying it, these rich fellas told him he could spend the rest of his life in the All-Niter Café, and they would pay him to do it.

Roy licked his lips. "The Sheriff is a tough one."

"Who you reckon is tougher, Deputy Rains?" said Forrester. He watched Roy's face some, then watched it some more. After a minute, he slapped Roy on the back. "Once again, Able was a good man. I know you and he was friends. We want you to know, we was friends with him too. And we take care of our friends. You go on in there and pay your respects. But we'll handle Lorne. You take the time you need, but you're our man here in Lake Castor. You're the man this town needs after this mess."

They each shook his hand and went on their way, leaving him to it. He watched after them until each was gone and stood there for a while after. He rubbed at his nose and figured he'd better start up the stairs so he did.

The inside of the funeral home felt nice and air conditioned, but anywhere would the way things had gotten lately and, even though his mind was on other things, his feet moved left then right until he got up alongside the divan where Frances Mabley sat. Old Joe and Sonny Byrum'd gotten to work setting up the viewing room, even though there wasn't nothing much of Able to be viewed, and thought it best to have the sister out in the lobby. Roy took the seat next to her on the divan, and they sat a bit, no one saying a word and Roy wondering should he even have come. But time passed, and in the end, all she said was "Oh, Roy" and put her head on his chest and clutched his shirt and let it all out. She sobbed and sobbed, but he didn't mind, because his head was elsewhere, thinking all the while:

I got away with it.

9

Roy spent the entire Wednesday at a funeral. Four of them, to be exact. Not since old Engine 4209 ran off its rails way back when had Lake Castor hosted so many services on the same afternoon.

First on the docket: Joseph Two Trees. The wily Injun's reputation took quite the hit. Lucky for everyone, his house burned during the ordeal or folks might have come round to do it themselves.

"How are things?" he asked Graham Maloney, the medical examiner over in Tucker.

"I can't wait until October," Maloney answered. He held what remained of Two Trees in a small box—a plain, brown box with a slot for a file card to mark him by. "Heat always gets to me, and you'd be amazed at the condition it leaves some of these DBs."

"DBs?"

Maloney nodded. "Dead bodies." He handed Roy the box. "Speaking of, this is Mister Two Trees here. The fire at the house didn't leave much. Seemed like he burned the most."

Roy took the box and held it under his arm.

Maloney leaned into him. "You can do what you want with him. Use him to litter your cat's box, or mix something in there when you bury him. You said he was Injun, right? Well if you mix him up with something against his religion, he might never make it to his happy hunting ground, and I think this sick fella deserves that, if you ask me."

Roy nodded, signed all the proper paperwork, walked out of the medical examiner's place, and put Two Trees on the dashboard of his cruiser. He got in and headed down the road to the funeral.

The Shanks boy's parents were a wreck. Both of them had been up a wall after the robbery, but since the discovery of what happened at the Injun's farm, they'd been inconsolable. The father drove a truck and had big hands and nothing to wrap them around and searched the horizons for someone to punish. He would find no one. Roy thought it best not to tell him what sat atop his dashboard in the tiny cardboard box. If he or anyone here found out, there'd be a mob to dispose of old Two Trees how they saw fit.

The mother erupted in tears at the sight of Roy. She staggered to him and fell into his chest and wailed. Roy stood like an idiot, arms akimbo until he realized they should go around her, so they did and he held her a moment until Mr. Shanks came to collect her.

"Thank you so much, Deputy Rains," said Mr. Shanks. "Thank you for finding that son of a bitch and sending him straight to hell where he belongs."

Roy nodded and removed his hat.

"Why did he do it, Roy?" asked the mother. "Why did he do it to my baby boy?"

Roy had no answer and word moved through that the services would be starting and folks gathered themselves and helped the mother to her seat in the pew up front. Mr. Shanks insisted that Roy sit with the family, on account of having solved the crime, and Roy declined not once, not twice, but three times, and the father wouldn't hear of it and marched the deputy right down to the front row with them.

They'd bought a nice casket lined with a bronze trim and a beautiful finish predicted to last decades, but they needn't have bothered. Roy knew not much rested inside that coffin, them not having much to fish out of the debris at the Two Trees farm. Roy lowered his head and figured little of anyone would be going into the ground that afternoon.

"Would you join us at the burial?" asked Mr. Shanks, a man who fought a losing battle hiding grief.

"I'd love to, but I've got another service to attend across town." Roy didn't care much to stick around and see Oliver Churchill enter the ground a second time and was grateful to have other funerals to blame. The father put his hand on Roy's shoulder to let him know he understood, to thank him for finding their son.

Roy got across the county in time for the start of Harmless Harris' service, coming in just late enough to grab a spot in back, while the other officers of Lawles County took their places in the front two rows. Sheriff Lorne Axel took a place at the head. This funeral stood in stark contrast to the Shanks boy's, with the pomp and regalia of a fallen warrior or soldier or something they fancied Zeke Harris to be at this one moment in his life. The preacher man lectured about service and sin and somehow made all that apply to Harmless, and not too many people shed tears over him. In the end, folks from the Lawles County Sheriff's Department helped him out the door and into the hearse, or what was left of him anyway.

Roy stood around by the back door for a bit and shook hands with all the folk who told him he did a good job killing that Injun and Harmless was a good man and all the while, he hoped he could elude Lorne. He didn't like the way the Sheriff would turn and look at him during given points throughout the sermon. So unsettling was the Sheriff's expression that Rains understood he should pay attention to what the preacher man said at each moment the Sheriff turned, as if he passively communicated with him through Scripture. However, Rains' mind kept wandering elsewhere and then would be brought around again the next time Lorne turned. One thing he managed to put together was the Sheriff didn't like things. Not one bit.

Yesterday, he'd had to tell him he wouldn't be taking him off the job after all, just hours after he'd told him he'd see him to the door without his badge. Lorne preferred that conversation handled via telephone, rather than in his face.

"You're a slippery son of a bitch," Lorne had told him. "I don't know how you do it, but you do it, and one day you're going to louse it up. I'll be there on that day, Deputy Rains. I'll be there, and no one else will. Just you and me." Roy got the message loud and clear.

"Something's fishy about all this," Lorne continued. "I don't know what it is, but I can smell it, and I'm going to root it out."

"In the meantime," Roy had said into the receiver, "if you'll just have Charlotte keep my badge for me, I'll be by to fetch it in the morning." They didn't need to say anything more on the phone, and Roy hoped to high heaven there'd be nothing more to say at the funeral. Lorne could sniff around all he wanted but, after today, if any evidence existed, it'd be six feet deep in the earth in various spots around the county. Secrets would be buried even deeper. Roy took a breath and shook the next fella's hand.

Next fella was Bubba Greene Junior who folks could say knew Harmless better than most as he owned the 809 out off the highway, and no one had more run-ins than he. Roy was surprised to find him tear-streaked and grief-stricken, seeing as how he'd figured Junior to have more reason to celebrate Harmless going into the hole than most others.

"He was a good fella," said Junior. "Real good fella. Would you mind if I bent your ear a second, Roy?"

Grateful to have him get to the point, Roy nodded.

"I been catching hell since this thing went down," he continued.

"How's that?"

"Lorne's been giving us grief over at the 809 on account of him saying it's a strip club," said Junior.

"Well, that's—"

Junior wouldn't let him finish. "My father ran things one way, but now I run things, and we ain't a nudie joint, Roy. Old Harmless knew that and took care of me, but he's gone now. He saw it right, you know. We're a bar, dammit. We're just a watering hole, serving drinks and playing music. Now, if Prissy Pierce wants to get up on the bar and dance, and maybe take off her top or whatnot, well there ain't much I'm going to do to stop her."

Roy studied the man's face.

"And them fellas sticking money in her britches while she's dancing . . . I've tried to stop it. Lord knows I have, but if they don't give it to her while she's dancing on the bar, they'll try to give it to her out back or in the corner or God help her in the bathroom, and that's a whole another mess of things, so I'd prefer that if they're going to do it, they do it right there where she's doing the dancing."

Roy smiled him, a public smile. "I don't know what you would have me do, Junior. I don't have much to do with the 809. You know that. I'm inclined to let you run things how you run them out that way, so long as there's no trouble."

"And I appreciate that, Roy. But I went to talking to folks yesterday, you know. Folks that would have a hand in getting shit done, and they told me I should come see you. They said you was in charge of Lake

Castor now, and if I went and made things right with you, you'd make things right with me."

The smile stuck to Roy's face. He looked around the parking lot. Amon Caldwell tipped his hat in Roy's direction before climbing into his Cadillac to head on South to the next internment. Tucker's mayor nodded at him and kept on kissing babies. Folks looked at him and whispered to one another. A handful of children played guns on the lawn in front of the funeral home, one unfortunate child taking on the role of Two Trees, the crazy Injun and getting shot by his classmates. That kid fell dead to the ground and twitched until his mother came around and popped him one good for being so disrespectful. Lorne studied him from beneath the canopy at the front door, barely paying attention as folks talked his ear off.

Roy drew a breath. "I'll see what I can do, Junior." He pat the fella on the shoulder and made his way to the cruiser. No easy task, as every fella he passed raised issue with one thing or another, wanted a hand or wanted to tell him what a good job he did over there, or just wanted to stand next to him as folks felt better about themselves being near someone so big. After much to-do, Roy slipped into his cruiser and started his car.

"This ain't the way I imagined it," he said to no one in particular, then reckoned he may well be talking to what was in that box on the dash. He nodded his head in its direction, watched Lorne through the windshield. "I guess this ain't how you imagined it neither."

He headed back to Lake Castor and over to Byrum's. All day that day and all the day before, he'd wanted to be anywhere else but Byrum's at that very moment. Cars wrapped along the streets stretching from the funeral home. He rolled his cruiser up to a space on the corner, watched as folk slouched toward the chapel, and wondered if he could pull this one off.

If years of playing dominos in the parlor out by the railroad tracks did nothing else, it populated Able Riggs' funeral. Old fellas from around the county dropped in to pay their respects, to see him off.

Frances asked him to sit with her and, although he didn't want to, she really wanted to, so he did. The preacher man told him some good ones, kept it lively, but talked to men about their deeds living well beyond their time on earth. He found some scripture to back it all up which gave it a sort of poetry, but the boiled-down essence of it said what Able done in Lake Castor would shape the town for the next generation and the one after that and he'd live in our hearts and in the trees and the air everyone breathed. All because of what he'd done and Roy knew better than most what he'd done and no, they didn't build statues for men like that. Most of them were just lucky to get out of this with their reputations intact and boy, had Roy sure seen to that.

Roy saw Able into the ground, going graveside and listening to the prayers and hearing more of the old guard remember him right and proud. He stood next to Frances, and she asked for a flask, and he felt sore he didn't have one, nor know where to go about getting one. She said never mind and went on with the show the way she reckoned she should, and in no time, they were back at her place where more merriment ensued. Folks brought casseroles and pies and dishes designed to keep Frances from her own kitchen for over a week. He ate a bit here and there, but Roy figured he was watching his weight now, whatever that meant, and after all, had shit to do.

"I hate to do it, Frances, but I'm going to have to scoot."

Frances had her hands full all day long. She hugged him. "Thank you, Roy." He started off, but she held him and looked him in the eye. Meant business. "I mean it, Roy. *Thank you*. For everything."

He thought to say something but figured he better not, instead stepped on out to his cruiser. Folks shut the hell up as he walked past, pretty sure he was torn up and best be on, but they loved him for what he did. He felt it. All across his shoulders.

He got into the cruiser and turned on the engine, got the air conditioner to humming, sat a bit. He watched Frances' house, which had been her mother's after her daddy died. Before that it belonged to a fella that went crazy and fed neighborhood strays and drove his car into Awaneeta Creek. After a bit, he pulled out onto the street and, for the third time that day, went to the graveyard.

This time he stood on the other side of the iron fence. From there he could see the grave of Oliver Churchill and the place where he actually rested in the hole marked for Odell Shanks. He could see the fresh dirt over the body of his old friend. He shook the bars and figured the rusty iron still strong enough.

"Last stop," he said and opened the top of the box. Inside was Joseph Two Trees. Powder and dust and chunks of bone. He knelt a bit and dumped the box onto the ground, kicked a bit of soil over top of it.

"Trust me," he whispered, "this is better than what anybody else has planned for you."

10

Roy stepped out of his cruiser and scanned the horizon. It looked nothing like rain. It hadn't in so long that the first gully-washer tearing through here would probably flood out the entire town. He removed his hat and wiped away a thin layer of sweat pooling inside his creases, then went on his way, up the side of the cruiser and toward the pickup.

"What in Sam hell you think you're doing, Roy?" screamed Danny Bandrow, the farmer from the other side of town.

"What are *you* doing, Danny?" Roy countered. "You blew right through that stop sign back there. Far as I know, you didn't even see it. If someone had been coming the other way, you'd have plum killed them."

"Oh, I saw it, you son of a bitch," spat Bandrow. "I saw the hell out of it, and you can write that in your stupid little notepad. I saw it today, and I saw it last week, and I'll see it every damn time I run it, you hear me, you fat bastard? I been living in this town for nearly sixty-odd years, and there hasn't been a stop sign there until two months ago. I didn't see a reason for them to put it there then, and I sure as hell don't now."

"It ain't a vote, Danny," said Roy. "It's a stop sign, and it's posted, so you have to stop."

"Says you, asshole." Danny slapped both hands at ten and two on the steering wheel. He no longer bothered with looking Roy's way. "And since I'm older than you and older than that stop sign and hell, older than that damn intersection, I say I don't got to stop. Listen here, I been driving that corner longer than you've been wearing that badge, so I say you can't just drop a stop sign where you want and expect folks to stop at it."

"I didn't put it there. I'm just the guy they pay to make sure folks stop at it. Now this time I ain't going to write—"

"No, you ain't going to do a goddamn thing," said Bandrow. "I'd like to see you try. Because if you expect me to give a damn about what you say or when you say it, then you got another thing coming. I ain't stopping at your damn sign. You got a problem with that, maybe I'll go take it up with Forrester. See what he has to say."

Roy drew a breath. Bandrow had cut him at the knees, bringing up Benjamin Forrester. Roy wondered how many people around town knew of the deal that had been struck, or if it even mattered. If it either bolstered any perceived power Roy had, or if it stripped it bare.

Later that day, Roy ran into the five-and-dime to pick up a pack of safety pins and on the way out, passed Sam McCarthy, who tipped his hat. McCarthy couldn't give a damn about him any other time, but here the richest man in town tipped his hat, and Roy's stomach jumped to action because, with that little movement, Roy understood he'd been bought. McCarthy went on his way, but at the same time, so did Danny Bandrow and so too would others. He knew that if he wrote a ticket for Bandrow running that sign, he'd soon get a phone call or worse a visit from Forrester or Amon Caldwell or Keith Bolanger or even Old Man McCarthy's smarmy son to tell him to stop causing a ruckus.

Roy figured he best head on over to the All-Niter to figure things out.

***

Frances smoked a cigarette out back and waved at him. His heart tugged at the corners.

"Some woman called over here for you from Tucker," she said, more than a little irritated. "She said she needs you to call the station right away."

"She say what for?"

"I ain't your secretary, Roy. You can use the phone and ask her yourself."

Roy reckoned that sounded fair enough. He stepped into the All-Niter and the bell rang, and he went straight to the payphone and dialed the station. While the phone buzzed, he waved at old Gil Tanner who lifted an eyebrow but not much more before going on with his coffee. The phone picked up, and Roy let Charlotte, the operator in Tucker, know he was on the horn.

"Yeah Roy, a lady down in North Carolina at a truck stop says she needs to talk to somebody about the case you've been working on."

"The case I been working on?" He ran through the files in his mind and could come up with nothing deeper than old Bandrow running stop signs.

"Yeah Roy, the deal with Odell Shanks and Maggie Hornbecker," she said. "She claims to have information on that."

Roy's heart started a bit. His stomach ran cold. "That case is closed, Charlotte. It closed about the same time as three coffin lids."

"Well, Roy, you're going to need to call this number back and follow up on it. You got a pen?"

Roy didn't know what to do. He fought off a panic. What on earth could a lady at a truck stop in North Carolina have to do with the Shanks ordeal? He wrote down the info and hung up the phone but decided he didn't want anything to do with whatever waited at the other end of that phone number. Instead, he dropped it into the trash can.

Frances came in from her smoke break and got to work refilling coffees. "Everything all right, Roy?" she asked.

"I'd say so," said Roy. But he wasn't convinced. He felt something tugging on him, and he hoped it was only guilt because that was something he'd lately trained himself to live with.

He'd been into his third cup of coffee about an hour later when Frances told him he had another call. He asked who it was again and she gave him a look that shot him up from the booth good and quick. It was Tucker again, Charlotte wanting to know if he'd contacted the woman at the truck stop.

"There was no answer," he said. "I left her a message."

"Well, Roy, she's returned it, I guess, because she said she wants to talk to someone. I told her you handled all the business in Lake Castor, but if you want, I can let Ellis or Coleman handle it."

"Handle what?"

"Whatever it is this lady wants," she said. "Do you want me to have them get a hold of her?"

"No," said Roy. "I'll call her back." *What could this phone call be about?* He shook it off and finished his business and figured he better roll around Lake Castor in the squad car, collect his thoughts.

He didn't yet have the driver door open. when the little bell rang behind him, and he turned to see Frances standing there. She fumbled some with her cigarette pack, but she didn't want to smoke. She looked this way and that. She kept her distance.

"You okay, Frannie?"

She looked up at him. The years peeled away from her. They were forty again . . . hell, *thirty*. Everything was in front of them and nothing behind. He half-expected old Able to come around the corner, thirty pounds lighter and still with all his hair, but Roy knew better. No, what he had was little Frances Mabley, tired and beat and needing somebody to hold her.

"Roy?"

"Yes, Frances."

She took a breath and held it. "My shift ends at ten tonight."

"How about I come back around about then?" The words left his mouth before he could do anything about it. Off yonder a crow laughed at him. A Mac truck powered down the highway toward Deeton. Otherwise Roy thought it entirely too quiet, and he found himself wanting to cup a hand to her face, to hold her by the chin, and stroke his thumb on that smooth cheek of hers, tuck errant strands of hair behind her ear, and he realized for the first time that he'd forgotten to breathe.

"Would you please?" she said. "I'd like that very much."

He nodded. Before he made further ass of himself, he turned on his boot heel and climbed into his cruiser. He raised a finger to her as he drove out of the lot, and she didn't move until he was well along his way and, for all he knew, that's where she'd stay until he came back around ten.

He tapped his fingers merrily on the steering wheel as he watched Stammy Peanucker blow through Pleasant Ridge Road at about fifty, twenty miles over the limit. He didn't mess with it, as folks predicted Peanucker to have a great year at quarterback, and the ticket would get him in deep with the coach. He saw Eugene Nash, Sr. crack open a beer and drain it while sitting at the light on Hampton, then throw the empty into the back of his truck. Nash missed and the can clattered onto the boulevard, but Roy didn't fuss with him neither. No, he hummed an old Milton Brown tune and checked his watch a time or two.

He later sat in his squad car in the old city park and could see across the overgrown softball fields that some kids took roost at the edge of the woods, passing a joint. He watched them a spell and considered more than once heading over there to rough them up a bit. There he sat, weighing the pros and cons, when along came a county car from Tucker, and out stepped Jack Coleman, the young kid who'd just made deputy. Coleman made his way to Roy's window and knocked.

"Been looking for you," he said.

"You solved the case, Coleman. Big things are in store for you."

"Sheriff wants you on the horn," he said. "He sent me out to tell you to call him."

"What on earth for?"

"That ain't my business. My business is telling you what I just told you. Now you been told." He started back for his car when he looked across the lot and pointed. "Hey, them kids smoking grass over yonder?"

"Get on back to Tucker," growled Roy. He sat there long after Coleman had left and long after the last of the dropouts disappeared into the woods. He couldn't shake the feeling that something waited for him.

Rather than return to the All-Niter, he stopped at the E-Z Go, the tiny convenience store across the parking lot from Maggie's Pizza Pick-Up where it all started and told the kid jockeying the register that he needed his phone. The kid didn't care. Roy dialed up the Sheriff.

"Why haven't you called that truck stop back?" Lorne wanted to know. Roy's nerves jangled. *Did Lorne sound happy about something?* Roy promised he would and asked for the number again. Lorne repeated his sentiment of never wishing to speak to Roy ever again and how much he resented having to do it at that moment. "Don't make me have to call you and remind you to do your job."

Roy scribbled the number down on the last remaining page of his notebook and thanked the Sheriff, but he'd already hung up. He told the kid behind the counter he needed to make another call and again, the kid did not give a shit.

After dialing the truck stop, Roy waited while they fetched the lady who'd been calling. She got on the horn and had an accent that couldn't be beat and told Roy what she'd been trying to tell him for some time now.

"I said I got some stuff that belongs to your dead kid."

"What do you mean by that?" asked Roy.

"I found it in our lost and found box," she said. "It's a cap and a nametag with the name Odie Shanks written on it."

"Must be some mistake," said Roy, his stomach aching to hell. *Must be all the damn coffee.* "Maybe there's more than one Odie Shanks."

"Sounds good to me," she said. "But his hat and nametag are from Maggie's Pizza Pick-Up, and the Internet says there's only one of them."

Roy closed his eyes. "Okay. So he left his stuff at your truck stop before."

"Yes, sir," she said. "But we clean out this lost and found box every Saturday day shift, and I was reading that the Injun fella up there kidnapped and killed that boy last Saturday night."

Roy lowered his head. "You read that, did you?"

"I sure did. I'm a big fan of the crime stories. I just eat that stuff up. Anyways, that means his effects must have been left after he was kidnapped or killed. Like maybe that Injun dipped down into North Carolina for something after he took him . . ."

Roy let her continue. Meanwhile, his stomach jumping-jacked inside his khaki uniform. There was nowhere to sit in the E-Z Go, so he stood there at the phone, taking it as this woman's words punched him relentlessly in his gut. Left, then right, then left, right . . .

". . . and one show I watch has folks from Langley analyze evidence like this. You know, if that Indian fella y'all killed was a serial killer, they'd be interested in this. You know, for the DNA. Is this something I should contact them directly about?"

"Beg pardon?"

"These effects?" she repeated. "Do you think I should holler over at the FBI?"

"No, ma'am," he said, maybe a bit too quickly. He scrambled for that last page of his notebook and the pen, licked the nib and held it at the ready. "Ma'am, I'll be out there to pick up those things . . . er, those *effects* right away. How does that sound?"

"Really?" She came off a little too excited. "Oh wow, do you really think what I got here is evidence?"

"We don't want to rule nothing out, miss." His stomach cramped. He checked his watch. *Dammit . . . Frannie.* He closed his eyes, and all he could see was Frances out back of the All-Niter. He did the math. If he hauled ass down eighty-five, he might be able to get there and back by ten.

But something told him he needed to do more than just pick up and destroy this hat and nametag. A sinking feeling within him said a crime-happy woman such as this probably had taken a few selfies with the evidence, probably would jack her jaws from here to FBI headquarters about her find.

No, he'd need more than a couple hours.

He let go a breath he'd held for quite some time. That soft image of Frances he kept in his mind—her green eyes, chestnut hair, weary smile—he let it go.

"How about you and me meet somewhere?" he said into the phone, checking his watch. "I'll drive out there, and you bring me that evidence, and I can tell you all about the case."

"Really?" He heard the woman jumping up and down on the other end of the line. "Are you serious? That would be amazing!"

"Just one thing," he said. "Be sure you don't tell nobody about this until I give you the green light. This has got to be top secret. Just between you and me."

She agreed. He asked her to pick out somewhere nice and quiet where they could meet and be alone, and she said she knew just the spot and gave him directions. He wrote it down and hung up the phone.

All the weight in the world was back upon him. He pursed his lips and scratched the top of his head. A crick festered nice and tight in the back of his neck, and he wished to high heaven there was someone who might rub it out for him. Again he thought of Frances.

"You want to use the phone again or something, mister?" asked that kid behind the counter.

Roy looked sideways at him. His shoulders slumped.

"No," he said. "I ain't got nobody left to call."

And with that he hopped on the Interstate and headed South.

11

The woman's name was Charmaine Mangum, and she worked part-time as a waitress down at the truck stop and part-time as a hairdresser in town. Town being Roxboro, North Carolina, about halfway between Lake Castor and Durham. She swore up and down she remembered the night the hat and nametag were left in the booth. She said she was willing to testify in a court of law, if need be.

"I don't remember nothing about the boy, bless his heart" she said. "I'm ashamed to admit it, after what happened to him and all. What I do remember is the man."

"The man?" Roy didn't care to enter her apartment, but she would have it no other way. She practically pulled him over the threshold and into her living room. "What man are you talking about?"

"The fella that was with him when he come in," said Ms. Mangum. "Older guy, about yay-tall. Hadn't shaved in a spell. Kind of handsome."

"What does that have to do with—"

"And not a lick of Injun blood in him, I must say."

Roy checked his watch. "You said you have, what was it, a nametag and an apron?"

"A hat, Deputy," she said. "Would you like some coffee? Tea, maybe?"

"No, I really have—"

She pushed aside one cat with a foot, then another, as she moved further into the bowels of her apartment, toward the kitchen. Roy sighed and massaged the bridge of his nose with his thumb and forefinger.

"Did you hear what I said, Deputy?" She flipped on the light to the kitchen, and immediately began to clamor about with coffee cups, sink faucets. Opening drawers and closing them. "I said, the man with the kid was not an Indian."

"Miss Mangum, I don't see what—"

She was a big woman. Not bigger than Roy, but big all the same. She pulled back her bangs and held them in place with a chip clip. "I remember it like it was yesterday. I didn't think nothing of it at the time, but after I went through the lost-and-found box the other day, it all came back to me, and I thought holy shit, I better get on the horn to you boys."

"Is that so?" Roy found another cat slinking out from under the sofa. "Miss Mangum, do you reckon to—"

"I remember him specifically because of how ornery he was about his food," she said.

"The kid was ornery about his food?"

"No, sir, not the kid. The older man." She leaned around the corner and looked at him over the rims of her glasses. "Did you say you take cream with your coffee?"

"No, I'm fine. Really." He did the math. If he got out of there within ten minutes, he'd only be fifteen minutes late getting back to Lake Castor. Perhaps he could stop at a payphone and call the All-Niter, tell Frannie to hang on a minute.

"I didn't think no more on it until the lady come in a couple days ago, looking for her glasses. I go to the lost-and-found box, and there it was."

"So, Miss Mangum, do you think—"

"I called you up first thing, on account of what I'd heard happening up your way," she said. "Like I said, I'm a sucker for the crime stories. I got my police scanner, I read all the papers that come through the station. Folks leave all kinds of . . . Deputy, am I keeping you from something?"

"As a matter of fa—"

"I ain't looking for no reward," she said. "Doing a service for you boys is reward enough. Whenever I read about the trouble people give the police, I often wonder where some folks get off. Not me. I know which side my bread is buttered on."

"Miss Mangum . . .?"

"Yes, Deputy?"

"You think it would be possible for you to retrieve the items . . . I mean, er . . . the *effects*?"

Her mouth formed a tight little circle. "Oh. Sure. Well, I suppose if you're in a rush, then fine. I know you have more important things to do, so why don't I just hurry along and . . ."

Her voice trailed off as she disappeared down her hallway, not bothering to turn on any lights, as she disappeared into a back room. Roy eyeballed her sofa and wished like the dickens he could fall into it, but didn't dare, for he knew not how many cats he might kill by doing so. Instead, he steadied himself against the wall and prayed she'd hurry along, when suddenly he heard a buzzing.

The sound came from her phone, lying like a turd on her coffee table. Normally, he would have paid it no attention, but the photo that popped up on the screen caught his eye. He stepped closer, then couldn't help but pick it up.

"I'll be goddamned," he muttered.

There on her screen was a photo she'd taken of herself and the very evidence he'd driven an hour to collect. Right there alongside her fat, smiling face was Odie Shanks' work hat and nametag, and Roy thought he might vomit right there in her living room.

"Do you think this means that the Injun was working with a partner?"

Roy spun around and found she'd returned to the living room, crept up behind him like an assassin. She carried with her a plastic bag with the truck stop's logo, hanging limp at her side. Roy's heartbeat kept time with the clock on the mantle, ticking ever louder.

"I'm afraid I can't comment on the case right now," he said. "I'm sure you understand."

She bit her lower lip and nodded her head. "Which means the case hasn't yet been closed." She pumped a fist. "Holy shit, I knew it."

"May I . . .?" He reached for the bag, and she handed it to him. Inside, he found the hat which said MAGGIE'S PIZZA PICK-UP and the nametag which read ODIE SHANKS. He turned it over and over in his fingers. Yes, it was genuine. He slipped it into his pocket and tucked the bill of the ball cap into the back of his waistband.

"I can't thank you enough, Miss Mangum, for your service to—"

He stopped short. Her mouth had dropped open, further than he thought possible. She took a step back and gasped desperately for air.

"You . . . Oh my god . . . *You* . . ."

Roy rushed to her. "What is it? What is the mat—"

"The *evidence!*" She pushed him away. She fell against the wall. "That is not how you handle evidence!"

Roy yanked the cap free from his waistband and scrounged back up the bag, but it was too late. She'd already lost her mind.

"You were supposed to preserve the evidence," she moaned.

"Miss Mangum," he pleaded, "there is no reason to—"

"I'm afraid I've had enough," she said. "I'm afraid this is all too much."

"Ma'am, if you'll please—"

She picked up her cell phone from the table. She tapped angrily at the screen.

"Miss Mangum, who are you calling?"

"Yes, hello. May I please speak to the Sheriff?"

Roy winced. He took a step closer to her. "Miss Mangum, I highly doubt—"

"Yes ma'am, I'd say this is an emergency. Of course, I will hold."

Roy checked his watch again. He sighed heavier than he'd ever sighed in his life.

"If you don't mind me asking, Deputy. Where is it you have to be that's so all-fired important that you can't do your job proper?"

Roy walked to the front door and closed it. Latched it locked. Before he pulled the nightstick from his belt, he looked one final time at his watch.

"Nowhere," he said, as he advanced upon her. "Not no more, that is."

12

Roy sat in his patrol car outside the All-Niter Café, not in the front lot but rather around the back way, so neither passing traffic on the highway to Deeton nor folks eating inside would see him. He'd sat in his car for a half-hour, maybe more, and stared out the windshield at the door, hoping he might will Frances Mabley to walk out for a smoke, maybe see him and decide all was forgiven. Ask to get in the car and for them to drive, just keep driving, don't stop until they were gone.

That would not happen. His face twisted into a somewhat permanent scowl. His eyes had narrowed, nearly squinting shut. He was becoming mean, which was something no one had ever in all his life called him, all things considered.

He wiped sweat from his forehead and thought of that air conditioner. He thought more than once how ridiculous all this was, how he should just swallow his pride and march across that steamy parking lot and go in there to explain himself. Not tell her the truth, mind you, but whatever else it was he could muster to have her forgive him and return her to what she felt the day previous when she asked him to meet her after work.

Hell, he told himself he would over and over, a million times even, if it weren't for Lorne. Yep, that was his county car parked right alongside the back wall of the All-Niter. Roy had sat there long enough to know there were plenty open spaces up front, and the only folks who would park out back that time of day were those who didn't want to be seen. No, Lorne didn't want it advertised that he lay in wait inside that building, and for whatever reason that gave Roy the fidgets.

What could that old bastard want? Honestly, Roy'd had it up to here with the Sheriff. He had half a mind to fork over his badge and tell Lorne where he could stick it. What was the point of keeping his job if he was going to be harassed every day? What was the point if Forrester couldn't run Lorne out of the county?

But it was more than just Lorne which had Roy on edge that afternoon. More than Frannie, too. He took a peek at himself in the rearview and put a busted finger to the cut just above his right eye. *Yep, she got me good.* He dipped his hand inside the jar of corn liquor he'd brung and touched the juice to his wound. It no longer stung, which offered him weak comfort. At least it wouldn't get infected. Sure, there'd be a scar but that wasn't so bad, because maybe he needed reminding of some of the shit he'd done.

Frannie . . .

Dammit, he reckoned there wasn't a bigger idiot alive. So many times last night he thought about what he should have done versus what he was doing. As the woman's screams for help became muffled pleas for mercy, he reckoned he could have been sitting on the couch back at his trailer with Frances, maybe watching a DVD and drinking on a six-pack. While he was washing that lady's blood off him in her shower, he wondered if he'd have tried to sneak a kiss by then, or if she would have let him.

***

Maybe it was lack of sleep. Could be. He hadn't gotten much to speak of. He dozed off some in that woman's apartment down in North Carolina. He found himself nodding off here and there while sitting in that parking lot. A commotion across the parking lot snapped him to, and he wondered how long he had been out.

Lorne was on the move. Him and two others in suits rang the little cowbell and quit the building, headed over to Lorne's county car. Roy hunkered down in the seat and watched them climb in. For a minute, nothing happened, and Roy started to think maybe the jig was up, and they'd seen him, but no sooner had he worked himself into a tizzy than did the county car start up, and soon enough, Lorne and the other two fellas were off and out of the parking lot.

He got himself out and watched the door. Again he prayed that Frances would come out and make it easy on him, but deep down inside he reckoned he didn't deserve nothing easy so he righted himself. He took a deep breath and let it out, then made his way across the lot to find that woman and tell her once and for all just how bad things had gotten.

***

But as luck would have it, Frances Mabley was having a shit day all her own.

She felt like an idiot.

First of all, there was no better word to sum up what went through her head all the night before, standing out back of the All-Niter, smoking cigarette after cigarette. She stood there until close to eleven before she finally gathered her shit and climbed into her own truck and took off for home. Stopping first by Roy's trailer to see if he was there and feeling even worse about doing it. Driving to her brother's place and letting herself in with her key and falling asleep on her brother's bed.

It wasn't until she woke up and looked in the mirror that she realized she must have spent most the night crying.

You are too old to be this stupid.

She went into work early. Tom the cook said something to her, and she said something back, but her mind was on one thing and one thing only: Absolutely nothing at all.

All that changed when Sheriff Lorne Axel came in. Sheriff Axel wasn't one to frequent the All-Niter. Come to think of it, she saw him in there rarely enough that she doubted she'd recognize him were it not for the big shiny star on his chest and the band on his hat which he removed like a proper gentleman. He carried with him something wrapped in a thin, ratty blanket, and she'd lived in Southern Virginia long enough to know it was a hunting rifle. He held it longways and waited for her to stop past with the coffee pot.

"No thank you," he said, waving it off. "I brung you something, Miss Mabley."

She looked at the rifle. "Is that my brother's?"

"It is," he said. "We're done with it, so we reckoned we'd release it to you. Unless of course you don't want it, which I'd understand. But to be honest, it's a real good piece. Maybe you could sell it."

"Maybe so." She only looked at it.

He handed her a Ziploc baggie. Inside rounds of ammunition clinked. She looked at them like they were poison. She took her time taking them from him, but quick as lightning slipped them into her apron.

"Listen, I'll set it back here behind the counter." He did so slowly.

"You want a menu?"

He shook his head. "Listen, if it's all the same, I'm meeting a couple boys from out of town. All three of us would like to have a word with you, if it's okay?"

"With me?" A part of her felt nervous. Still, she hadn't moved a hair since she and the Sheriff started talking. "What on earth would you need to speak with me about?"

"About your brother and how he died."

Frances reckoned it a miracle she kept herself together like she did. She squared away damn near everybody in the place and set checks on their tables and told Tom she needed a minute. Two fellas in suits showed up and took a seat with Lorne. She told them she didn't have long to talk because she'd have to get things set up for dinner.

"We won't need but a minute, darling," said Lorne.

And that's when Lorne and those two men leveled with her. They told her everything they knew so far which, they confessed, wasn't very much at all. They told her they didn't think Roy's story about what happened at the Two Trees farm was anywhere near the truth. They told her they didn't think Two Trees was the one who killed Harmless Harris. They told her they didn't think it was Odell Shanks who they found on that bed in the Injun's house.

"Why on earth would you say something like that?" she asked them.

"Because ma'am," said the man with the New York accent, "Odell Shanks is alive and well."

"That's impossible," she said. "We all seen him go into the ground."

The other fella in the suit shook his head. "Well, ma'am, we got a team out there at the Nokomis Cemetery digging up that grave. We don't know who went into that grave, but we know for a fact it wasn't Odell Shanks."

The bell at the door rang, and Frances Mabley shot out of her seat there in the booth like a black snake. Inside her apron, the bullets clicked together. She wrung her wrists and couldn't look nobody in the eye.

"I'm real sorry gentlemen," she said, "but I'm going to have to get back to work. I'd love to hear more about all this, but I'm going to have to get back to work."

Lorne stood. He put a hand to her shoulder which she promptly shook away. He returned it and held her to.

"Listen to me, Miss Mabley," he said. "It's real important you don't say nothing to Deputy Rains. I need to speak to him before anybody else does. I want you to call me the minute he shows up here. Understand me?"

She couldn't look away from the Sheriff's face. She couldn't nod, she couldn't shake her head. She couldn't get her brain past that one thought blocking all thought and action and any other synapse from firing.

Roy Rains had my brother killed.

With every coffee cup she filled that day, with every table she wiped, with every plate she served, all she could think was that one, solitary thought. It welled up inside her and festered, and she found herself at the register trying to add up some poor bastard's coffee and lunch special when she thought she just might scream, scream so loud she'd shake the windows and all of a sudden that little cowbell rang at the door.

In came Roy, looking quite a fright. He limped when he walked and something or another had busted his eye. His hand was wrapped in gauze tape and, as he hobbled closer, she swore she smelled corn liquor or something like it all along him. He twitched. She needn't look at him longer than ten seconds before any and all questions that she might or might not have had about him were good and answered.

"Hey, Frannie," he said. The words pained him coming out. He lifted a hand to wave but jerked it back down on account of the pain. His left leg wouldn't lift all the way off the ground. "Look, I'm real sorry about not coming around last night. You wouldn't believe what happened."

She opened her mouth but nothing came out.

"You think you could fetch me a cup of coffee?" he asked. He looked around. "Say, where are the boys today? Awful quiet, you reckon?"

There was no juke playing. Folks quit eating, talking. Even Tom quit fussing with the grill and left some hash browns on to burn.

Roy continued to slouch forth, looking for exactly where to sit. He stopped and stood square before her.

"Hey Frannie, what gives?"

It was as if she had a sixth sense. She saw it all laid out before her. She saw her brother or what was left of her brother six feet down and not joining her for Christmas. She saw this piece of shit with his shit-grin scowl. The one thing she couldn't see was just how he done it, but she didn't care so she leaned down to pick up the rifle.

When she came up from behind the counter, she thumbed in one shell from the Ziploc in her apron, then a second, and she put the rifle into action. She might not have been the best shot, but at that range, she sure could cut him in half, so she fired.

First one got him in the chest. He was plenty surprised even if it didn't register quite well at first. He stood there, arms still at his side, and he looked down. There was a hole. There was blood. Soon, there was more blood.

"This is for my brother," she growled.

The next shot took out half his face and all the cares he had in the world. He dropped to the tiled floor, first to his knees, then forward and onto what was left of his head. He was long gone, but that didn't stop Frances Mabley from standing over him, rifle still pointed down below and screaming hell fire at him. Screaming her brother's name and screaming her own name and screaming over and over until the words ran together and no longer made any sense at all.

#SWEET
MELINDA
KENDALL

1

Melinda Kendall saw the two headed her way and figured she was in no mood for this shit. *Not today*. She instinctively drew her legs to a close, but knew it was too late. They had seen her and made steadfast plans to fuck with her. Other days she could make sport of them, turn whatever nonsense right back on them. *But not today*. For today, she had begun to kick and her attitude on life could use some improvement.

And sure as the sunrise, they were on her. They took turns challenging and daring each other, arguing which would be the first to make an ass of himself. The taller one won and could barely contain himself as he approached her.

"Hey, little missy," he said, his Louisiana accent a gumbo of drawl and polished mumble. "You having some car trouble?"

Options presented themselves to her, although she'd prefer a proxy handle her decision-making, due to her condition. True, this car had gone about as far as it was going to go, especially with her in it. She'd ridden it hard since Nacogdoches and had no more money for gas. *But these guys had money*. Maybe they could even give her a ride. She had an arsenal of tactics at her disposal to get what she wanted.

But not today.

She'd sat outside the bait and tackle shop for over an hour after the car quit on her, at first trying to figure out what to do and then just trying to get her thoughts to quit racing. She was in a fix all right, and the only thing that would cure it was miles. Putting a lot of highway between her and her troubles. Running out of gas did a number on her plans.

Instead of acknowledging TallBoy and Pudgy, she only stared back from behind her sunshades. This threw fuel on their fire.

"What's the matter, baby?" asked Pudgy. "You need a ride? I can give you a ride." He fell over laughing. He'd come at her with his best material.

She weighed each and every one of her options. She could ask for help—beg, even. She wanted to give them the finger, offer a few suggestions to what they could do with their fancy, rich-kid fishing poles, but she couldn't see an endgame with an outcome in her favor. Guys like this had a violent streak in them that didn't mesh well with their entitlements. She also had a .22 in her bag and thought about a round bouncing in their skulls. But she knew her limitations and reckoned now wasn't the best time for her to make these kinds of decisions. She said and did nothing.

TallBoy sensed something. He popped Pudgy's shoulder with the back of his hand. "Let's get in there and get our stuff," he said. "Leave this one alone. She looks like she's been through the ringer and something ain't right with her."

"She's just how I like them: skinny and skanky." Pudgy wasn't ready to give in. "It don't look like that long ago since she's been hot."

Melinda lowered her head. They walked past her and up the dry, wooden steps of the bait and tackle shop, then disappeared inside. *Best thing for them*, she told herself. Actually, she knew it was the best thing for *her*. As much as she'd love teaching a couple of idiots a valuable lesson on how to treat a lady, she didn't need the attention. What she needed was to get as far away from Texas as possible and to do so quietly.

So for starters, she needed a ride.

The Oldsmobile Cutlass wasn't even hers. She'd stolen it from her boyfriend—*ex-boyfriend*—two days earlier. She needed to ditch the car and find another one. Sam would have someone looking for that car, and the sooner they found it, the sooner they'd be that much closer to her. For so long, avoiding Sam had been a game. She could dip in and out of his periphery, and the only consequence would be a shouting match, a little session of who could hurt who's feelings, silly revenge fantasies. Most often the result was angry sex, as if the public humiliation dramas were only foreplay. But she knew she had crossed a line, and the consequence this time would be more significant.

She'd been making mistakes for a while now, starting with skipping a Literature class during her Freshman year, which led to her running into Sam Tuley, and culminating into Friday morning, the day she'd high-tailed it out of Nacogdoches. With the wooded little college town in Deep East Texas in her rearview, she replayed the events of her downfall, wincing with each bad decision she'd made. She watched the horror unfold and knew there was no undoing what had been done.

*   *   *

She met the boy at the bar on Thursday night. He said all the right things. She was in the mood to do all the wrong things. She and her boyfriend Sam were going to the mattresses lately, and not in the good way. It never mattered what started these fights, or even what finished them really. All that mattered was how bad one could hurt the other before it was finished. And this time, Melinda was bound to leave a mark.

She let him buy her drinks, but that wasn't really necessary. Usually a bump or two of the stuff Sam sold these days killed any appetite she had for booze, but *when in Rome* . . . The boy figured out the score and asked if he could have some, she said sure, let's go back to my place and party. He was down, and she figured this would be the perfect way to show Sam he shouldn't have fucked with her.

And by *her place*, she meant the place she shared with Sam Tuley, her boyfriend of eleven tumultuous months. Ever since he started dealing, the place had transformed from a study pad to a drug den and, most of the time, the phone never stopped ringing. She unplugged the line and led the boy into the living room.

"You said you had a boyfriend?" the boy asked. "He won't like, come home and shoot me, will he?"

"He won't come home," she told him. "Not tonight, anyway. We got into a big fight, and a large part of him getting even—which is the most important part—is not coming home." The boy appeared to relax, but Melinda didn't buy it. He never seemed to lose control or get nervous. He seemed to have it all figured out. "I ain't worried though," she said, "because Sam Tuley will always come back for me."

"What did y'all fight about?" the boy asked.

"I really don't even remember." Melinda scooted over closer to him and pulled out some of Sam's shit, dropped a small pile of it onto the back of a CD jewel case—Skynyrd's *Pronounced*—and began to chop out some lines with her student ID card. "All we do is fight anymore. I think it's the drugs, honestly. All the damned drugs. When we met, I thought he was smarter than all the other boys I met on campus. We first tried crystal to help us during a late-night cram session, studying for a Poly-Sci exam, and then the next thing you know . . ."

"It happens to the best of us," said the boy. He watched her work the shit, the student ID chop and slide, slide and chop until four skinny lines snaked across the CD case. She offered him the first one, then took hers.

They got to talking.

"So he starts dealing," she said. "He swore it would only be for a little bit, to get us over a hump, but one thing Sam Tuley ain't all about are *promises*. It's good stuff though, ain't it? Real clean, not like the bathtub stuff you usually find out here in East Texas. So you go to Stephen F. also? I haven't been making it to class lately. I was Dean's List for the first three semesters, but not this year. Next semester will be totally different. I need to get things back on track. It seems like when we're doing all this damned crystal, things are much clearer than they ever were, but at the same time, it comes at you so fast . . ."

He smiled. "And then when you come down, it ain't no picnic."

"We won't have to worry about that tonight." She stood up and walked into the bedroom. He heard her shuffle around a bit, then she walked back out of the living room with two large baggies of snow-white powder. "Sam's buddy hides this shit over here when they're making a run."

The boy tensed a little. "And they aren't coming home? With all that shit in the apartment?"

"Relax," she cooed. She sat so their legs touched, snaked an arm through his, set the baggies down on the coffee table. "They're on the run, and he's pissed off at me. Trust me, as much as this is, they probably have another baggie this size or bigger. Last I heard, they had to drive clear out to Longview to move some of this shit to some rednecks. They won't be coming home tonight."

"He's that deep into it, huh?"

"Lately, he is." She rubbed at her nose, and the shit drained down the back of her throat. "At first it was fun. We made enough money to pay for what we put in our faces. People calling, knocking on the door all hours. People in and out of here and trust me, tweakers never know when to go home. Soon, they quit dropping by. Just one guy, JoJo, coming in and out. And JoJo and Sam would go on long drives, and Sam would hide these big bags in here, then be gone."

"How come you don't leave him?" asked the boy.

Before she answered, she took in his impossibly blue eyes, let herself be hypnotized. "I don't want to leave him. Not most the time anyway. I want him to quit treating me like shit. I want him to quit thinking I'm lying all the time. To always think I'm cheating on him."

The boy laughed. "Why would he think that?"

"Don't get me wrong, I'm not a cheater." She leaned and kissed him full on the mouth. "But right now, me and him are broken up. And he needs to learn to respect this. I'm always getting accused of cheating on him. Him screaming and throwing things and calling me names in front of everyone. So if I'm going to do the time, I sure as hell want to do the crime."

So she did and a half-hour later, they scrounged up their clothes scattered about the living room floor, did the other two lines, and she immediately began to regret it. She'd punched Sam in the face, keyed his car, once called the cops when he got a little rough, and set his schoolbooks on fire. She'd never fucked another guy and couldn't help but feel a line had been crossed. Her mind raced. *Could she repair this?*

Still, she talked: "It's the drugs. That's why he is like he is. Not just the meth, either. He gets so riled up on crystal that he needs a Rufie or a Xanax to get any sleep. You think that don't have side effects?" He held up her pointer finger, then let the finger droop. "He cries in his sleep. I wake up sometimes, and he's just sobbing and carrying on, and

I massage him and stroke him, and then in the morning, he feels like he has to even the playing field. He reads through my journals, listens in on my phone calls, follows me to class. We fight, then make up, then fight again. He tells me all the time he's going to leave me."

The boy put a hand on her shoulder, then both hands, and soon he was massaging. "Calm down, Melinda," he said, his voice velvet. "You're getting all worked up over nothing. This is between you and me and don't nobody ever have to know about it."

"That feels great," she said, trying like the dickens to relax. He could massage until Christmas, but they'd done too much crystal.

"We need to take the edge off," he said. "You got any booze?"

"There's some vodka in the freezer, I think," she said. He got up, and she heard him clinking around in the kitchen a bit. She looked around the room. Two giant baggies of JoJo's high-grade shit on the table, couch cushions tossed askew from their little bout of screwing. She thought she'd cry. Part of her was fool enough to wish Sam would walk in the door right now and make everything better, but only a very small part.

In came the boy carrying two cocktails. He set one in front of her. "Drink this," he said softly. "You need to relax a bit, okay?" He leaned in and kissed her neck.

"I don't think I can," she said. "It's hard for me to drink when I'm partying like this."

"Trust me," he said, "it will help."

So she took a drink and lit a cigarette. He watched her, his fingers caressing her arm. Her body had been going so fast for so long that the first swig of vodka did a number on her. If felt good to slow down, even if it was just a little.

"Thanks for listening to me babble," she said. "Sorry I've been so much drama."

"I've had a great time so far," he said. "Take another drink."

She smiled. "Are you trying to get me drunk?" He lifted the glass to her lips, and she took another drink. The vodka burned her tongue, but she forced it down. "You're really a sweet guy. I can't help but think that in another life, you and me, we could have had a lot of fun."

"We're having plenty of fun in this life." Now his fingers moved to her neck. Light strokes with the tips of his fingers. "This has been one of the best nights I've had in a long time."

"Really? That's so sweet. Sam used to say sweet things to me, but that was a long time ago."

"Sam's an idiot. He doesn't see what I see. If he doesn't come back, you'd be better off."

She looked to him. She wanted to hug his blue eyes, to live inside his lips. Each time his fingers made a pass across the flesh of her neck, her heart stopped beating until he began another.

"He'll come back. Sam Tuley will always come back to me."

"I don't blame him."

"I'm an awful person."

"No, you're not," said the boy. He lifted the glass to her lips again. "Take another drink, Melinda."

"If I take this drink, I want you to kiss me again."

"Finish the cocktail, and we'll do whatever you want."

She swallowed it down and melted into him.

2

Sam Tuley will always come back for me . . .

She awoke to the door knob rattling. Her mind was foggy, and she tried to slap the cobwebs free. Bar . . . boy . . . drugs . . . drink . . . She snapped to and sat up. She panicked. Her world was about to end. She was naked. She started to scream for the boy, but he wasn't there.

Was he in the bathroom? *Where was he?* She'd have to explain to her paranoid boyfriend why she was sleeping naked on the couch with all JoJo's drugs on the coffee table and—

She froze. JoJo's drugs were *not* on the coffee table.

And the boy was nowhere to be found.

Her stomach sank, and the kitchen door opened. "Melinda? Melinda, are you home?"

It was Sam. Melinda flew across the room and down the hallway to the bathroom. *You are so stupid, you are such a stupid—*

She slammed shut the bathroom door and locked it.

"Melinda? Baby, we need to talk." She could hear Sam through the door, making his way to the bathroom. She searched the room for answers. Her head was so foggy. They'd each done just two rails of meth, how in the hell did she pass out like that? The answer came to her as soon as she'd asked it. *Oh Melinda, you are such an idiot.*

She nearly crumpled to the bathroom floor. The boy had slipped her a mickey. Tricked her. How long had he planned on stealing JoJo's shit? When she showed it to him? Before? *Had he planned it before they'd even met, way back at the bar?* Her world closed in on her. Sam pounded at the bathroom door.

"Melinda, open this door, right now." He pounded some more. "We need to talk. I'm serious. Quit fucking around."

"Just a minute, Sam," she said, barely able to manage her voice above a whisper. What would he do? She knew what he'd do if he found out she'd banged some guy from a bar in their apartment. She had no doubt. She'd pulled all kinds of shit on him, but she'd crossed a line. At some point in the evening, it had made sense. It didn't now. He'd beat the hell out of her for that.

She choked back vomit welling in her throat.

He wasn't waiting. "Melinda, I'm serious. We need to talk. Look, I know we've been at it, and I don't care right now. I'm sorry for whatever you think I did. Whatever it is, I apologize. I'm really, *really* sorry, and I'll never do it again, promise. I love you, and you're the best I know. Will you please, pretty please open the motherfucking door?"

She grabbed the bathrobe hanging from the back of the door. It would have to do. If she didn't open the door, he'd kick it in again, and it could be an uphill battle calming him down after that.

"Sammy, I'm going to open the door," she croaked. "Please calm down now."

Her hand rested on the knob until she heard him answer, "I'm calm, honey. Please open up."

She pulled the bathrobe tighter around her and turned the knob. She expected anything. She expected to see him pointing his grand-daddy's .22 at her, then possibly pull the trigger. She even half-expected him to fly into a rage and jump atop her, beating her until she stopped moving. But she did not expect to see what she saw when she opened the door, and that was her boyfriend, Sam Tuley, covered in blood and looking all kinds of harried, her realizing then that, despite all the nights he woke her up crying, this was the first time she'd ever seen him scared.

"JoJo's dead," he told her. "He's dead, and I killed him."

***

He led Melinda out to the living room so he could tell her what happened. She stumbled in a stupor to the couch and sat, then remembered what had happened on that couch and scooted a little further down. Sam rambled on and on, chattering away at the events of the night before, and how JoJo and he had gotten heated, and how one called the other motherfucker this and cocksucker that, and soon they were slugging each other in the chest, and one took it a little too far, and they both were cranked out of their minds already. JoJo pulled a knife, Sam wrestled it away from him and stuck him with it, and here we are. Melinda wanted to scream, to get sick, to crack up laughing until someone took her away. All around was evidence of what she had done, what she let happen. She hoped nothing gave her away. She hoped Sam was too tweaked to notice.

And all the while, it kept running through her head. *Sam had killed someone*. She slashed his tires once, set his shit on fire, told everyone he couldn't fuck longer than fifteen seconds most the time, thanks to all the drugs. She loved getting him up in a lather, watching him lash out and scream, act like a fool even in public. But hearing that he'd killed someone put them in an all-new ballpark. It put her in a totally different sport.

"But I got good news out of all this." He smiled like a madman. "Are you ready for some good news?"

She could only nod.

"I dragged his body out to the Angelina River and threw it down an embankment," he said. "Wolves'll be real bad out there. Thick with buzzards in no time. There won't be nothing left of him for nobody to find."

She smiled weakly. What was she going to do? She felt time ticking. She probably didn't have a good five minutes before he went looking for the shit. Another thirty seconds or so before he realized it wasn't there. She needed to distract him, keep him focused.

"How come you didn't bury him, honey?" she asked.

"I couldn't bury him." His pupils glazed like donuts. "No time. I didn't have a shovel. I'd be out there all night. You don't think we need to go back and bury him, do you?"

"Maybe." She shrugged. "Just in case people start looking for him."

"That's the good news!" He snapped his fingers. "That's what I meant to tell you. I'm dragging him down the banks of the Angelina, and his phone starts up. Scares the living shit out of me. Then, my phone rings. I don't know what to do, so I answer it, and it's Noah. He's looking for JoJo, because he wants to score. I tell him JoJo went out of town to sell that ounce, like he was supposed to. He says, since he's out of town and all, then I must have the shit, and I tell him I do, and so he wants me to hook him up. Except Noah wants to hook up large, because he's got a bunch of people looking so I come up with a plan."

Melinda felt herself getting sick. She spotted her panties next to the magazine rack by the couch, where they'd landed last night.

He continued: "I'll keep selling his stuff like I'm supposed to when he's out of town. When the guys looking for that ounce out in Longview get calling, asking where's JoJo, I won't know, but I'll offer to bring it to them. Pretty soon someone will figure something's up, and I'll agree, and be the one organizing the biggest search party, trying harder than everyone to find him, only I'll know no one'll ever find him, because the wolves, fish, gators, and buzzards and whatever else won't leave nothing. He'll be gone. Disappeared off the face of the earth."

Melinda covered her mouth with her hand. Swallowed what tried to come up. She wanted to go home, to drop out and disappear. Sam knew where her parents lived. He'd drive up to Oklahoma and drop them down an embankment to feed wildlife. *Where would he put her*, she wondered.

He went on: "So I got to clean this blood off me and get selling this shit because, baby, while we're covering for JoJo and waiting for them to start wondering where he is, we can make a whole lot of money. A *whole* lot."

And she lost him. He spun on his heel and turned to go back to his room. She snapped to and realized what he was doing. *He was looking for the shit!* He'd be under his bed, jimmying loose the floorboard and reaching into the crawl space—

"Sam?"

"Mel, I'm real sorry about the other day. I haven't been myself lately, and it's because of this JoJo shit. He doesn't respect me. He never has. He hides his shit here, because he's too scared to get caught with it. Or he *was*. He ain't scared of nothing no more. He'd have me do all the driving, when we went out to Diboll or Huntington to get shit, or out to Tyler to sell it. You should have seen him mooch, when it was time to pay for gas or sodas or whatever. Anyway, my point is that I'm real sorry."

"Sam?"

He was half-under the bed, half-out pulling at the board with his fingernails. "I think that a lot of times I get real angry, and I don't know how to direct that anger. So I lash out at you. My dad was a real grumpy person when I was growing up, and that's how I saw him act around my mom and me. I think that's where I get it from. But I won't be like that no more, honey." She heard him pull free the board and set it aside.

"Sam, honey—"

"And we're going to make so much money. Believe me, babe. In no time, we'll be running JoJo's business and rolling in it. He made so many stupid mistakes and trust me, those aren't the mistakes I'll be making. Watching him this past couple of months taught me one thing, and that's you got to trust people—Wait a second . . ."

"Sam, please—"

He scooted out from under the bed and rose to his knees, turned to her with a look on his face. She'd never seen that expression in him before, and she took a baseball bat to it. One swing and he dropped. Never saw it coming.

The bat fell to the floor. He was still breathing, bleeding freely from a nose split in two. The grip of the .22 peeked from beneath his waistband. She vomited. He would have shot her. He would have thrown her down an embankment to rot with JoJo.

Time to go. She grabbed the .22, some clothes, the keys to his Cutlass and was out the door. She wouldn't stop until it ran out of gas. Because she knew it had to be true, the very thing that used to keep her sane when she was spiraling, now chilled her to her very bones: *Sam Tuley will always come back for me.*

***

That very same Cutlass sat idle in the weed-choked lot next to the bait and tackle shop clear on the other side of Louisiana, where the two fraternity brothers from Tulane barely considered it as they walked back to their ride.

They opened the trunk and tossed in their bait, weights and lures next to the cooler of beers and the rest of their gear.

They got into the car, the taller one driving, and started her up. Headed back up the highway. The stereo jammed some classic rock from a New Orleans station, but as they headed out of range, the speakers popped and crackled and fuzzed until the taller one could take it no more. He told his buddy to reach in back for a CD.

"Get me that Allman Brothers," he said, and the chubbier one turned in the seat to rustle around in back but stopped just short, suddenly not moving. "What's the hold up?"

"Uh, Todd—" stammered Pudgy as he sat back, resting against the dash with his hands skyward.

The taller one turned to look and stared into the barrel of Melinda's .22. She sat up in the backseat, holding the grip with both hands and pointing it into his face.

"Eyes on the road, frat boy," she said. "Last thing I need today is you cracking this car and putting me in the ER."

"What the—"

"Keep your hands on the wheel and do as I say and I won't put any extra holes in your head that don't belong there," she said. "Fatboy, you turn around and put on your seatbelt. And take a right at this junction up ahead. Your fishing trip has been canceled. You two are taking me for a little ride."

3

S ure, she could have left them duct taped to the car and stolen their money, but what if one of them had shimmied loose before she managed to get on down the road? Either one of them outweighed her by at least sixty pounds and would have worked her over and had no qualms about getting revenge and hiding the body so that not even Sam would find her. She thought about rapping the backs of their skulls with the .22 and knocking them out long enough for her to disappear, but then Pudgy, who just loved the sound of his own voice, got lippy.

"Stupid backwater cunt trash," he spat. "Filthy skanky bitch."

Melinda took a deep breath, but couldn't control it. She'd had it. All that shit she'd tolerated from Sam, months and months of it, and now this rich kid running his mouth, calling her names . . . She hauled off and punched him in the back of his head, then again, and then again and again. It hurt, but it hurt more to not do it. And she knew it wasn't hurting him, not doing nearly enough damage, not the kind of damage she wished to do. She knew the gun lay on top of her extra clothes in her backpack, but she tossed that idea out of her head right away. *No, don't do that . . . It hasn't come to that yet.* She kicked the back door open and got out of the car before she did more damage.

But she wasn't done. She looked around for rocks, sticks, something big enough to put an adequate hurt into them. Nothing. She kicked the back fender, but that wasn't doing it. Her cheeks flushed, her heart throbbed . . . she needed to break something. She wanted to hear something plead for mercy. She rounded the car and opened the trunk and saw all the fishing gear and tackle and broke fancy fishing poles over her knee. Both of them, then tossed them to the side of the road.

Nope, that didn't do it. She looked at the backs of their heads through the back windshield and felt the rage well up in her again. There was a gas can in the back—*Don't even think about it!*—next to the tackle boxes. She screamed profanities into the trunk and, once the last of her energy extinguished, she collapsed onto the back bumper and put her head into her hands.

I've got to think. I've got to slow down and think. But that wasn't working. Something had taken over her brain. Gone was the girl from Oklahoma with the 4.0 GPA, eaten alive by the junkie waif running from her tweaker boyfriend. Her only companions the pair of dirtbag frat boys tied up in the front seat of a stolen car. She brought her fist down on whatever she could punch, which turned out to be the tackle box, and she punched it right open, sending tackle and gear spilling out across the back of the trunk.

And she saw it. She smiled to herself. What she would be unable to do with power and force, she would compensate with depravity and terror. She fastened two fish hooks on either end of a short length of fishing line and slid back into the backseat of the car. Suddenly she calmed, seemed more composed. But she knew the truth. On the inside, her feathers were ruffled.

"Boys, I hate to disappoint you, but I've got to go." Her voice was soothing. Had she been able to think clearly, she would have realized this was much more disarming than screaming and punching at whatever she could reach.

"You're going to jail, you skanky cunt," growled Pudgy.

Melinda's smile bared teeth. She reached for the duct tape on the floor board and yanked off long stretches of silver. "See, there you go again. We're always on the verge of having a good time, right there on the edge, then you have to go and open your mouth." She slapped one of the strips of tape across Pudgy's face, covering his mouth. His muffled protests were lost to the afternoon. "Silence ain't golden baby, it's silver."

She turned to TallBoy. He said nothing, but watched her, his eyes flickering with fear. "I wanted to be a good person," she told him. "You understand, right? I so badly wanted to start all over and be good." She put tape to his mouth, smoothed it out across his lips. "But I'm afraid I'm going to have to wait until New Year's to make that my resolution, because I got other shit to do." She turned to Pudgy and held the hooks and line in front of him. His eyes narrowed, TallBoy's widened. They both began to squirm.

"I'd hold still if I were you," she cooed.

The hook pierced Pudgy's cheek. Melinda hadn't expected that, but she found a sinister solace to it. It popped going in, the barb passing the fleshy expanse, then popped coming back out. Her anticipation of enjoying a similar reaction to TallBoy's face surprised her. She made sure the line kept taut and TallBoy shook his head to and fro to keep her from catching him.

"I'm going to hold you still sweetie, one way or another," she said softly. "Why don't you be a good little boy and not move?"

TallBoy grunted from behind the duct tape. No use.

She moved her free hand down his chest, past his stomach, and rested it on his crotch. "If you want, sugar, I could find somewhere else to put this hook." TallBoy froze. His eyes watered. For a brief moment, she felt sorry for him. But she passed the off-ramp for sympathy a few miles back and let go of him down there to secure his face and this time, when she felt that first little *pop* of the hook penetrating his face, she closed her eyes and savored the silence.

4

Well, we made the news, thought Melinda Kendall as she slumped onto the motel bed. The mattress was tight as a prude and offered as much slack. She rustled around in her backpack and found a pack of smokes, grimaced when she realized she only had two left besides the Lucky. The newscaster on TV went on and on and couldn't believe what she reported. This was the crime of the century, right there in Southeastern Louisiana.

"—when authorities found the two Tulane students in an abandoned car in the small Mississippi Delta community early this evening. The two men have been identified as Todd Whitmore of St. Louis and Brett Likely from Dallas, both reportedly on a fishing trip—"

Todd and Brett. Melinda chuckled to herself.

She put her head in her hand. *This isn't me. When did this happen?* Long before she put that baseball bat in Sam Tuley's face, that's for sure. But after two days of manic confusion and instability, she'd found the clarity she experienced while handling those boys this afternoon quite . . . *refreshing.* But this couldn't be her.

Or was it?

She needed rest. She'd been going at it like this for days now—on fumes—riding the residual high from the last little bit she'd done back at Sam's apartment, but that was all but gone. She knew she needed a little help getting to bed, but that's why she'd stopped at the supermarket. Of course, she'd lifted the wallets from Todd and Brett and raked in quite a haul. The car had been what she really wanted, but she could never keep it, as it would lead the cops, or worse: Sam, right to her.

In fact, thanks to the news, she figured she'd have a difficult time of it for a while. She'd stopped at the grocery store before checking in, which was a good thing, but forgetting to buy smokes while she was out could be a bad thing. Very bad. She rustled through the paper sack for her sundries, each with its own purpose.

She knew from experience that sleep would be no easy feat tonight and despised the thought of tossing and turning all night. So she had made sure to get the meth users' two best friends: a bottle of Tylenol PM and a liter of Jack Daniels.

She had forgotten the last time she'd eaten, and even though actual hunger lingered nowhere near on her horizon, she had bought a can of tomato soup. It had the nutrients necessary for whatever, so she opened it with a pocketknife, careful not to cut herself on the ragged, sharp edges. She drained the soup into one of the motel's plastic cups and drank it raw. The thick, viscous tang of the tomato sliding down her throat and filling her belly. She popped two Tylenol PMs and chased them with a slug from the Jack Daniels.

It began its work immediately.

The news reporter kept it up: "—both men had been brutalized by their assailant which has been described as a woman of about twenty years of age. According to—"

Brutalized? Good lord, Brett and Todd. Have you no shame?

"—she approached them at a fisherman's supply store in La Porte, asking for help. After Whitmore and Likely gave her money, she pulled a gun and instructed them to drive her across the state line, into this sleepy Mississippi town. It was there that she began her ritual of torture and degradation."

Who watches this filth? She laughed out loud and pulled on the whiskey bottle again. It had a bite, and she considered cutting it with a little cola from the vending machine, or even some water, but that would mean getting off the bed, and she was way too comfortable. Besides, she didn't want to miss a second of this news story. Even though she'd lived it only hours before, their version of the story was infinitely better.

The television screen showed footage of the frat boys being wheeled into the back of an ambulance on stretchers. *Poor fellas.*

"—were unable to move from the car, as they were bound with duct tape, hands behind their backs and feet and legs strapped to their seats. What happened next is a twisted tale of terror straight from a horror movie as the woman used fish hooks, disfiguring the two men for life. According to reports, she then left the two men bleeding in their own car, and continued on foot. Authorities have begun a manhunt for this woman and issued artists' rendering of her likeness according to the descriptions given by Whitmore and Likely. However, the trauma experienced by both men have reduced their ability to agree on a description—"

Melinda nearly spit her Tennessee whiskey across the motel room. On the television were two artists' renderings of her. One portrayed her as an evil, sallow, gaunt woman with stringy hair, one reminiscent of a witch or a hag. The picture made her appear about fifteen years older, and she would have felt immediately self-conscious were it not for the second picture. This one showed a woman with smooth skin, piercing sexy eyes and full lips.

"Which one of you described that one?" giggled Melinda. "Your therapists will have field days."

"—if you encounter this woman, you are advised not to engage her. She is considered armed and dangerous, and if you see her, you are to contact authorities immediately—"

She changed the channel to a sitcom rerun. Her brain finally slowed. For the past twelve hours, it had felt like it was powered by a crackhead hamster running on its wheel, but now the little rodent ran out of gas. She leaned back on the bed and pulled again from the Jack Daniels. On the bedside table sat her wallet and the money left from the day's take.

But she needed to keep moving and, thanks to the frat boys and the TV reporters, hitching was off the table.

The bottle froze at her lips. An idea flashed before her, and she grasped at it to hold it still. *There are a lot of frat boys in this world,* she thought. *More than enough to get me where I'm going.* She took another pull and set the bottle aside, drank from the cup of tomato soup instead. She sat up. She now had her own full attention.

This had been easy, she told herself. Those two boys never knew what hit them until it hit them, and by that time, she'd already subdued them. And they deserved it.

She counted the money. Sixteen bucks. *Definitely won't last forever.* She ran her finger along the inside of the tomato soup can, scooping out the last of it, then sucking it off her finger. The solution now stood in front of her. She knew what she had to do.

There was only one small problem.

The rerun cut off, interrupted by *Breaking News* from the local affiliate. A grizzled TV anchorman rattled off her list of crimes and the horrible condition in which she'd left the two dirtbags. Once again, they warned everyone to steer clear of her.

"Shit," she muttered as her eyelids began to weigh a thousand pounds, "I'm goddamn famous."

5

The motel had a washer and dryer, so Melinda Kendall thought it best to take advantage and get after her clothes before they got out of hand. She went down in a pair of shorts and a T-shirt she figured she'd just throw away anyway. She stuffed every other stitch she owned into one of the motel's trash sacks and brought it down to the wash.

She'd called the front desk from the room and asked to stay on another night. After last night's newscast, she thought it best to stay off the road, hole up inside, and keep out of trouble. Out of sight. The last thing she wanted to do was step up to the front desk, let any more people catch wind of her. Maybe she could ride it out. Maybe this whole thing could blow over.

No such luck. A fella came into the laundry room looking for the vending machine, trying to get a soda. She didn't want to draw any attention, just pointed him down the hall. He left, but came back after a few minutes. She tried to convince herself that she didn't know he would.

And boy, was he slick. He was the type of guy who always had something going on. She had no idea what he saw when he looked at her, but she could tell he considered himself game.

"Hot out there, huh?" he said.

"It sure is," she said. She didn't care to look him full in the face so she kept her head turned sideways, hair down around her eyes. No telling if this guy watched the news. She'd much rather keep to herself, but she had a run of bad luck lately in that department.

"I'm in for a couple of days, until tomorrow at least," he said. She wondered what gave him the impression she cared. "Sales. Wine. I'm in wine sales."

"Ah." The washer buzzed and stopped spinning. She opened it, collected what she had and put it in the dryer.

"Are you much of a wine drinker?"

"Who isn't?"

"I know that's right." He stole looks up and down like he may not ever see her again, may need to remember her for later. "What's your favorite kind of wine?"

"Red." She slipped a couple of quarters into the dryer and got it to going.

"What kind of red? Merlot? Cabernet?"

"Cheap red," she said.

He smiled. He wasn't bad looking, really. A little older than most guys she'd go for. Definitely more *square* than what she'd consider *her type*, but he had a way. She watched his smile and supposed it nice enough.

"Do you ever drink Zinfandels?" he asked her. She shrugged. "They're real good. Especially if you like red wine. I've got one in my portfolio that's drinking very nice right now. It's from California. They've got some very nice wines out there. You ever been to California?"

She shook her head.

"You don't talk much, do you?" She didn't answer, so he went on: "If you ever get out that way, you have to see some of the wineries.

They're spectacular. Just rows and rows of vines, all making fruit for wines."

"That sounds lovely." She estimated her clothes were twenty minutes from drying and settled in for the long haul.

He popped the soda he'd been carrying and offered her a drink. She refused, and he sucked down a few gulps. "That Zinfandel I'm showing right now is one of those that you can drink all by itself, or with food. It's the kind of wine that you can enjoy in the middle of the day, especially one like this."

"I bet."

"Yeah." He was on the edge, peeking over, ready to leap. "Would you like to try a glass?"

"Why not?" She had nowhere to be.

"Really?" His sails filled with air. "Sweet. Hang here a second, and I'll go grab the bottle and a couple of glasses." He looked her up and down again as if she might vaporize before his return, then bolted for the door.

She giggled a little. *But this is a very bad idea. The last thing you need is to make any more friends.* The dryer knocked and clomped as the clothes rumbled round. She considered taking off, just grabbing the damp clothes and making a run for it. She could skedaddle, just scoot on out and get on the road, or she could retire to the room and keep the shades drawn. He'd never find her. Besides, she'd have to hitch and that wasn't a good idea.

How far are you going to take this? She didn't have time to think through scenarios before he returned sporting a half bottle of red and two plastic cups from the room. He poured the juice, gave her the glass with the larger pour.

"First, you'll get a little boysenberry on the nose, maybe a bit of chocolate," he said, sniffing into the motel cup. "But once you taste it, you'll get the pepper, spices, and a dry mouthfeel."

"Mouthfeel?"

"Yeah, take a sip. You'll know what I mean."

She looked at him like he had ten heads then took a sip from the cup. Followed it with a gulp. Then, what the hell, she drained the cup and set it down on the dryer.

"Mouthfeel," she said. She looked him full in the face, let him see her, figured *fuck it*. He couldn't look away. If he knew, he couldn't force himself to care. "Zinfandel's nice. What else you got?"

And in no time she let him talk her back to the room, or let him think he talked her back to room, because at this point she'd decided she was bound and determined to get in there. He was fun, and they were both out of town, and he had a mess of booze. She'd noticed the wedding ring earlier and never noticed when it came off, but it was off now so she reckoned him unlikely to raise a stink, fall in love, or want to go steady.

All of the bottles had been opened, been sampled around all the shitty restaurants in town. He told her over and over that all the joints out there were small-minded and knew nothing about wine and were still serving the same old stuff from the 80s. A couple of glasses got him to going, and she'd pour another, hoping to drink him tolerable.

He blushed. "I'm talking too much," he said.

"It's okay," she said. "It's very interesting."

And on that note, he leaned in for a kiss. It was clumsy and awkward, and since she'd been smiling, planted on her teeth, and before she realized what was going on, he stopped, unsure whether or not to go on. She kissed him back—proper this time—and he let her know right away that he'd run a yellow light. His tongue went every which way, mouth all over her and hands to grabbing.

Soon he leaned her back on the couch and started to work her buttons. He was all thumbs, so she helped him. In no time her shirt was on the floor, and he'd set to handling her titties. *Oh man, if this ain't a bad idea, I don't know what is*. But, no stranger to bad ideas, Melinda helped him off with his pants.

"You got a condom, sugar?" she asked.

"No, I don't," he panted. "You don't think I'm the type of guy who'd just happen to have a condom on him, do you?"

"You're about to sleep with a girl you met in a motel laundry room," she said, rifling through her knapsack. "You're exactly the type of guy who should have one." She scrounged one up, and they got to it.

Once all that was said and done, he hopped off her and skittered to the bathroom. She lit a smoke and looked through the wine bottles for one that still had some left. She threw back a jammy little number called a Pinot Noir and waited for him to return. He took his time in there. *Should I get dressed?* She felt shitty. Kind of. But nothing a shower couldn't fix.

She couldn't decide if she did it for the thrill or if she was just that horny. *No, it wasn't that*. Horny she could handle. *This was something different*. She wished Sam were still around. At least then she could get a bump. It was the last thing she needed, but she sure could use a bump.

He came out of the bathroom with a towel around his waist that was too small and kept all his cards on the table. He couldn't look at her. He busied himself around the room like he had a hundred other things to do. She began to get the picture.

"Sugar, you don't mind if I take one of these bottles back to my room?" He shook his head, and she lifted each one to find a bottle most full. They'd done some damage earlier. He grew impatient and went to his leather case and pulled out an unopened one.

"Here," he said, handing it over. His eyes looked at everything but her. He found his pants on the floor and retrieved his wallet, counted out forty dollars and handed it to her as well.

"What's this?" She only *played* dumb.

"Just take it," he said. "Get yourself something to eat."

Her cheeks burned, but hey, forty bucks was forty bucks, so she snatched it out of his hands without a second thought. She calculated how far that would get her, if she only ate two meals per day and figured no way, she worked way too hard, so she reached into her backpack again and this time pulled out Sam's .22.

"Oh, I'm afraid it's going to cost you a little more than that."

And to make sure he didn't cause any trouble, she tied him to the bed with him still wrapped in that too small towel, sheets binding each of his wrists and ankles to the posts and for good measure, one of his socks in his mouth. She found three hundred bucks and four credit cards in his wallet, as well as the keys to a Honda in the parking lot. The leather case kept four more bottles of wine, and she discovered a couple more cases in the trunk.

Not a bad day's work. She cleaned out her room, picked up her laundry and scooted on down the road in his Honda. *Not bad at all.*

6

M elinda Kendall's tears would not stop. A flood of emotion could be expected when a person was trying to kick, but this shit was uncalled for. Melinda'd always known it was not the day after, or the day *after* the day after, but the following day that was going to hurt. Meth left the system slow. It dripped and oozed through the bloodstream, like fat off meat. And when it was gone, it was gone.

And *it* was gone.

She remembered one weekend when she and Sam had really been at it. Not just run-of-the-mill, average Saturday night for the Jones's *at it*, but chalk-one-up-for Sam and Melinda *at it*. Both of them had sworn it off again and said *one thing's for sure: no more crank*, then found themselves following each other to the bathroom, thinking the other had something up their sleeve. Or were licking their driver's license. Or had saved some empty plastic baggies *just in case* and were holding out. Hell, Melinda had been known to finger through the threads of the shag carpet in hope for an errant rock.

That weekend in particular, they had been at DefCon One. Both desperately needed the other to fuck up, so they could point fingers and say *you did it first*, but stubbornness ruled supreme, and no one offered any give. He'd sat red-eyed, knees tapping, and she snapped at his every word, because he had a way of coming off like an inquisitor, and no one was getting anywhere. Things got hairy. She told him was a pussy, which he'd acquired a mess of childhood issues concerning, and he'd called her a cunt, which he'd done once too many.

She'd thrown a crystal ashtray at his head, which broke into a million pieces. He'd grabbed the copy of *The Satanic Verses* her dad had gotten autographed, locked himself in the bathroom, then tore out, page-by-page, the first two chapters. To his credit, he'd started with the blank pages, himself being a former bibliophile, but the anger welled up in him and, before he knew it, he'd flushed the dedication page with Salman Rushdie's scribble, and then started in on the text. Melinda lit into him like a fury, as she was known to do, and knocked the door plum off its hinges. She tackled him into the bathtub, where she operated on him with a vengeance. Fists flying, legs kicking, and teeth gnashing, but all for nothing. Sam was bigger and meaner and got a thrill out of her trying so hard. He got off on it. He had her clothes off in a heartbeat, right there in that tub and, when the cops came because the neighbors got twitchy, they received quite a show. And still, the cops said she needed to stay somewhere else, because it was technically a domestic disturbance, and they just had to follow rules, but Sam wasn't hearing it and threw a big fit, yelling at cops and saying, *hey, we were fucking when you got here, did it sound like she was in danger to you?* But the more he yelled, the more he proved their case. He screamed and cried and pitched a hell of a fit, but they still took her away and left her at a friend's house. He never got over the betrayal. That night when he cried in his goddamn bed, he cried alone and the next day they figured what the hell was the point in trying to kick? What point exactly? So they called JoJo and made a weekend of it.

Not since then had Melinda cried this much.

So why was she crying? Did she miss Sam? Of course, she missed Sam. Before him, she had one trajectory. She'd been beautiful, but smart. Guys didn't like smart girls in high school, but in college she found herself in demand. Not only hot guys, but dangerous guys. Sam wasn't her first, but as far as she was concerned, he could have been her last. Or at least, one of her last. He was handsome and funny and smart and *driven*. The drive alone sent her into a frenzy.

But that was not why she was crying. She considered herself not so foolish to remember exactly why she'd put that Louisville Slugger into his face, knew that he would want no explanations. She'd watched him rise up the ladder, knew that only JoJo would keep him still. No more JoJo, no more leash. He'd put her head on a pike and call it good business. *If you see what I've done to someone I loved, check out what I can do to someone who crosses me.* No, she didn't cry for Sam Tuley.

Did she cry because of the wine rep? That pasty fella with the funny hair back at the motel that called himself *Randy*? No, she reckoned not. Nor did she cry for the two frat boys now emblazoned with matching scars upon their cheeks, for no other reason than they were rude and insulting and in bad need of etiquette. No, she'd do that a million times, over and over again.

No rather, she cried because of the news broadcast. Once again, some pinhead with over-moussed hair told the story—getting most of it wrong—with an incredible backdrop of photos and videos and quotes taken out of context. They showed file footage of the frat boys being wheeled out of the car and pictures of the barbed fish hooks. He appeared on-site of the actual hotel room where Randall McVeigh had been bound, wrist and ankle, to the bedposts.

She cried because of what they said.

" . . .*a prostitute who authorities are calling 'Sweet Melinda'* . . ."

A prostitute.

"Sweet" Melinda.

A prostitute named Sweet Melinda.

She shuddered. If she had to figure which facet of the investigation peeved her the most, she'd have to spin a bottle or flip a coin or something, but there was no end to her despair. At first she dropped to her knees and wept, then threw herself across the bed and let it all out, screaming and kicking and calling the world a motherfucker, hanging hell in the balance. No outlet short of detonating a fission bomb would calm her sympathies, for she found the universe to be a whore, a whore with no shame who pointed a crooked finger in her direction and hissed, "*harlot.*"

They called her *prostitute* on the news. They said that authorities searched for a prostitute, and that sent her into a tizzy which resulted in the near-drained bottle of Jack denting the wall over the television and possibly a broken knuckle or two. She kicked the motel toilet a dozen times but that fucker wasn't breaking anything but her foot, so she gave up and figured this was not the way to go. She collapsed to the bed.

And to call her *Sweet Melinda?* Holy shit! How did they get that name? She'd been trying to blank it out of her mind for a while now, but she knew. She'd signed into that motel back at the Delta under the name 'Melinda Allman,' then went about molesting the seedy wine rep. They probably all figured it to be a alias, but newspapermen found poetry to a hell-bent prostitute named *Sweet Melinda*, and this thing was bound to catch fire.

"This ain't fucking fair," she said, then went to see if that bottle of Jack had anything left in it, but before she could get there, she fell to her knees and got to crying again. It got to be where she didn't think she'd stop crying. Tears might cease, but that lump in her throat never would, and until it did, she might never suck a full breath of air again. "This ain't fair at all."

But who would hear? Not the police. No, they were looking for a strung-out woman who lured men to bait-and-tackle shops or motel rooms, and would never hear the cries of the forlorn. Certainly not the victims. They would never hear her, for they didn't before, and why should they after? Her parents? No, she hoped they were never dragged into this. Sam? Any day now, he'd be putting two and two together. Any day.

Nope, it was just her. Her and the fella handcuffed on the floor in front of the television. Poor bastard thought he had it made, finding a girl at the truck stop who was going his way, and not just on the blacktop. He'd scored himself a gram of shit and wanted to find someone kindred to enjoy it, but instead wandered along Sweet Melinda Kendall and she'd figured instead of sharing, why not jack the whole sack, for there was very little left for her to have redeemed.

7

One of the things Melinda Kendall liked best about the shit was that it helped make light of a good, honest fix. That's what she reckoned she was knee-deep in right now. A good, honest fix. All the newspapers and bulletins and flyers posted at truckstops all told her the same thing, and that's she better make tracks and get out of Mississippi. Thanks to the shit, her brain fired quicker, which made events move in slo-mo, let her stay on top of the situation. That, in her estimation, about did it for the good news.

No motel in Mississippi would be safe. After the wine guy and the trucker guy, the cops gave her a *modus operandi*. The two frat boys back in Louisiana added heat in all the right places. She'd heard all the stories, added up all the facts or what got passed off as facts and came to one mighty conclusion each and every time.

She probably should swear off guys for a little while.

***

Getting out of Mississippi would be more difficult than she imagined. She sat atop a hill on the hood of a stolen Nissan and looked through the stolen binoculars at what represented her stolen and dashed dreams down on the highway below her. Just a Rapunzel's hair from the state line as a mile's worth of cars, trucks, minivans, station wagons, and the like snaked out from one hell of a mess of police vehicles. A uniformed officer checked each and every vehicle and driver, checked licenses and backseats. Family vacations were delayed, as were sales quotas and promises to be home for dinner. All because the state of Mississippi needed to find the evil tweaker prostitute known as Sweet Melinda.

And not just here. It had been this way out on 98, barring her from Mobile, on 42, and even on 84. She didn't dare fuss with the Interstate, heard tell they were getting them at the on-ramps. She figured to hell with it, if that's the way they wanted to play. Give her a little time, and she'd have it licked. She'd either divine a way out of the state on her own, or she'd wait them out until they figured her long gone, so they could go back to trapping speeders. She'd mosey out on her own. *The trick is, not to panic.*

Why panic? Why, when she could keep her head perfectly about her, thanks to the fresh bag of shit she'd swiped off the trucker. Ellis Wayne Gentry was what his driver's license called him and the folks on the news said he came from Arizona. Long-haul trucker. *Why couldn't I jack some fella who had something I could drive?*

She needed to think clearly. The shit helped, sure, but she couldn't afford to make any mistakes. She knew this was only a fugue, a temporary lapse of reason that soon would fade. She needed focus. No matter how on top of things she convinced herself she stayed, it could be so easy to slip and not even known she'd done it.

Which is what she told herself at the payphone. *What the hell are you doing?* She hung up, hoped she'd done it in time. *In time would have been after the seventh ring.* The seventh ring of the third attempt, maybe. The first couple of times she'd called, she said she'd hang up when he answered. But when he didn't answer, she'd gone into a frenzy and put all those quarters back into the slot and punched the buttons angrier and angrier and feeling a fury with each unanswered ring.

What was he doing? Why was he too busy to answer the phone? Was he fucking someone? Had he gone back to business as usual after she left, selling off shit to JoJo's customers and him, and some other whore rolling around in all that money? If she could, she'd pull the phone booth out of the ground like a withered gardenia and throw it into the highway, hopefully hitting a station wagon with a family of five that would never make it to whatever beach vacation they'd spent all year planning. *Why, oh why weren't you there Sam Tuley when I needed you most?*

She hung up the phone and took a breath. She knew exactly why he wouldn't answer the phone today, or tomorrow, or however many days it would take him to find her, do what he had to, then drive back to Nacogdoches where he could resume business as usual. Sam was a driven motherfucker, and hell would pity what stood between him and what he had to do and, for the life of her, she wondered just what that was. Louisiana? Half of Mississippi? If every badge in the state was on the lookout for her, every trucker, every motel owner . . . they'd all be in a race with Mister Sam Tuley, and she better get to hopping.

Time to play had passed. She considered her options, her brain not playing fair. Soup would probably do it, inject the necessary nutrients into her bloodstream, give her the whatever to counteract the what-ever sent her off to do the self-destructive and foolish things she found herself wont to do. Maybe soften the come-down.

She circled the little diner—Alma's Café on 63—for a bit, made sure no cops were inside, wanted to let the business die down a little so fewer people had the chance to see her, but no luck as the place stayed busy for so long that she finally figured that to be better, with everyone otherwise occupied and crowded and her more liable to blend in. She dusted off her jeans as if that made any difference at all and wandered in the diner.

A girl no older than she bustled past, arms full of dirty dishes, and said, "Just seat yourself where you can, hon. There's a table in the corner, and I'll be by to wipe it off in a sec." Melinda did just that.

She looked about the room and saw families, truckers, couples, folks eating and sipping coffee, living a life that felt so far from her own that she couldn't even imagine living in it or moving among them as one of them and wondered benignly if that was a choice made by her or some petulant God pissed at her for some shit she might never remember.

Melinda picked up a greasy menu spattered with something brown and looked it over. She found nothing sounding remotely appetizing but figured that's the state of things with her condition at the moment and settled on a chicken noodle soup with a cup of coffee.

Everything looked dirty to her. The urge to pick up a dishcloth and get after the menu manifested into a hankering to go at the booth itself, for it seemed coated in something slippery, and while she was at it, she could take on the walls, for someone had slung gravy or soup or sauce across the walls like blood spatter, and no one had seen to it in years or so, but first, someone would have to answer that damned phone. *How long had it been ringing?* She counted six rings just since she'd noticed it, but had only recently noticed it, instead focusing on a kid moodily rattling his glass of ice cubes while his mother impatiently waited for a cola refill. The waitress smiling and chatting up a trucker in the corner, not giving a shit that the world around her crumbled and burned, while one asshole at the counter watched skirts every time they passed but now wanted more coffee and kept saying *Miss? Miss?*

and waving his empty cup at no one who cared, and all the while, that damned phone . . .

Already chock full of issues that very evening with unanswered phones, she reckoned she'd had it. She up and stalked across the dining room, picked up the receiver and, even though the diner hummed at a billion decibels, without the phone ringing, it plunged into a vacuum of silence and she said, "Thanks for calling—" she looked at the front of a slimy menu "—Alma's Cafe on 63, how may I help you?" and the woman on the other end of the phone wanted to know if they were open. "Of course, we're open. Why don't you come on in?" Melinda answered, and then the woman wanted to know what the soup of the day was, but Melinda didn't know and looked about for help. Everyone had their heads down except the waitress in the corner, so she shouted over, "Hey! Hey, you! Yeah, you! If you ain't too busy, would you mind telling me what's the soup of the day?"

The waitress looked at her as if she had ten heads.

"Make time on your own time," Melinda ordered. "Why don't you bus that table over yonder, get that kid a refill, and see about fetching this pervy fella some more coffee? But first, tell me what's the damned soup of the day."

She caught a Mexican boy in a dish uniform and ordered him to wipe down her booth, and said while he was at it, see to the walls and seat. A man in a too-tight shirt and a too-small necktie came along and asked her did she want a job. In no time: equilibrium. First she refilled coffees and sodas and helped out with the bussing, but she soon saw more of what needed to be done than people doing it, so she got after them to do it. One thing women working in diners don't like is to be told by other women in diners what to do, but unfortunately for them, Melinda Kendall had recently faced obstacles more daunting than a stout woman named Dotty or a young waif with a nametag reading

EMMA and, to her own chagrin, had to use tactics other than baseball bats or the butt of Sam Tuley's .22. But things got done all the same.

And all I wanted was some fucking chicken soup and to do something sane for once.

But the universe turned against her and, with the rush well out of the way, she sat at the end of the counter while the waitresses counted through their money and the manager told her over and over that he believed Jesus Christ, friendly fella that he was, must have dispatched her directly to him, and she could work whenever she wanted and have all the best shifts if she'd please take the job. She blushed. When she'd left Oklahoma and waded through semesters at school in East Texas, she'd never believed she be as grateful as she was to accept a job in a joint like Alma's Cafe. Where better to wait out the Mississippi State police?

In fact, she thought, this could be exactly what she needed to turn things around. She stepped into the bathroom and looked in the mirror and wanted to cry something fierce. Her skin had gone to shit. Those circles around her eyes darkened, and she used to love her eyes, but now the green paled, and the whites rimmed with red. Her lips, dry and cracked. Her hair, once lush and vibrant and pert, now hung limp and stringy, and she wondered if any amount of washing and treating would ever make her young again. She told herself over and over that she was only twenty years old, but who else would know? She looked like someone who'd haunted Alma's Cafe for lifetimes, several lifetimes.

Remember: this could be what she needed. A steady paycheck buoyed by some hard-earned tips, a place to stay and get herself cleaned up, some sleep and some shampoo. Maybe rest up and get ready to make her way back to where she belonged. Just lay low in the cafe for a couple of months and become someone else for a while, just long enough for the police and Sam to forget about her, just long enough to string together a few paychecks and then figure it all out. This is how it's done. And she knew just what she needed to do to get it started.

One more . . . ?

No way. She put the entire baggie of the trucker's evil shit into the toilet bowl. Even after it floated atop the water, she fought the urge to fish it out and rub it all along her gums, put the paste in her however possible, but she didn't. Instead, she flushed the commode. It swirled and sucked down through the hole in the bottom and *voila!* she was on the road to recovery. Again.

Chicken soup will do it. She put her fingers to her hair and tried to gussy up but no use. She said *fuck it* and stepped out the bathroom to return to her job. *Her job.* As she rounded the back hallway and passed through the kitchen where the Mexicans smiled while pushing their brooms, she heard the ruckus in the dining room and knew in her heart of hearts what went on before the rest of her caught wind.

Two state policemen wanted to know who drove the stolen car out in the parking lot, for they had reason to believe it belonged to Sweet Melinda, the woman for whom they'd been scouring half the state, and the frumpy fella managing the joint said he had no idea because they'd been so busy all night, and the police saying they'd been watching it a little while, and it never moved, so Melinda walked toward the back door of the diner, all the way, hoping like hell they didn't have the place surrounded with guns drawn and orders to shoot her on sight.

8

Melinda woke with sticks, twigs, leaves, and the like stuck to her face. She'd rolled off her shoes sometime in the night, shoes she'd been using as a pillow. She could have slept for days had the sun not risen and brought with it gnats or mosquitoes or whatever the hell divebombed her face with little high-pitched zips. It hadn't been up long, barely straddling the horizon, but it meant business, and the mercury already began to climb. Melinda took a second to gather her bearings.

Riverside. Despite what felt like decades without respite from the sun and heat, the river rolled high and, rather than cross it last night, she'd decided to stop and rest. She felt like she'd pushed her luck enough tromping through the forest with nothing more than moonlight. The river felt like suicide.

Her lips were dry and surely cracked, but her throat needed relief the most. It burned and the air screamed across the lining. Who knew what floated or died in that river, but she needed something to drink, so she crawled to the bank and dipped in her hand, then drank voraciously.

"We thought you was dead."

Melinda whipped her head about and found the voice belonging to a small child, a kid about twelve or so, standing just behind her, fishing line in the water. Another younger boy stood beside him, also shoeless and brandishing rod and reel.

"What did you say?"

The boy pointed to where she'd woken. "You been lying there for so long, we thought you was dead."

"I was sleeping."

"We didn't know that."

Melinda looked them over. Simple little kids. She tried to remember what day it was, wondered if they should be in school. She couldn't. *How long had it been since I left Nacogdoches?* Nothing came to her. For a split second, she panicked. Not even knowing what year it was, but she collected herself and let things come back to her. She'd had a rough go of it lately. After a bit, she figured it didn't matter as it was still summer and school would be out.

"Why are you sleeping by the river?" asked the younger brother.

"Because I was tired."

The younger one accepted that, but his brother refused to move along. "Why don't you sleep in your bed?"

"You ask a lot of questions." She turned back to the river and cupped her hands, drank more.

"You ought not sleep out here," said the older brother. "There's lots of snakes and such. This river runs thick with moccasins in the summer."

"Thanks," she said, not needing to hear that at all. "Say, where are we?"

"What do you mean?"

"Where are we at?"

"We're at the river."

She took a breath. "What town are we in?"

The boys looked at each other. "Chicora's up this side of the river."

"And what's up the other?"

"Alabama, ma'am." The older one pulled his line from the water, fiddled with the hook, then cast it back yonder. "Where you aim to get to?"

"Good question," she said, thinking about it. "Other side, I reckon. You know how I can do that?"

"Why don't you try the road?" asked the little one.

She stood and watched the boys fish. They had an ice cooler at their feet. A tackle box and something to keep the fish, which she reckoned empty. They saw her looking at their stuff and asked if she was hungry. She lied and shook her head.

"We got sandwiches in there," said the older one. "Baloney and cheese whiz." She still didn't move. "You can have mine." He reached into the cooler and handed her a Ziploc with a mess of sandwich in it. She looked at it a long moment before unwrapping it then considered it a moment more before setting upon it. In less than three bites, there was no trace of it. The boys laughed themselves silly.

"What's so funny?"

"We ain't never seen a girl eat like that," the little one said. "You eat like our dog."

The older one reached back into the cooler and produced another sandwich, held it out. She shook her head, and this time, she meant it. The first one probably hadn't made it all the way down yet, but her dry mouth made choking down the bread near impossible, and the thought of more food gave her belly a fit. She dropped back to her knees and drew a few more gulps of water.

The boys laughed even more.

"Let me guess: I drink like your dog too."

She looked up and down the embankments, surveyed her situation. The sun cut through the pines at an angle and lit up the faded green clover, and the forest floor rusted by pine needles.

"How do you reckon I can cross this river if I don't want to use the road?"

The two boys looked at each other. "You can't swim it."

"You don't think so?"

The older one looked across it. "Naw," he said. "It's going too fast. You'd need a rope to go across, and maybe somebody on each side to hold the rope. Then I reckon you could ford it."

"How about the other way?"

The boys looked at each other again. "I don't think she gets shallow nowheres near here. And the river's up over the shoals back the other way. You're best to just use the road."

She looked up the river and back. The boys were right. The river flowed South at a pretty steady clip.

"Is this as wide as the river gets?" asked Melinda.

"I'd say so," said the boy. "But I wouldn't cross if I was you." He kicked at a pine cone with his bare feet. "We could ask my daddy to give you a ride across the river if you want."

"I don't think that's a good idea," she said. She considered all the pros and cons, then wondered what these two would tell their parents when they returned home. She looked them over and felt shivers racing up and down her body. There really was no way to convince these two not to tell their parents, was there?

Don't even think about it . . .

She thought of the two frat boys back in Louisiana. They'd been this age once. Had someone like her been around to teach them a few manners in their early years, they may have had a shot. These two looked her over like she was some kind of twisted science experiment.

She coyly felt around in her pockets, finding nothing but a dwindling wad of cash.

They're not even teenagers. What the hell has gotten into you?

She shook her head and put her fingers to the bridge of her nose. This was not who she was. Not at all. Someday soon, she'd get somewhere and string together a few nights of sleep and get her shit right. She'd get cleaned up, take a shower, figure things out. All of this would be put behind her, and she'd go back to being the person she was, the person she *was* before all of this . . . this *life* happened to her. She'd go back to being her parent's daughter instead of . . .

. . . Sweet Melinda.

"You should come up to our house and have dinner with us," said the older one. "Our momma's going to be home in a little bit, and you can meet her. We'll have dinner and play some games."

But for now, she couldn't see two little boys in front of her. Instead she saw the wine salesman, the two frat boys, the trucker. She saw two barefoot redneck kids who would no doubt grow up to be two redneck young men.

She felt tiny knives in the palms of her hands and realized for the first time that her hands had balled into fists so tight her fingernails drew blood and her knuckles purpled. She closed her eyes and let herself relax.

Maybe later this can be fixed, but for now you are a broken person. Truly, truly broken.

She did not look back at the boys as she turned on her heels and climbed out of the embankment. She heard them call after her, but she kept on, passing through trees and brush until she found the trail that would lead her out of the wilderness.

9

Melinda Kendall came upon the highway and wished it had been as shaded as the woods, but luxuries came and luxuries went, and this one was not to be afforded. She needed to put space between her and those boys, space between her and Mississippi. Space between her and East Texas.

He hadn't answered the phone.

He could be driving the next car that passed her on the highway. But then again, so could a highway patrolman.

She no longer cared. When she heard the car slowing to a stop behind her, she'd long ago decided that she didn't care if it was Sam Tuley or the Mississippi State Police. She'd keep right on walking until dropped by a hail of hellfire and bullets and be grateful to finally get some damned rest. Imagine her disappointment when she found it to be those two shoeless urchins from the river, both riding shotgun with their mother in a shitty, dented little Pinto.

Their mother insisted on being called Wanda Jean and wouldn't take no for an answer. The second her boys told her about the woman by the river, Wanda Jean had jumped into action. For Wanda Jean, there did not seem to be too many paths to heaven, so she made sure to leap at every opportunity that presented itself. She gasped and moaned at Melinda's wretched appearance, although she herself did not appear to be doing much better. Her clothes were older than a woman her age should be allowed to wear outside of the house, and her hair had thinned and run colorless.

Melinda tried like the dickens to not climb inside the rattling Pinto, but her efforts could not match those of the two boys and their eager mother. So in no time, she was aboard, and they took her back from where she'd come.

"Praise Jesus," said Wanda Jean. "Praise him up and down. It's just a miracle that you were led to that riverside where you come across my Gunner and my Tanner. It's a miracle, like baby Moses in the bulrushes."

"You think so?" asked Melinda.

"I know so." She had the smile of a woman touched by something, whether it be the hand of God or not. "I know it in my heart."

Melinda watched the road the entire journey, trying to make as many mental notes of the ingress to better facilitate the egress. If there were any on/off switches to all the Jesus talk, she couldn't find them, but figured her current situation and developments could possibly benefit from a little spirituality. So she let it slide.

Wanda Jean prattled on about being hungry and fed, lost and found, and a bunch of prodigal whatnot until finally they reached their house out near the river on a long stretch of lonely road. There was plenty of room about, some sun-baked crops out to the side of the house, a giant willow with a tire swing, a couple of outbuildings in disrepair. That Wanda Jean's biggest sin was being poor gave Melinda a bit of pause, if only because she'd considered robbing these Bible-thumpers one of the upsides to the detour.

"We're going to fix you up with a nice dinner," said Wanda Jean.

"You don't have to—"

"Nonsense," she said. "When I stand before Jesus at the gates of heaven, I don't want to be told I turned out one of his angels without first feeding her."

Melinda insisted on helping. She took hold of the sack of potatoes and set to peeling, while Wanda Jean fussed with a can of green beans.

"This is like a treat to me, as well," confessed Wanda Jean. "Used to, I had a lot of girlfriends. Before I met Robbie."

"Robbie's your husband?"

Wanda Jean nodded. "Robbie Early. He was something else in high school."

"Y'all was high school sweethearts?" Behind them, the children fought over a toy. "That's so sweet."

"He was the talk of the town, back in the day," said Wanda Jean. "You should have seen how all the girls wanted to catch hold of him."

"I don't guess they could hold a candle to your cooking, right?" Melinda scanned the kitchen. An old blender. Greasy metalware. An oil-spattered microwave. Nothing worth stealing. "You know what they say. The quickest way to a man's heart and all."

"You got a man?" asked Wanda Jean.

Melinda nearly dropped the potato. She fidgeted with it some, pretended not to hear.

"That's okay," said Wanda Jean. "I know how it is. I seen it plenty."

"It's just . . . It's not—"

"Don't fret on it." Wanda Jean stopped cooking and put a hand on Melinda's arm. When she took up the vegetables again, she had a song in her throat. "You know, back before Robbie, I was known to drink and cuss and lay with men who wasn't my husband."

Melinda opened her mouth, but nothing came out save a small choking.

Wanda Jean's eyebrows arched all the way up to her hairline. "It don't matter how we get to Jesus," she said. "Just so long as we get there."

They put dinner on the stove, and soon the boys dragged Melinda this way and that, and Wanda Jean spilled all the secrets of their little household like some long lost sister. After enough of this, Wanda Jean remembered her manners and ordered Melinda upstairs for a shower. Melinda couldn't have been more grateful and, in a matter of minutes, found herself a new woman.

She put on some clothes laid out by Wanda Jean and, when she came downstairs, found the husband had come home.

Robbie Early loved the Risen Lord. A man who worked as hard as he did and made so little to show for it really had no other choice. Given half the chance, most other men would have retreated into alcohol or gambling, but not Robbie Early. As he wiled the days away swinging his hammer or driving his saw, he felt a warmth from within that could only come in following the same occupation as the Savior.

"You must be Alice," he said, repeating the name she had given the family. "I am so pleased to make your acquaintance. Wanda Jean and the boys have told me all about you." He shook her hand with both of his. He led her gently to an empty seat at the table, already set with a paper plate and plastic utensils.

Fish sticks for dinner. Green beans from a can and lumpy mashed potatoes. A wave of hunger attacked Melinda's belly, but she fought it off, tried not to eat like a savage in front of them.

Inevitably came the questions she'd hoped to avoid. "Tell me, Alice," said Robbie, dipping his fish stick into a puddle of ketchup. "What put you out by the river this morning?"

Melinda didn't know how to answer. She toyed with her beans. She started and stammered, but said nothing.

"Are you hiding from your man?" asked Wanda Jean.

Melinda looked up and found Robbie had closed his eyes. His mouth whispered silent invocations, and she felt something welling inside her, something strange and familiar all the same.

"You're safe now, honey." Wanda Jean put a hand to Melinda's arm.

Robbie put a hand to her arm as well, but quickly removed it. At first, it seemed benign and innocent, but almost immediately self-aware. He went back to his dinner right away.

During the rest of dinner, Gunner and Tanner talked about how much fish they were going to catch. Melinda smiled and listened attentively, only occasionally stealing looks at Robbie Early, who she'd find looking back at her.

She pushed her hair behind her ear and smiled at him. She saw something in his eyes she recognized. Something familiar.

An agenda.

Finally, she told herself, she'd gotten hold of something she could work with.

10

After dinner, Melinda stepped back into the kitchen for a glass of cold water when she found Robbie Early with his hand in the pot which once held the potatoes. He'd run his finger along the inside to scoop up what little remained and stuffed it into his mouth.

"You caught me." He smiled.

"It ain't a sin to be hungry, is it?" she asked.

His face reddened, but his smile went nowhere. He put the tip of his finger into his mouth and left it there.

In came the boys. They each grabbed Melinda's hands and tugged, begging her to follow them to bed, to tell them a story. She said the only ones she knew were scary stories, and Wanda Jean suggested instead that Robbie read to them from a picture book. He agreed and escorted the boys upstairs, while the women stayed behind to clean up dishes from dinner.

"He's a great father," said Wanda Jean. "I got real lucky."

"You sure did." Melinda dried the next dish Wanda Jean handed her. She wanted to cry. She wanted to throw herself against the kitchen counter and collapse into a mess of salty tears, but held it back. She knew Wanda Jean would pounce at the sight of the first tear and inundate her with talk of Jesus and sin and redemption, and she found herself in no mood for that.

When time came, the Earlys put her up on the living room couch with a thin, ratty blanket and a flattened pillow. She tossed for a bit, wishing like hell they had a television. Wishing she still had some cough syrup or maybe some Tennessee whiskey. After an hour, lying there in the dark, she accepted that she'd never get to sleep and decided it was time to light out.

Before slipping into her shoes, she reckoned she'd investigate the drawers in the living room cabinet for maybe something she could take with her, when she heard a voice behind her.

"Going somewhere?"

Robbie Early didn't click on the light. He didn't seem to want anyone else to know he was awake. Melinda cursed herself for not thinking he'd be up and moving about after his wife had gone to sleep.

She'd wondered what took him so long.

"I was thinking of heading outside for a cigarette," she said. "I was looking for a lighter."

"I got matches," he said.

"Look at you," she said. "Quick with a flame." She took a step closer to him. "Would you like to join me?"

"I don't smoke."

"I don't care." She snatched the matches from him and led him out the back door by the hand.

She took Robbie Early out onto the front porch and closed the door gently behind her. It was a still night. Hot as the devil, same as nearly every other night she could remember before it. Muggy and sweaty and ripe for sin. She lighted her cigarette and looked over the flame at him.

"You been looking at me all night," she said.

Robbie Early stuffed his hands into his pockets. "You caught me."

"You got something you want to tell me?" She drew smoke into her lungs. "Maybe some kind of secret?"

Robbie looked behind him, direction of the house. Mischief lit his eyes, and he whispered, "Why don't we head around back?"

"Sounds good to me."

She followed him into the backyard. He led her to that scraggly willow tree and leaned her against the trunk. Her hands lifted themselves to his waist, and she drew him to her. He removed her hands from her and set them at her side.

"I want to show you something," he said.

She batted her eyelashes.

He motioned toward the cigarette. "Why don't you put that out?"

She took a final, long drag and dropped it to the grass. "Now, what do you want from me?"

"I wanted to get you alone all night," he said.

"What else have you wanted?"

He smiled. He cleared a spot in the grass below them and sat, leading her down with him. Again, she made her move, allowing herself into his lap, but he eased her gently onto the lawn. She blinked a couple times, then leaned against the willow. The tree's drooping drapery covered them from the house. She held her breath, wondering about this fella's game.

Robbie Early sat across from her, drinking her in with his eyes and then closing them and, while down on his shaggy lawn, he brought himself up to his knees, then put both hands on her shoulders. The weight of them bore mighty, and she reckoned it more than necessary as she lowered herself dutifully to his midsection.

"No, dear," he said.

"Relax," she said softly. "I got this."

He held her at bay with locked elbows.

"What gives with you?" she asked.

"Let me ask you something."

"Then get it over with," she said, her hands still reaching for the drawstring on his pants.

"Have you been saved?"

"Have I been what?"

He brought his face right alongside hers, leaving about an inch of give between the two of their lips and asked again.

"Have you been saved?"

"Oh, hell. You've got to be—"

"I want to bear witness to you, Melinda. I want to help you."

She convulsed. "What did you call me?"

"It's not too late," said Robbie Early. "You know, before I found Jesus Christ, I myself was a sinner. You wouldn't believe what kind of hitches the devil led me to."

"This isn't why you brought me out here under this willow tree." She scooted back from him, but the trunk would only allow her to go so far. "You sure you wouldn't rather me just work it some with my hand?"

"That ain't you talking, Melinda," said Robbie Early. "It's Satan."

In the South, there is nothing noisier than a silent, summer night.

"Why do you keep calling me that?"

He told her, "Because I know who you are."

"Jesus Christ."

She'd never seen a smile like the one bestowed on his face at that moment. She looked both this way and that for some kind of respite then decided no, she didn't need to escape. She'd done enough running and hiding, and that which went down right there beneath that willow tree wasn't nothing but further bullshit, so she reached for that fallen cigarette and took it in her hands. First, the cherry burned her, but she ignored it and plucked it from the grass and put it straight to Robbie Early's eye.

He fell backward onto the lawn and scooted like a crab, wailing all the way. She rose to her feet and walked slowly after him. All the while, him screaming and carrying on while she looked to his left and to his right until she found what she needed.

Picking up one of the heavier branches from what must have belonged to one of the loblolly pines over yonder, she advanced upon him with a grin far from heaven-sent.

"Maybe you shouldn't worry so much about saving other folks, Robbie Early," she said to him. "Maybe rather you should worry about saving your own damned self."

And she brought down that loblolly branch upon his forehead.

11

When she left the morning after, Robbie Early and the rest of the family were tied to their chairs at the kitchen table. She'd ransacked the place and found the keys to his pickup. An old Ford that had seen better days. She hadn't so much as untied them or said goodbye or even closed the front door when she left. She just left, got that truck out on the road, and had found herself driving west.

She told herself it was because there weren't any use driving east, not the way they had her bottled in. She told herself she'd run out of options. She told herself in order to go east, she should turn around the other way, sneak up 61, and break into Memphis, then resume her route toward the Atlantic.

But she knew, deep down inside, why she'd turned the car around.

It picked up after the seventh ring.

"This is Sam. Leave a message or hit me on a text."

She hung up the phone.

Dammit, Sam . . .

She picked it back up. Scooped her coins from the change slot and slipped them, one-by-one, back into the phone.

"Ma'am . . ." said the security guard.

"Just a minute," she hissed. "I'm almost done here."

He crossed his arms. "I said you could make one phone call."

"He didn't answer." She punched the number with her index finger. "So technically it's still one phone call. Let me try one more time."

"Ma'am . . . I'm sorry, but I'm going to have—"

"*Please.*"

The security guard sighed. He looked up one side of the casino corridor and down the other.

"All right," he said, "but make it quick. I ain't supposed to have you in here. You know the rules."

Any other day, she might have kicked and screamed and told him no, she didn't know the rules, because she'd never been there in her life. Told him whatever it was he thought she was—homeless, a prostitute, whatever—he was wrong. But today was not like any other day, so she thanked him kindly and waited for Sam to pick up the line.

"This is Sam. Leave a message or hit me—"

The security guard walked a ways down the corridor to offer her privacy. She tucked herself closer into the phone. She softened the fall of the coins by sticking two fingers into the slot and catching them. His back remained to her. Ever so softly, she reinserted them.

You should call your mom and dad.

She shook her head. Kept eyes on the security guard.

Seriously. Call your father and tell him what is happening. You know how fast he'll be here? You'll be in your own bed tonight—

"This is Sam. Leave a message or hit me on a text."

And it all came rushing out.

"Sam . . . it's me." She tried to swallow the lump in her throat. "Sam . . . are you there? I can't talk long . . . I only have a minute . . ."

The security guard turned, pretended not to be watching her from the corner of his eye.

"Sam . . . Sam, I'm sorry. I made a mistake and, listen to me . . . Listen to me, I think I want to start all over. That's what I want to do,

I want to start all over. Sam, if you please . . . I believe it's possible, and if you please forgive me, Sam, I want to start all over and you'll see . . . I can be a better girlfriend. I'll be a better person, and I'll do whatever you want, Sam. Just . . . please . . . If you'll just—"

Beep. An operator with no accent whatsoever told her if she wasn't satisfied with the message, she could do this or that, but she never heard. She never heard any of the offered selections, because she'd collapsed to the floor in a heap of sobbing and choking and saying over and over *Sam . . . Sam . . .* into the phone, which she dropped and let dangle alongside her as she lay her head into her hands.

"No, you don't," said the security guard. He was on her quick and had her up by the arm. He was rough with her, which Melinda did not appreciate.

"Take your hands off me!"

"I done told you once." He didn't so much as wait until she was on her feet before he hauled her toward the front door of the casino. "I could lose my job letting you whores in here. I got a goddamn family, and you miserable—"

"*I'm not a whore!*"

She planted both feet and wrested her arm free from the man's grip. She turned and ran back to the phone. She picked up the receiver and jammed a finger into the coin return.

This time, the security guard was far less patient. He snatched her at the elbow. She smashed the receiver at his temple. Then followed with another blast to the phone, then another, and another.

"I'm not a whore!"

Next thing she felt was his fist to her face. Caught her high in the cheek, and she wasn't expecting it. She fell to the floor and covered her head with her skinny arms.

"I done told you, bitch."

He grabbed her by the arm and dragged her the length of the hallway, then pushed her out the casino door, into the white-hot sunlight.

12

Her ass wiggled, much like bait would upon a hook. She stuck it out beneath the hood of Robbie Early's pickup, parked at the far end of a suburban shopping mall. She hoped to land a big one. One like the fella who first walked by. Acted like he didn't see her, but he did, and not two seconds later did he turn around and fetch a second look. She counted her blessings on earning that much.

But down the mall parking lot came a police cruiser, and the fella acted like maybe it scared him more. He ducked his head, lowered his ballcap, and kept right on moving. Melinda ducked further between the engine and the hood.

This was it.

Good for her, it wasn't. The cruiser kept on about its business. Driving slow. Keeping an eye out.

No sooner had it gone its own way, than did she hop off the bumper and slam shut the hood. No sense sticking around there, she thought. She thought it as long as thirty seconds, because up yonder came another cruiser. Driving just as slow.

Jesus Christ.

Melinda turned toward the bookstore. Another cruiser.

Shit.

She turned the opposite way. The restaurant. The first time she looked over her shoulder: Nothing. The second time, she saw the cruiser had stopped just shy of the pickup. A second one rolling towards it.

So they're looking for the pickup.

She bit her lip and focused on the restaurant doors in front of her.

***

"If you're going to stay, you're going to need to order something."

She didn't care much for the bartender's tone. Melinda pulled a crinkled twenty from her pocket. She'd stolen it and another just like it from Wanda Jean's underwear drawer. Cleaned her out. She dropped it onto the bar and held up three fingers.

"Whatever that will get me three of," she said.

"I'm going to have to ask you to leave."

"Fine," she said. "Make it two of them, and you keep the rest."

The bartender, young and sunny and equipped with far too many buttons on his short apron, scooped up the bill and brought her a shot of whiskey.

"Finish it, and get the hell out of here."

Melinda kissed the edge of the glass, took barely a sip. The bartender put both hands on the bar and waited. Let her know he didn't have time to wait.

Outside, a third car parked behind Robbie Early's pickup. They'd gotten out of their cruisers. About five or so of them circled it. The sun was on its down, so they'd brought out their flashlights. They buzzed the rusty panels. The bumper. Tires, and then they were inside it.

If she left now, while they were busy . . .

Melinda finished her drink and waved to the bartender with her middle finger. Stood to leave, but stopped short. Up on the television, a news report. The sound was off, but didn't need the sound. She remembered it.

Cell phone video of her at the casino. The security guard picking her up off the floor. Her being dragged toward the door. The text at the bottom of the screen. Some clever graphic artist, using blood red words with a splatter font.

SWEET MELINDA VISITS CASINO!

Melinda got a move on. She threw open the front door and hooked a quick left. Toward the mall. No. the other way. Another cruiser. She bit hard on her lower lip, but kept walking. Moved between two cars and crouched while another passed.

She crossed her arms, ducked her head and kept moving. Toward the street. The car on her left, locked. Up another row. Car on her right: locked. Another cruiser. Moving slower. Up another row of cars. Passenger door locked.

I should run. I should run . . .

Driver door to the sedan was locked.

Another cruiser.

Just run, dammit.

The backseat door . . . *unlocked.*

She threw it open and climbed inside as yet another cruiser prowled past, just behind her. Driving slow, but not stopping.

Not stopping.

13

She hunkered lower into the floorboard at the first sounds of gunfire. Then, shouting. Tires screeching. More gunfire.

The driver door flew open.

Melinda made to scurry to her knees, but they'd given out on her. Instead, they popped and cracked, and she found herself face-down in the floor mat. The car roared to life.

More gunfire outside. Something sounded like a rock hit the back window. It did not shatter. The car didn't so much as slow down.

Melinda gripped tight the .22. She looked skyward to say a prayer, but realized she no longer remembered any prayers and reckoned they'd fall on deaf ears anyway. She counted to herself *one, two . . . three*, then came up—gun first—to the driver's seat.

"Don't move a muscle, motherfucker," she said. "I got a gun."

The bloody mess in the driver's seat looked at her through the rearview, moving only his eyes. He'd gone pale already. He kept both hands fast on the steering wheel, continued his trajectory forward.

"You hear me?" She rapped the butt of the gun against the back of his head. Behind her, she heard sirens.

"I don't think that's a good idea," said Odie. "You want to rob me, you can do so after we put distance between us and that Office Supply, ma'am."

"You ain't the boss here!" Her voice went higher than she intended. She didn't want to sound scared. She looked at this guy and thought he looked worse for wear. Right ear looked as if it had been chewed off, and the side of his head and shirt covered in a gallon of blood. Bedlam behind him, but he kept eyes front, as if he didn't care.

She licked her cracked lips. Wanted to look out the back windshield, but didn't dare take eyes off the driver. Watched as he sped out of the parking lot, tore up the highway. Exited. Took a right, turned left.

"Pull over up here," she said.

"Listen, we can't—"

"I told you to pull over." She held the gun up to the reflection in the rearview. "You hear me with that bum ear?"

He took a steady hand off the wheel and touched his ear. Brought a bloody finger up to his eyes.

Put his hand back on the wheel.

"Jesus." He slowed the car to a crawl. They were near the woods.

"This will do," she said.

Odie pulled over.

"What happened back there?" she asked.

He stared at his bloody fingertips.

Melinda hit him again with the butt of the gun. "Answer me when I'm talking to you."

He turned around in his seat. First thing she noticed was his eyes, how they didn't give a shit in this world that she held a gun on him or that she'd stolen his car or that the entire fucking world had erupted in gunfire behind him only moments before. How dead were his eyes. How dead they were to everything until they met hers. Until he looked at her, then suddenly a spark, and that spark lit a fuse and then, well, and then *boy howdy*.

"Holy shit," Odie whispered. "You're Sweet Melinda."

Her insides corroded. "That's right," she said. "And if you know what's good for you, you won't give me any lip."

"You're Sweet Melinda." This time when he said it, he said it slower.

She cursed her luck. She'd gone to great lengths to get out of Mississippi, and when finally she did, more folks knew her in Memphis than had known her anywhere else. She wanted to empty the contents of the .22 into his slack-jawed face. Better yet, she wanted to club him with it, hitting him until he simply stopped moving.

"Listen," he said, nice and easy. "I'll do anything you say, anything at all." His eyes were deep green, same as hers. The blood spattered around them had begun to dry. Something in her wanted to touch her fingers to her tongue and wipe it away. "But first," he said, "I think we need to find somewhere to lay low, you and me."

"You and me?"

"Yes."

Wasn't a single lie in those eyes of his. Her finger twitched at the trigger.

"You drive," she said. "But know this gun is at the back of your head. You said you know who I am, right?"

"Yes ma'am," he said.

She leaned back in her seat. "Then you know I won't hesitate to shoot you if you fuck with me."

His only answer was slipping the car back into Drive and getting them the hell out of there.

14

No sooner had they got inside the motel room than they were at it. First on the bed, then rolling off the bed and around on the floor, wrapped like a burrito in a blanket. Then they took a break and ended up on the couch, then back on the bed, and she thought soon her body would explode.

Sex, good not because she was horny and needed it, but because she feared for her life and needed it. The boy didn't seem to mind. He kept up with her, not as rough as Sam, but still willing and able. She felt guilty, because as of late, she'd started to itch and only thought it fair to let him know, but he didn't seem too concerned with conversation for the first hour or so of their acquaintance until suddenly he said, "Let's turn on the news."

"Lately I haven't found any solace in watching television," she told him.

"That's ridiculous. Since we got to Mississippi, nine times out of ten, they've been talking about you."

"My point exactly." She sighed and fished through her paper bag for that part-empty bottle of Jack Daniels. She noticed the bed was a bloody mess, thanks to him aggravating that torn-up ear again.

"If you got it," said Odie, "you got to flaunt it." He looked for the knob on the set but, not finding it, searched instead for the remote.

He clicked it on and surfed like mad until finding the local news. They were not talking about Sweet Melinda. They were not talking about fish hooks or truckers found hogtied at truck stops.

No, she'd been bumped for a hotter story.

Odie recognized everything. The front of the Office Supply, with the windows shot out. Bullet holes. Stretchers. The manager, hooting and hollering, his arm in a sling. The CoinExchange machine, looking like it had been hit with a bazooka. Dollar bills, fluttering in the breeze. Blood on the concrete.

"Holy shit," breathed Melinda. "What the hell did y'all pull in there?"

"We was just going to rob it."

"Y'all did a bit more than rob it," she said. She scooted closer to the television and said he should turn up the volume. The first reporter told them there was no known motive for the attack. The second reporter said they suspected three gunmen and two of them had been killed. Odie took offense that no one so much as mentioned his name and pissed and hollered.

"They said one got away," she said. "So that means they're looking for you."

The kid furrowed his brow and shook his head. "There was four of us. I was on the door, standing inside. That's where I got this." He pointed to that useless ear of his.

"Some luck," she said.

"Luck?" That same kid who'd been all too eager to please only moments earlier, now crawled over to the second, unrumpled twin bed to sulk. "I don't even know what kind of luck you mean. This is probably the biggest thing to ever happen to me, and don't nobody even know I was there."

Melinda shook a finger inside her ear, as if she'd just gotten out of the pool. She fought the urge to slap him.

"Listen, kid," she said, "you're in it something bad. You know what will happen when this is over? There will be a heap of protests and NRA speeches and Congressional hearings on gun control, and everybody's going to be looking for someone to blame. You and your friends just shot up an Office Supply. You are going to want nothing to do with this."

Still, he sulked. "That's easy for you to say. Any other time besides right now, and it's you on that television. It's a story they're doing about you."

"Well, you're on TV now," she said. "Be proud of it, but do it from a distance."

He opened his mouth to say something, but thought better of it. He scuffed at a tobacco-colored stain on the carpet with his shoe. Melinda wondered where he kept his own gun or what he'd done with it, why he had yet to show it. She wondered if she'd have time to get hers if needed, or where exactly she'd left it. Probably in her jeans on the other side of the room, near the door. She felt shitty again. Tried to think of anything at all besides inhaling and exhaling.

He said in a low voice: "At least you got a hashtag."

"What do you mean?" She scooched a couple of inches across the bed. A couple of inches closer to her jeans.

When Odie went for his pocket, she stood and halved the distance of the door. He raised a hand and showed her his palm, told her to calm down, not to worry.

"I'm just going for this phone."

This time, when reaching for his pockets, he moved slower. He tucked only his thumb and the tip of his forefinger into the back pocket of his jeans and out slid a phone. He held it, screen out, toward her.

"You ever get on Twitter?" he asked.

"I never have time to get on Twitter."

"You should do it," he said. "One of the things they got is called hashtags. It's the old pound symbol from regular keyboards—"

"I know what a hashtag is." For lack of anything better to do, she bent over and slipped into her britches. "What the hell does that have to do with you or me?"

"At least you've got your own hashtag." His shoulders slumped and he listlessly slid his thumb this way and that across the phone screen. "See? Hashtag Sweet Melinda. There's a bunch of them."

"That's people talking about me?" She stood up straighter. "What are they saying?"

Odie nodded. "They're more than talking about you. They got this little game they play called *Hashtag Sweet Melinda Says*. It's stuff they tweet you say when you're sticking people up and taking their shit."

"How do they know I said it if they weren't there?"

"No, not what you really said. It's just a game to guess what you would have said in a certain situation."

She snatched the phone from him and started looking for herself. As she found more of them, her eyes began to bug, and she felt her chest getting tight again.

"There's hundreds of these things."

"Yeah. Don't rub it in."

"This is what normal people do with their spare time?"

"Some of them." He picked at the dried blood on his ear. "I reckon."

She nodded over her shoulder toward the television set. "That shit you did back at the office supply store, it's going to have one of those hashtags?"

"It don't work like that," Odie said. "And even if it did, they don't know I was there. I mean, I got a hashtag too, but there's only seven hits."

"Really?" She looked up from the phone. "And what's your hashtag?"

"Hashtag Charming Bandit."

"That's you? The Charming Bandit?"

He shrugged, then nodded. She returned to the phone, all thumbs as she hunted-and-pecked across the screen. She squinted at the search results. She looked up.

"Yep," she said, "seven of them. Nice. They're all from the same account. Odie_Shanks." She felt it more than her imagination that the air had suddenly sucked from the room. She looked up from the phone to find him swimming in even more shame.

"Is that you?" she asked. "Odie Shanks?"

Again he nodded.

"That's so precious," she said.

15

She hadn't slept like that in forever. Certainly not since leaving Nacogdoches, maybe not since before even then. She thought of all those nights—those when they'd actually kicked for a few days—that maybe they could catch a couple hours sleep. Those when she'd wake up and figure maybe she should go back to class. Maybe she should turn things around. Maybe she should call her mom and dad.

But not even those nights. No, somewhere in the middle of one of *those* nights, she'd hear it, then suddenly come to. Eyes popping open in the darkness and taking the time to figure where she was . . . finding herself in her own room, or maybe Sam's . . . That alien weight on the bed alongside her. The noise. His silent sobbing. Sometimes shaking the bed, it got so bad. And each time, she'd fall for it. She'd wrap an arm around him and pull him tighter to cover him with all her warmth and love, and he'd wake up and, just like she, realize where he was and what was happening, then detonate a fission bomb.

She'd tell herself never again. Never again would she love him when he needed it. Never again would she sleep at his place or have him over. Never again would she take him into her arms, instead to do anything, go anywhere . . . So long as he wasn't there. Never again.

Then he'd show up with the shit, and they were in it for the long haul. Again, they were tethered at the waist.

The motel outside Memphis was a different story. Huddled up with Odie on the twin bed weren't like anything she'd done with Sam Tuley. Never once did Odie wake her in the middle of the night, awash in tears. Nor did he explode and call her a cunt or a bitch or any set of names determined to send her to a tizzy. Instead, he slept soundly and late into the morning.

She smiled to herself. Normally by now, she'd have him bound and gagged and pleading for mercy.

"First, you go into the gas station with a big bill," he told her.

"Do what?"

"Like a fifty," he said. "Or a hundred.

He'd coaxed her out of the motel room and into the booth of a greasy spoon. The last thing she had on her mind was food, but the smells of frying eggs and sizzling sausages sent her to a tizzy and, before she knew it, she had a plate full of hash browns that weighed more than she did.

"You take a fifty dollar bill, and buy something small." He finished the rest of his coffee and slid his mug to the edge of the table. "It don't matter what you buy, but today, I'd like you to pick up a newspaper."

"Won't it piss them off? Me buying a newspaper with a fifty dollar bill?"

"More than likely. But what you're trying to do is see how much change they have in the till. When they open it, look over the counter and see if maybe the register is stuffed with cash, or if they've been dropping them into the safe all day, like they're supposed to."

She nodded. The waitress refilled their mugs for the fourth or fifth time, and Melinda wondered how anyone could be so perky without a big, fat rail of—

"If they got the money, you come give me the signal, and I move in to do my half." Odie held his thumb and forefinger like a gun. "Easiest cash you'll ever see."

"Where'd you learn all this?" she asked.

"An old friend," answered Odie.

Once inside the car, she considered lying across the backseat and never waking up, but instead sat up front. She leaned her head against the passenger's window glass and watched the sun-scorched landscape. Dead cotton fields. Dead rows of corn. All briefly interrupted by a Dollar store or strip mall. She lazily half-listened as Odie told stories of his old friend Jake, on how to rob a gas station, on how it was better than robbing banks or credit unions or, god forbid, an Office Supply. He kept the radio on, but turned down low.

"Your plan is to rob gas stations from Memphis to Hollywood?" she asked.

Odie smiled. He didn't seem to interested in the road before them. "There are two things meant to keep a guy like me on the True Path," he said. "Damned if I can't remember the first one, but the second is the struggle against stagnation. We all need a touch of adventure in our lives."

She wondered to herself if maybe, over the past few hours, she hadn't fucked the sense out of him.

"And Hollywood?"

He caught a small chuckle before it got out of hand. "Ain't you been listening? We don't need Hollywood no more. Thanks to the Internet, we can be big-time celebrities right here, doing what we do. No more gatekeepers. No more begging to be let in the door when we can dynamite an entrance all our own. What, with a hashtag like the one you got and the one I aim to get . . . That's your Hollywood right there. That other shit's for suckers."

She crossed her arms. "Gas stations."

"I'll show you." He cocked his head to the side like he was thinking up lyrics to his favorite song. "You think maybe I'd look good with a moustache?"

She closed her eyes and didn't open them until he slowed the car to a crawl, then a stop. They had no idea if they were still in Tennessee or if maybe they had inched over into Arkansas. They hadn't seen but a smattering of cars on this particular road in a while. Odie found a Texaco. He lined the car up alongside two things that used to be payphones. He didn't kill the engine.

"There ain't nothing to worry about," he told her.

"I ain't worried," she said.

She made to open the door, but he put his hand to her elbow. She turned and his face rushed at her. His mouth missed hers and instead, hit a cheek. That stopped him none. He found her lips in no time, and suddenly it was hands this way and that and things could have gotten hot plenty fast had she not cooled him off.

"That's a sure-fire way to get the cops called," she told him, fire far from extinguished. "Don't you reckon we should have our mind on other things?"

"Impossible," he muttered. He moved in again, but she held him at bay, her hand to his chest. She popped open the door and moved herself to a safer distance. He bit the insides of his cheeks. "What do you say we hurry this along and find ourselves another motel?"

"That sounds nice," she said. "I have to tell you, I've never slept like I did last night. I'll credit you for that."

"Really?"

"Yes."

"I didn't want to say nothing about it this morning," he told her, "but last night you woke me up a couple times. I thought you were talking in your sleep."

"What was I saying?"

"You weren't saying nothing." Above them, the sun passed behind dark, demon thunderheads. The first rain in quite some time. "Turns out you was just crying."

Man . . .

Melinda took a step back from the car. When had she gotten out? It wasn't until the little bell rang on the filling station door that she realized she'd entered. She couldn't remember walking across the lot. Her feet taking her to the newspaper rack, to the freezer for a Diet Coke, the candy aisle. But her mind took her somewhere completely different.

Her mind felt every inch of her body. Felt the food she'd eaten that morning and every morsel she'd eaten since leaving Nacogdoches. Felt the air in her chest—not that panic attack, not that tightness—but rather a *surplus* of air, as if she couldn't exhale enough. Felt it all the way to her extremities, like if she didn't keep it in check, lightning would surge from her fingertips and send the entire world straight to hell. Her throat, as if a lump had been there for who knows how long had been suddenly excised and discarded.

And she could feel it somewhere below her belly, in that cranky canyon of a womb. Not just how bad things were, but how bad they weren't. Which could only mean they stood to get much worse.

"Looks like it might finally rain, you think?"

The cashier: friendly enough. Fat, fleshy man, looking over a pair of bifocals.

"Looks like it," she said.

She scraped change off the counter into a cupped palm. Never thought to look in the till, had no idea how much money was in there. Had mountains of things on her mind and couldn't be bothered with a stick-up.

They passed each other in the parking lot. Odie reached out a hand, and she stroked it. Behind her, she heard the bell ring as he opened the door. She got behind the wheel and waited.

She didn't deserve this. If she told herself enough times, it would be true. Melinda could rattle off a long list of sins she'd yet to commit. She'd never taken a screaming baby into the movies or a grocery store. She'd never used a racial epithet, not even when she was a little girl. She was certain there were others, but she couldn't think of them right then, just all the shit she had done, and she put her head to the steering wheel and tried her best to exhale.

A thousand sighs . . .

She took a look inside the plate glass window of the Texaco and saw Odie leaning on the counter. Talking with his hands and using his gun as a prop. Hashtag Charming Bandit.

Yes, things would soon be as bad as she reckoned, but maybe not for a while.

Maybe he did love her. And perhaps she even loved him back. But didn't nobody need to say what didn't need saying, and that's how they could fuck from there to Hollywood, and he never would change how she walked after, not like Sam Tuley. For all the gentle moments with Odie, she'd long for one or two a little rougher, but she knew it wouldn't be the same. Without a doubt, she knew Odie would never raise a hand to her and, well, that just wouldn't cut it, because she'd traveled quite a ways over the past week or so and learned a bitter lesson, like it or not, and that's how she wasn't half what she should be—half of what she *could* be—without Sam Tuley inside of her.

Odie, oddly was never concerned with the fate of his compatriots back at the Office Supply. How quick he was to shrug off the last fella he rode with. That on one side of the scale and, on the other:

Sam Tuley will always come for me.

Lightning, and then thunder.

A final push of heat, but it was no match for the front sneaking in. Suddenly a breeze blew through. She felt it, but didn't waste much time thinking about it.

Instead, all she heard were the words she spoke back at breakfast. Telling Odie, "The only way anybody's ever going to know that you done half the stuff you done is if they catch you doing it. Pity, that's what it will take to fetch your hashtag."

The car was running. She held down the brake pedal as she slipped it into gear. She blew Odie a kiss and lifted her foot off the brake. She pointed the car toward the setting sun and, for the next several hours, listened to the *whup-whup, whup-whup* of the window wipers, beating like a metronome to the words she'd heard so often:

Sam Tuley will always come for me.

Truth was, she reckoned he never left.

#EPILOGUE

The docent stood at the front of the tour bus and fiddled with his scarred-up ear. He held the microphone just shy of his chin, but he didn't need it. He had a booming voice and used it well. He could do all sorts of accents and imitations and allowed rarely a dull moment.

He had a story for everything.

Want to hear about the time they found actor Mitch Leavelles passed out drunk or whatever in the front yard of a teenage scream queen's house? Want to hear about what happened and how they hushed it up? The docent had a marvelous tale. Want to hear about the time the bigshot producer of your favorite blockbuster action film barreled his car into the the side of yonder burger stand, and who all was in the car with him? There was only one place in town to hear that one.

The docent didn't need a microphone, because folks knew this guy could tell a story.

So, when the doors to the tour bus slid shut, the people leaned forward and waited for him to speak. The bus parked outside the luxurious home of Tanya B. LaMarr and lately her name had been in all the papers, and if anyone knew the skinny on the scandal, it would be the docent.

If anyone had the inside dirt . . .

He opened his mouth to speak, but stopped short. Sure, he had stories. He had guys here and there who told him things other docents couldn't possibly know. He spent his free time on sets, helping his buddy who ran a catering gig or maybe selling pot to a grip, gaffer, or sometimes even the screenwriter. He picked up shifts in a bar where industry types got shit-faced and ran their mouths. He roomed across town with a dirty cop.

The docent knew things other folks didn't.

But that day in particular, the docent had other stories on his mind. Stories didn't anyone know all the pieces to. Stories that maybe a guy here or there knew of, and maybe even someone over yonder knew most of, but only one person knew all of it, and he stood right there at the front of the bus, and all anybody wanted to know about was the bad habits of a contestant on a reality show.

What most people wanted to hear was how these people got to Hollywood. In the case of Ms. LaMarr, that answer was easier, since most of America voted her to celebrity via text message or Facebook poll. Tweeted her straight to the stars. Others had a more interesting story, and the docent traded in those tales. He collected them.

Harrison Ford had been a carpenter on the set of *American Graffiti*. Stallone wrote a part for himself into his *Rocky* script. Mitch Leavelles wandered drunk onto a film set in his hometown back East, and a star was born. A certain child actress who shall remain nameless was the product of a lost bet between two film producers . . . always a juicy story on the bus.

However, every so often someone would ask that inevitable question.

"How did you get to Hollywood?"

The docent smiled to himself. He looked into their eyes and saw them for who they were. Saw them for where they came from. Maybe some shit town somewhere in the middle of the country. Maybe some place he'd once read about or driven through or maybe even stopped.

He'd been lots of places over the last year.

No, those stories the docent couldn't tell. Couldn't tell them about how once he sat in a room about yay-big with two of the meanest Federal agents ever to drink Virginia tap. How they pointed their fingers this way and that and hollered to the rafters that he'd be going away for a long, long time. About how any hopes he'd ever have of living as a free man or breathing fresh air or seeing stars of any kind were all but squashed. How he'd never see the outside of a jail cell for as long as they saw fit.

Unless . . .

Or another story, somewhat more action-packed, about how the docent ended up in Nashville. Yes, Nashville of all places, and carried with him a resume a mile long and mixed in with all the right people in the right circles and before long fell into the employ of one Frank "Butchie" Gregory. About how he and Butchie talked about people they both knew, none of who were still alive to counter any versions the docent might offer.

About how he got Butchie to put him to work. And how, one night, when Butchie was about to make a deal of a lifetime, the cops miraculously appeared and did what they'd tried for decades upon decades to do, which was catch Butchie red-handed.

Or, even still, a story about the last meeting the docent had with those federal agents. About how they found themselves back in that room about yay-big, and the one with the Yankee accent said:

"You'll have to go into hiding. Butchie's got some kind of reach, and he'll stop at nothing to make sure you're handled."

The other Fed, the one with an accent more down-home, asked if there were anywhere he might want to be placed.

"Anywhere?" the docent had asked.

"Anywhere at all," said the Yankee.

The docent had nodded his head after little deliberation. "There is one place I'd like to go."

And they agreed upon it and gave him a little spending cash to get there and warned him not once or twice but three times that if he so much as looked sideways at a gun or gas station or any sort of trouble, he'd be locked away for the rest of time.

They all agreed he could never again use the name given to him by his parents. He would no longer need it, since it had long ago had been buried in a cemetery back home.

So he caught himself there on that tour bus, tugging his pulpy ear and lost in thought about old friends he'd made and lost and would never see again, when one of the tourists brought him round again. Lifted high their hand and repeated the question.

"Mister Tour Guide, can you tell us?"

"Tell you what?"

"How it was that you came to Hollywood?"

The docent checked his watch. Nearly one year to the minute. One year since walking into the All-Niter after his classmate's funeral. One year since dropping the quarters in the juke and ordering up some Stevie Ray. One year since making a new friend, best one he ever had.

One year since he'd started for Hollywood.

He raised the microphone to his lips.

"That would be a story, all right," he said in a near-whisper. He tapped his fingers on a thick, wire-bound sheaf of papers he kept at the front of the tour bus, always by his side.

"But I reckon we best save that story for another day."

ACKNOWLEDGEMENTS:

I am powerless without my friends, especially Lana Pierce, Nick Karner, Alex Maness, Monique Velasquez, Piper Kessler, Tracey Coppedge, Meredith Sause, Jeffrey Moore, Michael V. Rollin, Raia Mihaylova, Todd Keisling, Zachary Walters, Julie Malone, Jana Whiddon, Dan Morrison, The Mission Creeps, Bob Walters, Rudy Kraul, Bobby Gorman, Natalie Pruitt, the Regulator Bookshop in Durham, Mel Melton, Mike Bourquin, Michael Howard, Brian Centrone, and Khalid Patel. You all mean more to me than I could possibly express.

Portions of this book have appeared elsewhere in some form or another.

"Further South" (*Severest Inks*, 2012)

"Rather a Nice Finish" (*Pantheon Magazine*, 2012)

"The Return of the Red Hot Mississippi Hot Mess" (*Swill*, 2014)

ABOUT THE AUTHOR:

Eryk Pruitt is a filmmaker, novelist, and screenwriter living in Hillsborough, North Carolina. His films have earned top prizes at film festivals around the world, and his novel *What We Reckon* was a finalist for the Anthony Award. His latest novel, *Blood Red Summer*, is available wherever you buy books. He can be found either at his desk, hard at work on another story, or mixing drinks at his bar, Yonder.

ALSO BY ERYK PRUITT:

Continue reading for an excerpt from Eryk Pruitt's
follow-up novel

What We Reckon

Coming soon from Rock and a Hard Place Press

An Excerpt From:

Eryk Pruitt

1

It will end much like this, thought Grant as the fire flickering up his nostrils gave way to a slow, mellow drip down the back of his throat. No sooner had he chased away the sweats, the whispers, the steady but fevered panic that so often wrapped its fingers tight around his windpipe than did he eyeball the rest of the kilo—still shrink-wrapped with only a jagged hole, hardly big enough—and consider into what further mayhem he might find himself.

It was good coke, sure, but Grant had no reason to think it wouldn't be. Back in South Carolina, Bobby had been his best friend and would hardly look sideways at shit that wasn't of a particular quality. *You want to put bullshit powder into your face,* Bobby used to say, *then go down past Decker Boulevard.* Bobby had a reputation. Folks around town knew he had the good shit. They knew how to get a hold of him night or day. What they didn't know was where he stashed it, but Grant did, so a fool and his narcotics were quickly parted.

The only thing better than good cocaine, he thought as he plucked another pinch from the hole in the package, *is stolen cocaine.*

Any tranquility, perceived or otherwise, came crashing to a halt with a knock at the motel room door. Grant quickly shuffled away the brick of cocaine into a hollowed-out King James Bible, then scooted it beneath the bed. He perked an ear. Listened. Held his breath.

"Hey, Grant," called a voice from outside. "Open up. I ain't standing out here all day."

Craig.

Relief.

Grant reached into a paper bag for a brand new bottle of brown liquor and two plastic cups that came with the room, then set them on the tabletop where once sat the contraband.

Craig did not enter when the door opened, but rather stood at the threshold.

"Thanks for coming," said Grant. "Means a lot."

"You look like shit," said Craig. He nodded his head to Jasmine, sitting on the bed, not looking up from the television set. "Both of you."

"And you've lost more hair since last I seen you," said Grant. "Come in. Have a drink. Been a while."

"Not long enough." Craig took a step into the room. Only one.

"Jasmine, say hey to Craig," called Grant. If she heard him, she didn't let on. "You remember Craig, don't you?" When still she said nothing, Grant narrowed the distance between the two of them and said, "Jazz, you are being rude."

She turned only her head, made perfunctory eye contact, then returned to the television. The sound was off and the picture looked like shit, but still held her full attention.

Before Grant said anything more, Craig waved a hand and called him off. "Don't worry about it," said Craig. "I ain't staying long."

Grant rounded the little table in the corner and sloshed whiskey into the plastic cups. About two fingers' worth. He swallowed one before pouring himself another, then handed one to Craig.

"How you been?" he asked.

"Got divorced," said Craig. "About six months back, I reckon."

"Real sorry to hear that. I thought you two made a good couple."

"You never met her." Craig sipped from his cup. "We married long after you skipped town."

"What I mean is, I seen photographs of you two. One of y'all dancing. I thought she was hot enough, even for you."

"Our wedding," said Craig. He shifted his weight from one foot to the other. "Look, if it's all the same—"

"Why don't you sit down?" Grant kicked out a chair, but Craig only looked at it. "Seriously, take a load off. This here is a fresh bottle and I already tossed out the lid. The least we should do is throw a dent into it. Talk old times."

Craig crinkled his nose like he smelled something funny. "I'd rather not talk old times, to be honest. It took damn near an hour to find this place and I ain't looking forward to the hour back."

"I sure appreciate it." Grant held out his palms. "Really, I do. It means the world that you'd do the work and make the drive. I'd come to you if I could, but it's best if I steer clear from Lake Castor for a spell, if you know what I mean."

Craig nodded. He looked across the room at Jasmine and watched a single tear quiver across her cheek. He watched it a long time, then turned back to Grant.

"This is it, you hear me?" he said. "This is the last time."

"Craig . . . buddy, I—"

"I'm serious. You ain't an easy person to say no to. So, after this, you'd best forget my phone number. Forget about me and anything I ever done for you."

"That's a tall order," said Grant. "Without you, I'd probably be dead. Dead or in jail, so forgive me if I don't up and forget everyth—"

"I'm not joking around." He wasn't. He'd hardly touched his corn liquor. The cup rattled as he slapped his hand against the table. "This is the last time."

"Okay."

"I need to hear you say it."

Grant licked his lips. "This is the last time."

Craig let the moment linger. Silence hung between them like a sinner. He let it linger a bit more before he reached behind himself and tugged a brown envelope from the waistband of his work khakis. He set it on the table between them, minding the liquor. Grant held his breath a bit before snatching it. He tore it open and dumped the contents onto the table.

Drivers licenses. Two of them.

Social security cards, also two.

A pair of birth certificates.

Two entire lives, scattered across the scuffed tabletop alongside a cheap bottle of liquor.

"Dear Christ," Grant whistled, "this is great work." He picked up one ID, then the other. He held each to the naked bulb hanging between them, then lowered them to the table. He couldn't take his eyes off them. "I mean, this is really good work. Jasmine, come check this out."

She didn't move.

"This time, you outdone yourself," said Grant. "Jack Jordan. My name is now Jack Jordan. Will you get a load of that, Jas—I mean, *Summer?* From now on, I'm Jack Jordan and your name is Summer Ashton."

And so it became thus.

"Who are they?" asked Jack.

"Jack Jordan was just a kid," answered Craig. "Grew up around Amarillo, in West Texas. Ran his car into a tree a few days shy of graduating high school. The girl, she died of leukemia about six months ago. These should pass an ordinary traffic stop or credit check, but if I were you, I'd stay out of the emergency room or anywhere asking after medical records."

Jack pat his old friend on the shoulder. "You are wasting your talents down at that copy shop. I've met some folks who'd pay a pretty penny for a fella like you."

"From what I'm to understand," said Craig, "they'd pay a pretty penny to get hold of you too. Both of you."

Jack let that settle a bit before he up and poured himself another shot. Dropped a jigger's worth into Craig's cup as well.

Said, "If that's the way you want to play it, then fine. I won't call on you no more. After you leave here, you and me is done. But I won't forget you. Not ever." He cocked his head toward the cup. "Now, drink with me and let's get on with our goodbyes."

Craig eyed him over the top of his cup as he slowly sipped. Immediately, he coughed. He choked down what he could, then broke into a clumsy laughter.

"Should've known the stuff you drink would be shit." He took another swallow. "I swear, I don't think you could surprise me anymore."

"I got a kilo of cocaine stashed beneath the bed."

"Goddammit, Keith . . ." Craig stood, knocking over the chair.

"You want to see it?" asked Jack. "I'd never seen that much blow before. We hollowed out a Bible and jammed it—"

"Hell no, I don't want to see it. I don't even want to be in the same room with it."

Jack tried to block him from leaving. "Craig, wait . . ."

Craig stopped. Looked his old friend in the eye.

"I need you to help me sell it," said Jack.

"Go to hell, Keith, or whatever your name is. You know, for a short piece of shit, you really—"

"I ain't kidding around, man." Jack put his hand on the knob before Craig could reach for it. "I need to move this shit kind of quick. I could use the cash. Hell, who couldn't? You stand to earn a nice chunk of change for yourself if—"

Craig slapped Jack's hand off the knob, then opened the door. "I'm leaving," he said to the room, "and I don't want you calling me. Not for cocaine kilos, not for fake IDs . . . not for nothing."

Jack followed him into the parking lot. The night had turned cool, as the promise of autumn set upon them. Craig stopped shy of his pickup truck, then spun on his heels to face his old friend.

"How much longer you going to keep her on?" he asked.

"Jas—I mean, Summer? She can leave anytime she wants."

"You and her fucking yet?"

Jack laughed through his nose. "No, we ain't fucking, and we ain't about to start." He scratched at the asphalt with the toe of his shoe. "That's the last thing I need right now."

"Then maybe you ought to see about cutting her loose," said Craig. "She looks like she could use a little break."

"She's fine," said Jack. "If you remember, she always had a flair for the dramatic."

"It's really none of my business, but I mean it when I say the two of you have seen better days. Y'all been eating?"

"Things got a little messy, leaving the Carolinas." Jack rubbed at the scar alongside his hip, still amazed at the feel of it. "I'm afraid our girl, she didn't—"

"I said I don't want to hear nothing about it," said Craig. "You asked me to get you some Texas IDs, so I imagine that's where you're headed next, if I wanted to imagine anything at all. Which I don't. But if you plan to get lost, then I recommend you stay lost. I don't want to know nothing about where you're coming from, and I damn sure don't want to know nothing about where you're going."

Yonder, a stray tomcat emerged from the brush and crept silent and slinky across the parking lot in search of food. Jack watched it a spell longer than he'd planned and snapped out of it only as Craig opened the driver's door of his pickup. Jack shuffled after him.

"Remember how you and me and Davey used to stay up all night drinking coffee in the truck stop on the far side of town?" asked Jack. "What was it called, The All-Niter? What if I told you I saw a joint just like it about two exits up the highway? We could head up there and fetch us some hash browns and shit coffee and—"

"Man, I've got to go."

"Say, how is Davey? You ever see him anymore? He still around Lake Castor? I ain't—"

"Keith, I've got to go."

Jack's hands dropped to his side. He took two steps back and stared at the truck tires. He shrugged.

Craig climbed behind the wheel, then rolled down the window. He nodded toward the motel door and said, "Look, I don't plan to get in the middle of nothing. But if I were you, I'd clean up your act. That girl in there ain't nothing like the girl I met, what, four, five years ago. You ain't neither, but you've always been a smart fella. Too smart, sometimes."

Jack bit his lower lip.

"What I'm saying," continued Craig, "is maybe you two ought to take some time off. I can't help but think this whole mess you've brought down on the both of you is going to do one or the other of you in. If you care about her as much as you say, maybe you ought to think about that."

"You're right about all of it." Jack touched each of his fingertips with his thumbs, popping several knuckles in the process. "That being said, it'd be a lot easier for you to sell off an ounce, were you just to ask around—"

Craig threw up a hand. "You've got a way of dragging people down with you and, if it's all the same, I want to be left out of it. One day or another, someone's going to get a hold of you. The law or worse, and I can't have it leading back to me." He slipped the truck into gear, then didn't so much as nod as he backed out of the motel lot and, in a spray of gravel and rock, got himself onto the freeway.

Jack stood there a spell. First, he felt awful. Craig's words, like rico-chet, pierced him and knocked him senseless. Then, up came the fury. He'd become quite skilled at starting anew and wasn't accustomed to someone popping in from his past to throw fast a finger in judgment. It was all he could do to keep from climbing into the shitty Honda they'd just bought and chase down his old friend to run him off the road, give him the what-for he'd probably had coming since they were little.

Eventually, all of that settled and left him standing alone with only the florescent hum of the street lamps and the faraway din of traffic. It was easy to hate, thought Jack. It was easy to fly off the handle and take your eyes off the prize.

More difficult was to keep focus.

To learn from one's mistakes.

Perhaps Craig had a point. Perhaps things had run somewhat off the rails. Perhaps time for a change beckoned. Perhaps it was time he shed himself of Summer or Jasmine or whatever her name was, lest she drag him down.

But he had many things to do before that day came. For one, he had a stolen kilo of cocaine to unload. For another, he had to carefully map the quickest backwoods route into East Texas. And, more pressing, he had about three-quarters of corn liquor left in that bottle back in the room.

He slapped his palms against his thighs, as if brushing them clean, then headed back inside to see if maybe Summer would snap out of it long enough to help him finish it.

2

The smell of gasoline.

    Cicada, whip-poor-will, and the sweet symphony of late August.

Summer came to in the passenger seat of their shitty Honda, on the far side of a gas station parking lot. Maybe three, four in the morning. Roadside, but not another soul to be found. No one in the driver's seat.

Alone.

No Jack.

No keys in the ignition. If he'd finally up and abandoned her, he would have left her the keys. A little bit of money. Perhaps even . . .

In a bluster, she thrust her hand beneath the passenger's seat. Rifled through empty go-sacks and plastic soda bottles.

Not there.

Summer dove into the backseat and cast aside one trash bag full of her clothes, then a knapsack. Kicked errant books and CD jewel cases to the floorboard.

Still nothing.

In a fit of desperate inspiration, she reached beneath the driver's seat and didn't realize until finally her fingers found it, that she had forgotten to breathe.

There it is.

She exhaled.

Jack would never leave without it.

Summer leaned her head against the backseat window glass. There were lights on in the gas station. Streetlights, florescent and throttled with flies and moths and gnats swarming in angry spasms.

She wiped sleep from her eyes.

Summer had been dreaming of farming. Of raising carrots and beets and cabbages and wandering fields of produce. Rows upon rows, sprouting from good, honest dirt collecting between the toes of her bare feet, then sprinkling back to the earth to birth more plants. She had been dreaming of the barn, of the farmhouse, of the chickens and cows and even a rooster, which she named Gordon. In the end, it was Gordon who woke her. Gordon's crowing, telling her and the rest of the world to wake up, lest they sleep through End Times.

Jack . . .

Maybe he'd gone into the gas station to shake a leak. Maybe he'd gone inside for another bottle of those trucker pills he often thought he could hide from her.

Maybe he'd only be a minute.

Summer housed no doubt that Jack Jordan would one day make a run for it. She also assumed there'd be no ceremony when finally it happened. She could very well find herself ditched roadside far, far from home. Cold, alone, and in some state of disarray. But she also knew he'd come running at the first sign of trouble. He'd fall in with another girl, one who couldn't keep up with his shit—they never could—then realize what he and that girl had wasn't love at all, not anything like what he shared with Summer. He'd get around the corner and finally believe all the hype he'd been spoon-feeding himself didn't mean a hill of beans, because he was nothing without Summer. Nothing at all. Then along he'd come, tail tucked.

Not even Jack Jordan could convince himself he could move a kilo without her.

If she'd done anything, it was prove she could make it on her own. She could live on the street, if push came to shove. One night, a year or so back, she'd taken off for a couple days with some guy and, just to see if they could, they camped beneath a bridge. They'd lit fires and ate hot dogs and stood out on the off-ramps, holding signs and asking for money. They'd spanged[A1] [A2] eighty-six bucks in three hours. That's $25.50 per hour, and they weren't even trying. On the third night, it got cold, so they went back to his apartment and tried black tar heroin.

Best she knew, Jack had never noticed her gone.

Summer leaned forward, between the driver and passenger seat. She thought more than once about wandering into the gas station to see what he'd gotten himself into, but didn't so much as pop open the door to the backseat. Instead, she sat still, staring at the dashboard and trying like mad not to get lost in her thoughts but losing, losing desperately until she noticed a commotion yonder and found Jack, shuffle-stepping across the parking lot, holding his britches bunched at the front. Behind him, a fat older man chased him to a spot shy of the gas pumps. A man holding a baseball bat.

Jack threw open the driver's door and slammed the key into the ignition, started the car, then got them on the road. He never once looked at her through the rearview, never once asked why she'd climbed into the backseat. He was a mess of sweats and shakes and kept both hands firm on the wheel, lest he vibrate out the door. All that cacophony, yet how still were his eyes. How still and even. Summer watched him a long moment to make sure he was okay, but soon bored of it and returned her dead stare to the dashboard.

"Slow down, Jack," she said. "Speed limit is fifty through here."

He did, a little. Summer couldn't see past the high beams, the twin yellow lights stretching into yonder night.

"Where are we?"

"Texas," said Jack.

She blinked. "How long have we been in Texas?"

"Too long, it feels like."

Summer squeezed into the front seat. Craned her neck until it nearly touched the windshield, then turned her head upward to the heavens. Or what she could see of the them.

"How much further we got to drive, you reckon?"

"Another hour, at most," he said. "We'll get another motel and hole up for the morning. Tomorrow, we'll grab some lunch, then go check out a place I found on the Internet."

She sighed. "Another place. You know, I really liked the last place we had. The one in Columbia."

"The duplex?"

"Yeah, that was real nice. Washer, dryer . . . dishwashing machine. I think of all the places we've stayed, the duplex was the nicest."

"You were hardly there at the end."

She drew a half breath and held it. "That doesn't mean I didn't think it was nice."

The air soured and Summer could tell he was sorry to have brought it up. He knew it'd get her thinking about Scovak. She'd thought plenty on him since leaving South Carolina, and very little on anything else. Mostly, she thought about the last time she saw him, how his eyes narrowed to slits when she told him she was only going to be gone an hour, that she'd be back as soon as she could. How he'd squinted and gently stroked his beard, pointed at the chin, and said nothing as he looked away and returned his attention to his brand new tattoo. The one with her name on it. Like he knew she was lying to him, like he knew she could never lie to him. He allowed it. If for no reason other than he was certain she'd change her mind, he allowed her to leave, and no sooner had she driven over the Savannah River had—

"Hey, you in there?" Jack snapped his fingers, inches from her nose. "Stay with me. It's late and I've been driving, what, nine hours now? I've been going nuts and you've had enough time in that little head of yours. Come on, wake up. Talk to me."

"I miss him," she said.

She could hear his eyes roll in his head. He said, "Summer . . . don't—"

"I'm not, Jack." She turned in her seat. Her breath fogged the passenger window glass. She reached out a finger to mark it, but stopped short. She had no idea what to write. "All I'm saying is I miss him."

He sighed. For the first time, he took his eyes off the road, hands off the wheel. Summer didn't know if his trembling hand reached to stroke her hair or pat her shoulder or possibly even strangle her neck, but instead, reached inside the breast pocket of his flannel shirt and wrestled free a wrinkled pack of smokes. He tapped one out and offered it to her, but she refused. The driver's side strobed furious orange as Jack fussed with the lighter, finally sparking it. He drew and blew deliberately on his cigarette. Drew and blew.

"You know," she said, "I'd prefer not to say his name again either. In fact, as of this moment right here and now, I will never again utter his name. You hear me?"

"I'd be more than fine with that, if it were true."

"It's true and you'll see." She sat still, as long as she could. She watched the road a good while, the names of the towns on signs popping up alongside the road. Names like San Augustine and Macune. Chireno and Etoile. Towns that could only be gas stations at highway intersections, open or closed, but mostly closed, and billboards that should have long ago been painted over. Pine trees sentinel and stretching well into the night like crooked fingers, blocking out moons and stars and letting through no light, nor any out. Summer watched it all and wished there were more, but there wasn't, so she spoke.

"But one thing the man whose name I won't say used to tell me was there weren't no use in being sad when there were so many other things on the planet to be."

"Weren't he just a poet, then."

"It may sound simple to someone like you," she said, "but it's actually very wise if you break it down."

"I'm sure it is."

"I know you never did like him," she grumped, "but you didn't know him. Not like I did. He said I was the only person he'd ever met who wasn't afraid of him."

"I wasn't afraid of him."

"You can't even say it without cracking your voice."

"I'm telling you, I wasn't scared of him." Outside Jack's window, the world whipped past in a blur of starlight and streetlamps. "Part of my act was pretending he intimidated me."

"You did a mighty fine job." Her voice could have been draped with tinsel. "Especially the parts where he came in the front door and you slipped out the back."

"Half the things they said about him weren't true, I'd bet."

"How much?"

"How much what?"

"How much would you bet?"

Jack licked his lips. "I'd bet that entire kilo under the seat that he never did time for killing nobody. I'd bet that's all something he dreamed up so folks would take him serious. That one tattoo he had above his elbow . . . You remember it?"

"I remember his every inch."

"He said it was how they mark someone in the Aryan nation after they'd killed somebody for the cause. And by *somebody,* what they mean is—"

"I know what they mean."

"I'll have you know I googled it and that weren't no Aryan tattoo," said Jack. "It's some bullshit he and a couple drunk peckerwoods carved into his arm with a safety pin and some India ink and now he's trying to play it off like he's hard, and all you kids lapped it up. People can be full of shit sometimes."

She crossed her arms. "He didn't let a whole lot of people close, not like he did with me. That's why a lot of people . . . Hey, Jack, will you please slow down?"

"Will you please not tell me how to drive?"

She said, "There's a kilo of cocaine under your seat and you're going twenty over the speed limit."

Jack did. He pushed his sweat-mottled hair out of his face with a twitchy hand. Summer noticed for the first time he had yet to buckle his belt and zip his fly. She studied him through eyes squinted.

"You were having one of your fits back there, weren't you?" she asked. "Back in that gas station bathroom?"

"Summer, please . . ."

"You act like it don't affect you none, that I'm the odd one for getting sore about things. That all the sneaking out in the middle of the night and changing names and the lies and looking over our shoulders, all that rolls off you like water off a duck, but these fits you get say something quite different."

"If it's all the same," he said, voice cracking, "I'd rather think about something else. Anything else, to be honest."

Summer nodded. "Fine. Not talking about it don't make it go away, but suit yourself."

"You ain't the only one who lost someone," muttered Jack.

"Oh ho!" It was Summer's turn to roll her eyes. "I bet if you tried, you couldn't remember her name."

"Her name was Michelle and I miss the ever-loving shit out of her. I had something awful special with her and I'm afraid I might have broke her heart. You never know how something like that could affect a person."

"She's young, she'll get over it." Summer twiddled her thumbs. Through the windshield, the sky colored purple and resplendent. Up came the sun. "Besides," she said, "if what you two had was so special, you wouldn't have lit out with her student loan money, would you?"

Jack took the last drag from his smoke and tossed it through the window. He didn't bother to roll it up, instead let the wind roar through the opening.

"Summer," he said, when finally he spoke, "all that mess is in the rearview, and that's where it should stay. We have a unique opportunity lying before us. We each can start anew, a clean slate. How many people get a chance like this? When we cross into Lufkin, I suggest we drop all our troubles and burdens at the border, leave all those hard times behind us. Because from here on out, it's going to be roses and sunshine."

"You think so?" Summer asked with a whisper.

"I know so."

Jack leaned back in his seat and slipped an arm around her shoulders. She tucked herself into him, suddenly warmed. But at the door there beckoned yet a chill. One that nobody, not even Jack Jordan, could ward away. So she sat silent and filled herself with his smells: the cigarette, his sweat, the fresh stench of panic. She matched, best she could, the rhythms of his unsteady breathing. For even if she couldn't say it out loud, even if she wouldn't allow it past her tongue, she'd still say it over and over in her head.

Say it so loud in there that sometimes, she could hear nothing else.

Just his name.

Over and over.

Scovak.

Scovak.

Scovak . . .

www.ingramcontent.com/pod-product-compliance
Lightning Source LLC
Chambersburg PA
CBHW050518110726
47899CB00005B/1504